TOGETHER WITH YOU

"My heart is, and will always be, yours."

— JANE AUSTEN

First paperback edition November 2025

Cover design by Alt 19 Creative

www.authorlesliemcelroy.com

paperback: 979-8-9926505-8-7
ebook: 979-8-9926505-7-0

This one is for my readers who are afraid to let love in again.
Believe in the magic of love.
Believe that lives converge for a reason.
Believe in the messy masterpiece that is true love.

And when you do find that love, let them love the hell out of you.

AUTHOR NOTE & CONTENT WARNING

Dear Reader,

I appreciate that you wanted to take a second chance at love with Noah and Evie. For the majority of the book, I have written it to be lighthearted, cozy and full of comedic and chemistry-fueled banter. However, the story also discusses heavy topics of cancer, anxiety and panic attacks. It also contains adult language and explicit sexual scenes. If you prefer to keep their love story closed-door, please mind the spicy chapters listed below.

XO, Leslie

Spicy Chapters:
Chapter 21
Chapter 22
Chapter 23

TOGETHER WITH YOU

A NOVEL

LESLIE MCELROY

1

Evie

I've never known a love like Noah Pearson.

And I don't know if I ever will again. It was a once-in-a-lifetime kind of love and over the past seven years, I learned to accept that I will never see his face again. But no matter how hard I try to forget him, the town of Hollybury won't let me. Even something as simple as the first snow of the season reminds me of him. That's what prompted my thoughts of him today. The snow. Those magical flurries silently crashed into my windshield, just like the images and sounds of Noah's voice silently crashed into my mind when I least expected them to. The windshield wipers scraped excessively against the glass. At some point I must've cranked the setting to high and the snow was letting up as I took the only exit to Hollybury.

"Get it together, Evie. It's just memories. He's never coming back," I mumble to myself. Michael Buble's *It's Beginning To Look Like Christmas* starts to play and endorphins immediately release. I swear that man could sing his own rendition of *Wheels on the Bus* and I would swoon every time.

I slowly make my way through my quiet little town. Tourists say that visiting Hollybury is like stepping into a snowglobe. There's a family medicine office building next to a coffee shop. Across the street, there's a diner and hardware store, both owned by old Mr. Dorsey, who loves to be in everyone's business and is a stickler for town ordinances and rules. Miss Lizzie, owner of the bookshop Novel Bound – and local wannabe matchmaker – always loves to give Mr. Dorsey a run for his money. Conveniently, the bookshop is located right across the street from Dorsey's Diner, so it is inevitable they get into some sort of argument every day just to ruffle each other's feathers. I think they are secretly into each other, but are too stubborn to admit it.

I come to a complete stop in the middle of these two buildings. Right in front of me is the gazebo, a landmark that indicates the heart and soul of Hollybury. My hands grip the wheel a little tighter because the gazebo was a special landmark for me and Noah once upon a time. It's where he officially asked me to be his girlfriend.

Suddenly it is hard to breathe.

I'm the one who burned us down. I didn't want to do it to him, but it was the easiest way to let him go. With everything going on with my mom, I did not want to drag him into any drama that would stop him from pursuing what he really wanted. Especially since one of his dreams got taken away from him within seconds. Now, I know in my gut that he is for sure never coming back. Not with all the fame and fortune he has acquired since becoming a world-renowned chef. His face has been plastered on *Food Network Magazine*, *Food and Wine* and *Bon Appetit*. He's been a judge on multiple cooking competitions and has traveled all around the world. He is living his dream and it's bittersweet for me. I was supposed to go with him. Until everything changed. Until that phone call I got on the empty football field the week before graduation that shattered every dream I once had.

A text comes through, bringing my awareness back to the present. The name Gerard with a heart emoji pops up on my screen. I roll my eyes and smile. There is some sort of drama happening at the bed and breakfast no doubt and Gerard, my best friend since college and now employee, cannot wait until I am at the inn to tell me. I turn left down Evergreen Lane and take an immediate right down the winding driveway toward an old historic inn. We just had the exterior painted white and decided on evergreen shutters to highlight its charm. We are less than a month out from our soft opening on Christmas Eve and have been hard pressed to find an in-house head chef to run our kitchen.

Once I park behind my parents' truck, I actually look at my phone and read the message:

> You need to get here. NOW girl.

I shake my head and smile. I text back:

> Seriously, G? You couldn't wait the two minutes from the town square to the inn to tell me in person what's going on? You have my location! I was on Main when you texted me. Getting out of my car now.

I unbuckle my seatbelt. Ding. "Ok, brace yourself."

Nerves infiltrate my stomach. We have yet another interview today for a resident chef and I am worried this one is also a dud. My parents are getting annoyed with me for nixing every candidate so far, but they would never in a million years tell me so. My parents are Hallmark parents. It's like they were written by a happy-go-lucky romance writer who never wrote any type of angst and happily-ever-after was always a given. They do not have a mean or negative bone in their bodies. Even after all we've been through, they never lost hope. I can't say the same for me.

I pull down the visor and open the small mirror. I need to touch up my makeup before I walk into this interview. I just drove an hour back from Hartford, where I gave a talk at my old college about opening up a historic inn and all the ins-and-outs of permits and renovations and formulating a business plan. I reach into my purse and grab my travel bag of essential makeup items: concealer, mascara and a blush that can double as a lipstick. I flatten out staticky hair that resulted from my beanie and run my hands through my loose ash-blonde curls. I huff,

"That will have to do for now. I'm sure this interview won't last long anyway."

The snow has slowed, so I forego my umbrella and run up the old stairs to the front door of my pride and joy and current, unshattered dream: the Evergreen Inn. Now that Thanksgiving is over and all the renovations are finally finished, I can start decorating for Christmas.

Awaiting me once I open the large walnut door is a wide-eyed Gerard, who nearly tackles me as he reaches for my trusty red scarf.

"Gerard," I muffle under my red scarf that temporarily is covering my face. "What is the emergency?" So much for fixing my hair in the car because now it is standing up at all angles from the erratic way Gerard took off my scarf.

Gerard places my scarf on the coat rack. "Why are you moving at a glacial pace? Girl, do you not understand the definition of NOW?"

"I literally just walked through the door. You need to calm down. Whatever it is, I'm sure it can wait."

"Oh you mean a 6'4" hunk of a chef could wait for little Miss Priss to get her act together?" Gerard crosses his arms and bats his eyes sassily.

"You know I hate that nickname. And who is acting like little Miss Priss now? You are extra sassy today. Did you have too many shots of espresso?" I take off my coat and hang it alongside the dilapidated scarf.

Gerard scoffs. "Okay, first of all, rude. Second, you are doing a whole lot of yapping and not enough getting your pretty little ass in that kitchen to meet this god of a man. And you know that if I say he is a god of man, it's true."

"You think that every man is a god of a man. Who do you think you are talking to? I know your track record. For years you thought Harry Styles was the hottest thing to walk this earth."

Gerard starts pushing my back toward the kitchen, where I hear my mom laugh at whatever our interviewee just said. Oh, she must really like this person. My mom is genuinely laughing. I can easily tell between her fake laugh and real laugh and that is for sure a real laugh. "I stand by Harry being the hottest man on this earth," Gerard says. We stop right before the swinging door to the kitchen and Gerard turns my body to face him.

He rigorously fixes my hair and pinches my cheekbones.

"Ow, what the hell?" I rub my cheek, probably making it redder.

"Oh stop being such a baby. I want you to look hot before you walk into that room because girl...let me tell you. I may still think that Harry is hot, but I don't know, this specimen of a man might just rival him. The rolled up sleeves. The scruff. The green eyes. The tattoos. Lord help me."

"Okay, well why don't *you* hit on him then if you are so infatuated?" I gasp playfully. "Or better yet, why don't you ask him out?"

Gerard scrunches up his face. "Girl, that man is as straight as they come. My gaydar was not registering any ounce of gay in that man. And something tells me that you are going to think he is *so* fine. Not to mention, how long has it been since you've got some?"

My mouth drops to the floor and I cross my arms. "That's none of your business."

"Um hmmm. I think this man is going to make you want to get some. Soon." He waves his eyebrows like he knows a juicy secret and I have a feeling I am going to find out the exact secret he is keeping in about two seconds. I hear a muffled voice and I get this strange sensation that I have heard that voice before. Goosebumps cover my body and before I can try and figure out where I might know that voice from, Gerard sneaks up behind me and pushes me forward through the door.

I bump into the back of our interviewee and fall straight to the ground. Gerard was not lying when he said he had muscles. I feel like I crashed into a brick wall.

"Oh my! Evie! Are you okay?" my mom exclaims. I see her feet make their way toward me.

"Yeah, Mom. Just blame Gerard for pushing me into our guest," I grunt.

"I got her, Lydia."

My heart drops to my stomach and the goosebumps come back in full force. His voice ricochets through every inch of my body. His strong, veiny hand grabs my wrist and that's when I see the start of a sleeve of tattoos run along his just as veiny forearm. Once I get some sort of stable footing, I finally have the courage to look up at his face. His sharp jawline is covered with the perfect amount of scruff, his green eyes still kind as ever under his thick eyebrows. He let his hair grow a little longer on the top compared to the almost buzz cut he had before. The tattoos are the only new feature about him, though. I can tell right away. It's Noah. My Noah.

Instead of embracing him in the biggest hug or kissing the life out of him like I imagined I would all these years in all the scenarios I conjured up in my head, my fears and hurt and guilt take over and my walls spring up in a matter of seconds.

"Hi, Evie." His deep yet soft voice fills the silence. Part of me wants him to scoop me up and resume where we left off seven years ago. The other part of me wants to safeguard my heart so it can't be destroyed by love again. I am feeling everything all at once. Most of all, I don't understand why he is back in Hollybury and not in New York.

"What are you doing here, Noah?" It comes out sharper than I intended. It is the hurt talking. It may not be fair. It's just where I am at this moment. I am suspended in such disbelief that he is actually here, standing in front of me, in this kitchen, in the inn that I renovated and refurbished. Years of my blood, sweat and tears I poured into this place. I may not have wanted to admit it then, nor I am going to outwardly admit it to anyone now, but this has been the ultimate distraction to my broken heart and broken dreams. I worked my ass off because I needed something to work out. I needed one of my dreams to come true.

I never expected my other dream to be on the other side of the kitchen door. Looking like a damn snack. If I thought that his quarterback and captain of the football team look was hot, his chef look takes the cake. Noah's emerald eyes dart toward my parents and he almost growls, "She didn't know about this?"

I shoot a look at my parents, who look like toddlers who just got in trouble for coloring on the wall with permanent markers. *Yup that's right. You are in trouble.* "Mom. Dad. Know about what?"

"Well, you know, Evie girl..."

"No, no. You can't *Evie girl* your way out of this one! What the hell is Noah talking about? Why is he here?" I can hear my voice raise. I pride myself on being pretty mild-tempered, but when the situation calls for it, I make sure people can hear me clearly. This is one of those situations.

My dad chimes in, "Evie. We knew you wouldn't approve of this new hire. Given everything."

"You think?" And then it registers. "Wait, what do you mean new hire? I thought this was an interview!"

Noah now looks intently at me. "I moved back to Hollybury, Evie. I'm here for the foreseeable future."

"But not forever, right?" A flicker of hurt glazes over Noah's face as I turn to my parents. "No. As co-owner of this inn, I don't approve of this hire."

"Evie, be reasonable." My dad wraps an arm around my mom. I notice the tired lines that have developed over the years around my dad's eyes. His hair has turned gray in response to the worry and stress he had to endure. "There's no reason, other than your obvious history, to not hire Noah. He needs a job and we need a chef. And from a business standpoint, it's a good decision. He is a great chef and he will naturally drive in business. Plus, he is from here. It will be nice to have someone who is already acclimated to the area and I'm sure the town is going to be thrilled about the news."

My parents are right, but I am in no state to admit that to them. All I can think is: *No, no, no, this can't be happening.* He is not about to swoop in here and pretend like the last seven years never existed. We fell apart and for so long, I wished we could fall back together again. But I have finally started to feel okay without him. I shake my head and say, "Nope. I can't..." Tears begin to form and almost escape before I turn and run past Gerard, who has his hand over his mouth and eyes wide in disbelief at the soap operaesque scene that just unfolded in front of him. I grab my coat and scarf so fast that it causes the coat rack to crash to the floor.

I fail to grab my keys but I don't think I can operate heavy machinery right now. I start jogging down the winding driveway and finally the tears break through.

2

Noah

Evie Hawkins has never looked so beautiful. Even when she is mad, she is still the most beautiful girl in the world. She is pure fire underneath the facade of tailored, muted perfection and my heart is happy that nothing has changed. She is still the same Evie I fell in love with when I was seven years old. A twinge of guilt comes over me as I look at Bill and Lydia. Evie was blindsided and I was a part of it unintentionally.

Bill is the first one to speak. "Noah, I am sorry we didn't tell you that Evie didn't know. We were about to and then she bulldozed in here and..." He takes a deep breath and forces an optimistic smile. "She'll come around, I promise."

"Yes, she will. We are nothing but convincing. We were the ones to convince her to pull the trigger on this old dump." Lydia gestures to the beautifully redone kitchen. One of the things that made me fall even more in love with Evie is her ability to see the beauty in the wreckage. She found the beauty in me once upon a time. "You are the last piece of the puzzle. She is just too scared to have you back in the picture." Lydia touches my arm. "She's at her spot. Go talk with her."

I sigh and nod. I know exactly where to find her. I stride toward Gerard in the doorway, who I had the pleasure of meeting before Evie arrived. He just gives me a nod as I sliver past him and run after my girl.

The cold breeze has definitely picked up since I got here. In my rushed state, I forgot to grab my coat, so I resort to unfolding my sleeves all the way down to my wrists. There is something different about Connecticut winters compared to New York ones. I missed these winters. Where everything is blanketed in white and not turned into muddy sludge on the busy streets.

I just want Evie. I want to hold her. Make her listen to what I have to say. I want this job so bad because I want to be near her. The snow crunches under my feet and I see remnants of Evie's footprints. I smile because my one stride covers two of hers. She always thought she could outrun me. I remember training for football and she challenged me to a race. *One lap around the track. I bet I can beat you. The winner gets to choose whatever movie we're going to watch on our date.* I knew how much she loved choosing the movies. The way her face lit up when the opening credits would start. The way she would throw her gorgeous blonde hair up in a messy bun and let little tendrils fall and frame her face. The way she tucked her legs underneath her butt on the couch as she draped a blanket over herself. The way she would pour the entire bag of peanut M&Ms into the tub of popcorn. Pure happiness. Her happiness made up my entire happiness. That's why I let her win. Every time.

It was the small things about Evie that I fell in love with. I was ready to give her the world. I am still ready to give her the world. I need her to know that and, God, I hope I'm not too late.

I finally make it to the steps of the gazebo and hear soft sniffles. Evie's leg is frantically bobbing up and down. She's in her head, processing everything that just happened, and if I know her as well as I think I do, she is completely freaking out.

I slowly take each step up toward her. When she doesn't acknowledge me, I say, "Evie."

She wipes her nose with the sleeve of her teal coat. That color always brought out the green in her eyes. My heart skips a beat when I see the red scarf burying her neck. She still has the scarf.

"What are you doing here, Noah?"

"I wanted to make sure you are okay. I promise I didn't know that your parents didn't tell you about me. They assured me on the phone that they would tell you about me coming back and potentially being the in-house chef at your inn."

"But what about your new, great, big beautiful life in New York?"

I slowly step toward her and put my hands in my pockets. "It wasn't enough."

Even though she is looking straight out into the windows of Dorsey's Diner, I can tell that her eyes have turned misty again. "I don't understand how that isn't enough."

I shrug. I want to tell her all the reasons why it isn't enough but now, in the middle of the whole town, isn't the time. "It just isn't." I am about to sit down when Evie pops up in a fiery rage.

"You have everything you have ever wanted, Noah! Why the fuck would you give that up to come back to this sleepy town? It doesn't make any sense! Especially when I haven't heard from you in seven years!!" She paces on the creaky wooden gazebo floors. "I was finally learning how to be lonely. I was finally learning how to live my life without you!"

I am taken aback. A fire inside of me swiftly develops. *What the hell?* She is rewriting history and it's not fair. And she doesn't even know the whole story. "You told me not to contact you again, Evie!" Now I start to yell because as much as I want her to win this one, as much as I want to see her smile, I also want her to face the truth. "Don't put that on me. I was just doing what you wanted!"

"What I *wanted*? You think that I wanted to get that phone call about my mom? Do you think I wanted to throw it all away? Do you think that I wanted to try and forget about you so that my heart wouldn't break every fucking time that I saw you on a magazine cover or on the *Today Show* or whatever else you were being interviewed for?!"

I sense that we aren't alone anymore. Stares are coming at us from every angle. Whispers are filling the air and circulating like the falling snow. Shit. Now all eyes are on us. This whole argument is going to spread like wildfire. I want to carry Evie over my shoulder and take her back to the inn where we can have a proper sit down and talk things out, but I don't think that is going to happen. She is too hurt and pissed off and blindsided that she can't see straight. And honestly, in her presence, I can never see straight. She has this ability to throw me off-kilter while also grounding me when I am spiraling out of control. She is the only one who could ground me. Through all the noise, she was the one who cut through it like a knife. Silencing the world around us. Silencing the critics and the naysayers and the people who said my future was over when I blew out my knee. She was the one who helped me submit my application to culinary school. She was the one who jumped up and down and screamed when I opened my acceptance email. She was always there.

I was finally learning how to be lonely. I was finally learning how to live my life without you!

Her words make me shudder and are colder than any breeze that can touch my skin. "All I know is I didn't want this." I look at her up and down, and it takes all my strength not to hold her while I say the next words to her. "Evie, I never wanted you to be lonely."

"It happened anyway, didn't it? Shortly after you left, when I realized that you weren't coming back, it was hard for me. It broke me that despite living in what is virtually a magical snow globe in a magical small town, there was no magic strong enough to bring you back." Tears are streaming down her face.

"And what do you have to say to that notion now, Evie? Because I am back. And we are going to be seeing a lot more of each other since I am your new head chef."

She backs away from me. I didn't realize how close our bodies were until she did that. I missed her being that close to me. I ache for it. I am so distracted that she is in front of me at all. "Don't get ahead of yourself, Noah. You are hired on a trial basis."

"But, your parents said..." I'm confused.

"I never agreed to this. I still hold fifty percent of ownership. So we'll compromise. You will be our head chef in a probationary period, if you will, until our soft opening on Christmas Eve. This is part of the interview process they didn't disclose to you. I would have done this to any other person we considered. Plus, you still have ties to New York. You say you are back for now, but I need to protect my business. This is important to me. I want to make sure you are a good fit for our inn and the vision I have for Evergreen. If you accept these terms, then you start tomorrow, Mr. Pearson."

It sounds so wrong for Evie to call me Mr. Pearson. No one calls me that. It's either Noah or Chef or Noah Pearson. Never Mr. Pearson. She is putting up a wall, but I am determined to break it down these next few weeks. I know how much this means to her. This is her dream. Other than becoming a photographer one day, she told me that she always wanted to make something that looks run-down and ugly and unsalvageable, beautiful. Anything she touches turns beautiful. If she wants to keep it professional between us, so be it.

I reach out my hand and wait for hers to finally touch mine. I want to feel the spark that her touch always ignited. More importantly, I want Evie to trust me and depend on me again. I am now the one in the stands cheering her on. The tables have turned and I am completely okay with that. I am her number-one fan.

Her cold hand meets mine and we seal our agreement with a handshake. "Okay, so for the next few weeks, you will be under observation. After I debrief with my parents, we will make our final decision. And Mr. Pearson?"

I raise my eyebrows. "Yes, Ms. Hawkins?" I am fighting off an entertained smirk. She is so damn cute.

"We need to keep things professional between us."

That is going to be the tallest order of my life, but I will happily agree to this silly request only if it means I get to see Evie's face every day for the next month. I say, "Professional is my middle name."

Evie rolls her eyes before letting go of my hand. "I see you haven't let up on your dad jokes."

"Never."

I glimpse a small smile on Evie's face and my insides twist in all different directions. She starts to descend down the rickety old steps. I'm surprised this thing hasn't collapsed yet. It's hundreds of years old. I say, "So the gazebo is still your favorite spot, huh?"

"Yeah. It is. Probably always will be. I'll see you tomorrow at work, Mr. Pearson."

I am treading on unsteady ground. Every move that I make for the next month can make or break this relationship—and determine whether or not my future with the girl of my dreams can be a reality again. I am going to prove to her that what we had is worth piecing back together.

"See you tomorrow, Ms. Hawkins."

3

Noah

I approach the Hawkins' residence and suddenly my palms become sweaty. I have not been here since the day I left Hollybury. I could have waited until tomorrow to talk to Lydia and Bill, but I've been having a hard time breathing. The whole ordeal in the center of town, at the gazebo that meant so much to me and Evie, is eating away at me and I need to confront her parents about the fact they did not warn Evie of my return. I guess I could have reached out, too–I just didn't think that Evie wanted to hear from me. I know I fucked up by not reaching out to her all these years, but I honestly was scared. Just like she didn't want to hold me back, I didn't want to hold her back either. Regardless, I am praying that she did hold back and hasn't been with anyone else. I don't consider myself a selfish man–except with Evie.

I knock a few times and place my hands in my pockets as I await for someone to open the door. I rock on my feet and exhale. Just as I am about to knock again, the door opens and I am greeted with Lydia's smiling face. Her smile can light up any room–Evie definitely inherited that from her.

"Hi Noah. We weren't expecting you but I am glad you stopped by."

"Who is it?" Bill's voice booms over the TV. I hear his trusty recliner close and those springs sound like they are about to snap.

Lydia calls over her shoulder, "Come and see for yourself."

When he reaches the front hallway, Bill's face lights up just as bright. A sliver of pride travels through me because despite me and Evie's breakup, despite essentially breaking their daughter's heart, they are still welcoming me back with open arms. They are kind of like a second set of parents. Parents that I wish I had. My parents passed away in a car accident when I was five years old and I was raised by my grandpa. Bill and Lydia represent an image of a relationship I saw with Evie–still see with Evie.

"Ah, nice to see you Noah," Bill says.

"And look, he found the front door." Lydia beams up at Bill.

My face flushes. I guess I wasn't as sneaky as I thought

when I was a teenager. All I can do is continue to rock on my feet and shrug while my hands stay in my pockets.

"I see that. We thought that with all those years of sneaking into Evie's room from the tree in the front yard, you had no idea where the front door was located, son."

"We're kidding." Lydia opens the door wider. "Come in, Noah."

"Thanks." I beam at her this time. "I don't mean to interrupt your evening."

"Nonsense. We just finished eating dinner and are about to start one of our many shows. I swear it is impossible to catch up with all the new shows coming out or even catch up with shows that have been out for years that have won so many awards! We got into this binge-watching when I was recovering from chemo. Are you hungry, dear?"

My heart tugs at the word "chemo." I feel guilty for not being here through it all. I am happy I get to be in the same room with her now and we can have this conversation. My anxiety was at an all time high when I first left Hollybury because of all the things I was leaving behind. Cooking was a great distraction. School was particularly grueling. I didn't have time to sit with my feelings or dwell on what could happen to Lydia. What was happening in Evie's head. How she was dealing with it. I kept my anxiety at bay. That is, until I started to get noticed. Once I received offers to be on shows or do interviews for magazine articles, my attacks came back in full force. I didn't have the one person who knew how to calm me down. I did the best with the tools I learned.

"Um, no thank you. I already ate." I stand by the couch Bill and Lydia have had for years. I nod toward the television. "That's great. I wouldn't know half the shows that are out now. I've been so busy."

"We've noticed and we are so proud of you, Noah. Please sit." Lydia gestures to the old beige couch. I sink immediately into it and settle in.

"So, what do we owe the pleasure?"

I clasp my hands together. "I want to talk with you two about what happened today. I had no idea that Evie didn't know. And now she is pissed at me. That's not how I imagined my homecoming would go. That's not how I imagined seeing Evie for the first time in seven years. She aired out our laundry in front of the entire town."

Lydia and Bill exchange a knowing look. Then Lydia says, "Yeah, she is pretty upset. But don't worry, Noah. She will calm down once she knows that this is about business more than anything. We want someone we can trust to provide great food and service to our customers and hiring you is a no-brainer. You have the experience, obviously, and the status in the culinary world, but more importantly, you are like a son to us. You know that. No matter what happens between you and Evie, you will always be like a son to us. We can't turn you away."

I nod. My fingers are interlocked so tight, my knuckles are turning white. "While I appreciate that, I want to make things right with your daughter. She even put me on probation and I am in a trial period," I use air quotes when I say "trial period."

Both Bill and Lydia burst out in laughter. Bill places his hand over his face. "Oh, that girl is so headstrong and stubborn."

"She gets it from you, you know." Lydia points to Bill,

whose face is turning red. She turns her attention to me. "You are not in a trial period with us, Noah. Don't worry."

"No, it's okay. I want her to feel like she has some control in this situation that blindsided her. I'll play by her rules. She needs to see that she can trust me again. I'll do whatever it takes to make her feel secure." Even if that means adhering to whatever guidelines or rules she has for me. I know I am in for a wild ride with her and she is going to try and make it impossible for me to get close to her.

Bill's laughter subsides. "That's why we loved you for our Evie. You always made her feel secure. That's important in a relationship."

"Look, I want to make things right because I want this opening to be so successful for you all. Especially for Evie. I always wanted her to live out her dreams."

"Well, she is downstairs in the dark room developing some photos she took today after your little not-so-meet-cute, if you want to talk with her in a more private setting." Lydia gestures to the basement door. Years ago, Evie begged her parents to transform the basement into a dark room so she could practice developing photos.

I press my palms against the sinking couch, stand and adjust my old gray Hollybury Husky hoodie. I have worn this sweatshirt so much that it is developing little holes throughout, but I can't bring myself to throw it out. It acted as my security blanket away from home and it is perfectly broken in. "I don't know. I think she prefers if I keep my distance."

"I know my daughter. She doesn't want distance. She wants to see if you will fight for her." Lydia practically pushes me toward the basement door. Despite her petite frame, she sure is freakishly strong. "Go fight for her."

I slowly and hesitantly make my way down the creaky steps into the basement. A red light fills the large room and I see my girl meticulously using tongs to transfer photographic paper from one bin to another. Her hair is pulled up in a messy bun and she looks so in her element it makes my heart leap. I know how much she loves renovating and making things that are broken whole again. She did that with me. She found all the scraps from my childhood and developed me into the man I am today. She influenced me in the best way.

I also know how much she loves photography. She was the one who captured all the big moments of my high school football career. She was always on the sidelines cheering me on behind the lens. Now it's my turn to cheer her on.

I clear my throat to try and get her attention, but there is no response from her. The last thing I want to do is scare her. I clear my throat again. Still no response as she clips some photos onto a string above her workspace. Even though it is nearly completely dark, I can still make out the curves of her ass as she tip-toes to clip the photos. She turns her head slightly and that's when I see a white earbud secured in her ear. Damn, she will never hear me. She is probably jamming out to a Christmas playlist. I chuckle as I approach her because of the small sway of her hips, I can tell she is totally in the zone. It is then that she takes the tongs she is working with and transforms them into a microphone and lip syncs to, by the looks of the way her lips are moving, *Christmas (Baby Please Come Home)*.

Classic Evie. After all these years, she is still the same

Christmas-obsessed beautiful goofball. I love this Evie. The one who did not care what the world thought of her.

Here I am, falling even more in love with her, which I didn't think was possible. There is a new layer to her that I am dying to scratch the surface of. I know that Lydia's cancer jaded her. Hurt her. Just like my leaving town hurt her. There was a whole lot of hurt and not enough time for healing. This is one of her ways of healing. Christmas music always got her in a better mood.

Evie finally turns around when I am about a foot away from her. The next thing I know, I feel the metal tongs hit my left eyebrow.

"Oh my god! What the hell are you doing here? And why didn't you alert me that you were behind me, you weirdo?!" She takes out her earbuds, which are still blasting with Darlene Love's vocals. "I thought you were a murderer!"

I start chuckling as I wipe the blood from the small cut on my eyebrow. "And you thought your best line of defense was a pair of tongs?"

"It stopped you from advancing on me, didn't it?" She sets the tongs down. "Are you okay?" Her fiery eyes look up at my cut eyebrow and her hand starts to reach up to inspect it. She stops right before her fingers actually touch my skin, realizing she is about to break some sort of boundary she set in her head about us.

Disappointment floods me. My skin is ablaze from the anticipation for her touch finally on me. I need her to touch me again. It has been too long.

She squares her body toward mine. I cross my arms and say, "I'm fine."

"You didn't answer my question. What are you doing here, Noah?"

No beating around the bush. I'll get straight to the point. "I didn't like the way we left things at the gazebo. It felt too formal and I guess... a little disconnected." She opens her mouth to protest, but I hold up a hand. "But I get it. There has been a lot of hurt between us. A lot of history that cannot be erased. That being said, I think that in order for this trial period to work, I need for you not to give me the cold shoulder. I want you to be successful, Evie. If we go into this with a contentious relationship, it's never going to work. Even if you don't think I am the right fit at the end of the day, I'll respect that and we can move on. If, however, you feel like I am the right fit, I want it to be a somewhat positive relationship to begin with. I don't want to call you Ms. Hawkins and I definitely don't want you to call me Mr. Pearson. Mr. Pearson is my granddad. I'm Noah and you're Evie. Let's keep it simple."

She slowly nods as she assesses my request. She still responds with a cold tone. "Deal. Anything else? I'm really busy with processing all of this."

I take a beat, trying not to push her so she doesn't close up on me completely. "Processing all of what? Your photographs? Me coming back? You opening up an inn? What?"

She places her hands on her hips and looks down. "Everything, Noah."

At least she is calling me Noah and not Mr. Pearson. That's a sign she is letting me in a little.

I nod and walk around her to take a look at what she is working on. It's a series of black-and-white photos. A bird on a snowy branch. An old couple on the bench next to the gazebo, looking in each other's eyes like nothing in the world can phase them. A table outside of Dorsey's diner that is set up with a single flower in a small clear vase.

I get to the final photo hanging on the line and it shakes me. It's the football stadium covered in a blanket of snow. Cold. Empty. Still. Everything a football field should not be. Yet, it represents everything that football means to me now. The ache in my knee activates, but I distract my pain by saying, "You still got it. I'm happy you kept up with photography. I know how much it means to you. Have you taken pictures anywhere else?"

Her voice is shaky when she responds, "Oh some places here and there. Nowhere special. I mainly stay in town or in the nearby cities."

I go back to the picture with the old couple. The way she captures the little moments in people's lives always astonished me. "I always loved the portraits you would take. Some of your best work. You did a portrait series on me when I played once upon a time. You remember?"

Evie stands next to me and it takes all of my self-control not to grab the back of her neck and kiss her senseless and make her forget everything that happened. To forget that we were ever apart. Who were we to think that we couldn't have it all? "I remember." She finally exhales. I look over at her and see a tear roll down her face and I know immediately that I am starting to enter territory she isn't ready for.

She's calling the shots right now. The ball is in her court. I need to go.

"It's getting late. I'll let you get back to it then. See you tomorrow, Evie."

"See you tomorrow, Noah." She puts her earbuds in and turns her body toward the bins, avoiding any kind of eye contact with me. She's not ready to go there yet. I will wait as long as I need to for that day to come.

I quickly give my goodbyes to Lydia and Bill and head out to my old Chevy truck that my grandfather gifted me when I was sixteen years old. I kept it in a garage in New York and would periodically maintain it and drive it around the city so it could stay in tip-top shape. I slam the heavy door and turn on the ignition. My hands rest on the large leather steering wheel as I look at the front door of the Hawkins' residence. It's an all too familiar feeling, driving away from Evie in the truck. The only difference between now and then is that this time, I'm not going anywhere.

4

Evie

Seven Years Ago

"Noah, what are we doing here? Are we going to get in trouble for trespassing?" Noah removes his hands from over my eyes and that's when I realize we are on the green turf of the football field. This place feels different now. Ever since Noah collapsed to the field after getting tackled, clutching onto his knee, knowing that his career was over at that moment, he did not want to walk on the field. I didn't think he would ever come back. Other than for our graduation.

He wraps his arms around me from behind,nestles his head in the crux of my neck and secures my arms, which are holding onto a fluffy maroon blanket that he instructed me to get from his truck before we left my house. His lips press lightly on my skin. I am in an oversized white t-shirt and grey sweats–my usual go-to on Friday nights lately. Summer is right at our fingertips but I can't help but miss winter. And I suddenly want it to start snowing. Nothing bad happens when it snows. It brings all the magic. But right now, Noah is the one bringing all the magic. And the gorgeous sunset isn't so bad either.

"Your hair looks pretty like this. It looks golden in this sunset." My hair is down and curled in loose waves. Noah is brushing it away from my neck and laying small kisses up and down my exposed skin. Goosebumps travel along my body and I can't help but smile. He may be expertly avoiding my question, but he is so damn good at it.

"You are such a charmer. But seriously though, what are we doing here?"

He grabs my hand and leads me onto the field. "I figured I wanted to come back before we graduate next week. I want to make a new memory here. One that is filled with my forever future rather than my painful past." We make it to center field and he gestures for me to hand him the blanket. I oblige and he spreads it across the face of the husky at the 50 yard line.

I beam at him. He is now almost fully recovered. After moping for a few weeks about all the physical therapy he had to do, and after a stern talking-to from his grandfather, he pulled up his big-boy pants and killed it at every session and did everything the doctor recommended for him to do. He worked when he needed to work and rested when he needed to rest. He is free of the crutches and the cast and everything that was holding him back. He also looks extra hot tonight with his dark maroon backwards hat. His taut muscles are protruding under his white short-sleeved shirt and jeans. He is so devastatingly handsome that I still sometimes wonder why he is with me in the first place. But then I remember that he is literally my best friend in the entire world and nothing can tear us apart.

My heart skips a beat when he pushes behind my knees, causing me to fall into his lap. He maneuvers my body and I am in the very compromising position of straddling him on the ground. We have only slept together a few times, but each time is more magical than the last. Less awkward. Less scary. I feel completely safe with him.

Noah reaches his hands up my shirt and I place my hands alongside his neck. I bring his lips to mine and his hands start exploring my body, electrifying me. A rebellious smile appears on his face as he plays with the clasp of my bra.

"Noah Pearson. You better not start something you cannot finish."

"Who says I am not going to finish? I have learned the art of discretion over the years."

"And what if we get caught?"

He continues to fiddle with my bra, his rough fingers grazing my sensitive skin. "Then we get caught." He kisses a line down my throat, talking out what the consequences may or may not be of our very public display of affection. "It's not like they are going to expel us. We are graduating in a few days."

I sigh. "You're right."

"I know I am right." He smiles, revealing his delicious dimples. I will never tire of them.

I tug the small amount of hair underneath the bill of his hat. "You're lucky you're cute."

"I love getting you all fired up. Fiery Evie is a good look for you. But then again, so is Sweet Evie. Reserved Evie. Shit, even Hangry Evie is fucking adorable." He kisses my jawline. Shivers travel up and down my body. I swear this man is trouble in all the best ways. "I'm so happy you are mine and soon we will leave Hollybury behind."

"I am so happy you are mine, too. And soon we'll be jetting off, or rather driving off to New York." I look into his bright emerald eyes, "Speaking of. Have you heard back from culinary school?" I got my acceptance to many colleges, but the elation I felt when I got the acceptance email from NYU was unparalleled. The only missing piece was Noah. He has been waiting to hear back for a few months now. He did apply on the later end of the application window, but that shouldn't really matter.

I can feel his pulse quicken in his neck and his breathing shifts. He swallows hard. "I got the email a few hours ago. I just haven't opened it yet."

I feel around his jeans for his phone. "What?! Oh my gosh, Noah why not?"

He grabs my hands and holds them close to his chest,

"Because I am fucking scared of not getting accepted. I applied the latest I can possibly apply and what if they looked at my application and just saw that my only extracurricular was being football captain? They are going to paint me as the dumb jock and totally not qualified to be in the same room as really talented chefs and..."

"And what?"

"I am scared that I won't be able to go to New York with you."

I cradle his face and give him the softest kiss to calm him, "No matter what is in that email, I promise that we will still have a future together in New York. We can still start our lives together. We can explore the city and go to so many Broadway shows that you are going to become a converted musical theater junkie. We are going to find a crazy expensive apartment that is probably 500 square feet and we are literally going to be on top of each other." His eyebrow cocks at my last comment and I press my forehead to his. "I'm here for you. Always. Now give me your phone."

He smiles and pulls out his phone from his pocket and hands it to me without protest. I smugly smile and unlock his phone. I click the blue mail icon and scroll down until I see the message. I click on it and read, "Dear Noah Pearson...We are pleased to inform you..."

"Oh my god! No fucking way!" He snatches the phone from my hand and reads the email for himself. His face lights up. Then he squeezes me and kisses what seems like every inch of me.

I laugh uncontrollably and say, "You did it, Noah. You did it, babe! And I am so proud of you!"

He lays his hands on the sides of my face and looks at me so intently and lovingly, I swear my insides are molten. "New York isn't ready for you, Evie Hawkins."

"Well, the world isn't ready for you, Noah Pearson."

"I can't wait to start my life with you, baby girl." He grabs the back of my head and crushes his lips to mine and I realize that not everyone has a great love in their life. I am so lucky that Noah Pearson is my great love. His kisses are toe-curling and leave me wanting more every time. There isn't enough time with Noah. Even when we spend the whole day together, I miss him the second he drives away in his old Chevy truck. We have our whole lives ahead of us and it seems like nothing can ever tear us apart.

He is it for me.

Before I realize what he is doing, he unclasps my bra. I gasp, "Noah..."

"Yes?" he asks, pretending to be oblivious to what he just did. He tickles my sides and I begin laughing again. That is one thing about Noah, he always knows how to make me laugh. Another thing about Noah, he is not stingy with his kisses and I have never felt any doubt about his love for me. We get tangled in each other, and suddenly I don't care that we are out in the open, in the middle of a football stadium. I am going to kiss him like it's the last time because he deserves those kinds of kisses. This man is magic.

I feel my phone buzz in my back pocket and Noah's hands cup my ass. "Are you going to answer that?"

"I am kind of busy making out with my boyfriend right now. Whoever it is can wait." I resume kissing him, pulling on his hair, making him moan against my mouth.

About thirty seconds after the call gets sent to voicemail, my phone buzzes again. *Dammit, who is calling me right now?*

I pull the phone out of my back pocket, leaving my lips glued to Noah's. I see the word *Mom* flash on the top of my screen. For some reason, I feel this slight panic in my gut and I can't shake the feeling that something is off. "My mom knows I am with you. I better answer this." And just before I slide the answer button, I press a finger to Noah's lips, "Behave yourself."

"I can't make any promises. Not when you are looking the way you do right now." He deviously continues to lay kisses on my skin, slightly sucking on my neck. *How in the world am I supposed to concentrate on this conversation with my mom while he is doing these things to me?*

Regardless, I swipe to answer. "Hey, Mom. What's up?" Noah squeezes my side and I use all my willpower not to squeal in response. Noah deviously smiles and continues his very thorough exploration of my body with his mouth and hands.

"Evie? Um, I know you are with Noah but um... can you come home?"

That uneasy feeling gets stronger in my stomach. Tingles rush through my body and I feel my face get really red. I press my hand against Noah's strong chest and he immediately stops, sensing something is wrong. A serious look takes over his face. All playfulness from a few seconds ago is gone.

I tuck some hair behind my ear. "Yes, of course, Mom. But is everything okay?"

"Just come home please." There is no confirmation that everything is okay, which is unusual for my mom. She is the one who makes it a point to make me see the beauty and light in life. She is so bubbly and personable and honestly, the most optimistic person I know. But then again, both of my parents are optimists.

"Okay. I'll see you in a few." Then silence.

"Is everything okay?" Noah studies every inch of my face.

I shake my head and my eyebrows furrow because what I say next to Noah are the truest words I've ever spoken, even though they are laced with so much uncertainty. "I don't know." I stand up, both bummed that we cannot continue our little makeout session, but also extremely scared of what awaits me at home.

Noah probably breaks every traffic law to get me home in record time.

"If my dad ever finds out that you ran all those red lights with his daughter in the passenger seat, he is going to kill you." I reach for the silver door handle and Noah covers my hand with his.

"Don't you dare, Evie. You know that when you are in my car, you will never open your own door."

"Noah, I appreciate the chivalry and the old man-ness of it all, but I need to get inside."

He exits the truck, slams his heavy metal door and takes about three large strides to get to my side. He swings open the door and I practically speed walk to my front door. My hands are shaking so bad that I am fiddling with my keys. There is something wrong, I know it.

"Here, Evie. Let me." And just as Noah inserts the key into the door, my dad opens it. His eyes look distant and a little puffy. My heart drops. The last time I saw my dad like this, my grandpa died.

"Hey, you two. We feel terrible we interrupted your date." My dad can barely muster up a forced smile.

"No problem, Mr. Hawkins." Noah presses his hand against my back and guides me into my own house. I guess my feet cannot move on their own.

"Gosh for the thousandth time Noah, call me Bill."

"Okay, well, Bill. We knew we had to come when Mrs. Ha... I mean, when Lydia called." I feel his warm hand leave my back and he starts to back away. "I'll just be on my way."

"No, Noah. You need to sit down, too." I see my mom come out of the kitchen with a tray full of hot chocolate with a heap of whipped cream on the top and cinnamon covering almost the entire surface of the whipped cream. "Unless you have a curfew."

"No, ma'am. I can stay." Noah takes my hand and leads me to the couch. My mom crouches down a bit so that the tray is at our eye level. "Here."

"Are you okay, Mom?" I say, my voice cracking a little. Noah squeezes my hand as I reach for the hot chocolate. I don't even take a sip, just set it on the end table next to me.

My mom and dad finally sit down on the couch across from me and Noah. My heart is beating so fast, I am convinced that it is echoing off the walls.

My mom clears her throat and wipes some tears from

underneath her eyes. "No, I'm not." My pulse blocks out all the sound and I zero in on my mom's voice. "I'm sick."

Noah's hand squeezes mine even harder. It's like he already knows what the news is.

"I have cancer."

I don't even remember collapsing onto the floor and scooting over to my mom. All I can say is, "No, no, no." I nestle in my mom's lap and just say, "But you are going to be okay, right? You have to be okay, right?"

I glance over at my dad, who has tears streaming down his face. And then look over at Noah, whose hands are clasped together and pressed against his mouth. I can see his eyes also getting watery.

"They found a lump during my mammogram and they suspected cancer. And it is. They caught it pretty early–stage 2, which means that it has unfortunately spread to a few lymph nodes. It's going to be a long road of testing and chemo and recovery and hopefully I can reach remission." She turns my head towards her and cradles my face, "It's going to be okay, Evie. We just have to be strong."

As much as I want to be strong, I can't right now. This can't be real. I am waiting for my mom to wake me up from this nightmare and for her to be perfectly healthy. "Why didn't you tell me sooner?"

Her pained eyes meet mine. "I wanted to know all the information before I told you. I didn't want you to worry and assume the very worst."

How can this not be the very worst? "I am worried, though. I don't want to be strong for this, Mom." Tears run over my cheeks. "I can't be strong for this right now. This is not fair." I lean into my mom's lap as she caresses my hair. Then I feel the touch of the three people I love most in this world on my back, comforting me in the worst moment of my life.

How can the best day of my life become the worst day of my life?

5

Evie

Gerard and I open the door and exit the Pilates studio that just opened up this summer. It was a massive deal and was the most talked-about topic for weeks. We rarely get any big chain anything in Hollybury. Sweat is dripping all along my back and my legs are shaky as I walk down the steps and head across the street toward Dorsey's Diner. That small protein bar was not enough to keep my hunger at bay.

I hear a groan next to me. "Oh my gosh, girl, my entire body is shaky and I am famished. Why the hell did you convince me to do Pilates? It's a special kind of torture."

I look both ways before crossing the street. "I needed to blow off some steam. And have you ever done hot yoga? Now that's a special kind of torture."

"Let me guess. You are still mad at your parents for keeping Noah their dirty little secret?" Gerard wiggles his eyebrows and I can tell he has all these dirty thoughts running through his mind about Noah. I do not want to talk about this right now. I just want to eat because if I don't get food in my system in the next five minutes, I will turn into my alter-ego of a hangry monster. No one wants to see that.

I pull open the door to Dorsey's Diner and hear the bell chime above our heads. The smell of coffee fills the air and the familiar sounds of the hustle and bustle from the kitchen, the clinging of forks and spoons against porcelain plates and mugs and the constant chatter among Hollybury residents is comforting. The breakfast rush is definitely underway, but luckily we find a small table for two near the window.

I already know what I want but Gerard insists on taking the longest time known to man to decide on what he wants to eat, a trait I discovered while we were in college. It doesn't matter if he has been to the restaurant before, he insists on taking his sweet time and perusing every inch of the menu. "So, are you mad?" Dammit he will not let this go, but I still don't want to have this conversation in a restaurant filled with the world's biggest gossipers. I swear the sign for Hollybury should read: *Welcome to Hollybury Population 9,813, Home of the Gossips.* And I know everyone is still reeling from the gazebo show

Noah and I gave them a couple days ago. It was not my finest hour.

"Let's order," I say to hopefully distract Gerard from pressing the subject.

Gerard flips over the menu and pretends to read it. "You aren't getting off that easy, Little Miss Thang. Okay, I get being upset that they kept a secret from you and low-key hired him without talking to you about it, but if I found out that my ex-boyfriend, albeit the love of my fucking life, is now back in town and working with me to fulfill my dreams, I would fall head-over-heels without question."

Even though Gerard hit the nail on the head, I can't help but be cautious about letting my heart accept Noah back into my life. I let him go for a reason and I am scared of what him being back in town means. I don't even want to think that it's permanent because if I have learned anything in life, it is to let go of any expectations. Because the moment I had expectations, that's when life dismantled them. I want to free Noah from any expectations about him being back. The implications. The sheer memories that come into my mind is too much to bear right now.

But damn if he doesn't look good as hell.

The queen bee of town gossip, Miss Lizzie, comes over and says, "So I saw that Noah Pearson is back in town." Her fiery dyed red hair and matching red lips block my sight of the chalkboard with the daily specials.

"Nothing gets past you, Miss Lizzie." I pretend to look at the menu even though I have had it memorized since high school and basically get the same breakfast every time I come in here. Mr. Dorsey comes over with some coffee and water and I start chugging down the water. I was fresh out of water in the middle of class.

"And I forgot about what a tall drink of water he is. If I was thirty years younger, I would climb him like a tree." Water goes down the wrong pipe, giving me a coughing fit. Lizzie and Gerard start giggling like they are in on an inside joke that I am not privy to.

"I'm with you there, honey," Gerard chimes in. "The amount of times I have run into walls or typed the wrong thing in the system at the inn because I was distracted by him, is too many times to count. And that has been just the past couple of days. I regret nothing though. Oh and that chef's uniform!" He wiggles his eyebrows and I roll my eyes because dammit, he isn't wrong. "It's a sight to see, let me tell you, Miss Lizzie. I wish I was the dough he is kneading."

Miss Lizzie smiles deviously and heads back to her table. I feel myself getting extremely hot. The image Gerard is painting is eliciting a very strong reaction from my entire body, especially my core. "Okay, can we please change the subject?"

"Hell no. That man is fine and I need all the details of your past. Including how big his d–"

"G! Stop, we are in public and at Dorsey's Diner, no less. This is hardly the place to talk about how big *that* is." I can feel myself turning even more red because I remember exactly how big he is. I am so happy I have the excuse that I am flushed from my workout class, instead of getting hot and bothered by the very detailed scenario playing out in my brain.

"Oh stop being such a prude. I need details like yesterday."

"What can I get you all for breakfast?" Dorsey comes over and I have never been so relieved to see him.

"Yes, I'll have my usual. Two eggs, overeasy, with hashbrowns, sausage, and some sourdough. Oh can I also have some slices of avocado on the side?"

"Ugh girl, now you are making me feel bad. I really want the cinnamon bun pancakes."

"Then get them."

"You are over here being all healthy and shit."

"Oh my gosh, just order what you want, G. If it makes you feel better, I will have a bite of it. I just like to get any sugar fix from my coffee or better yet, my hot chocolate, which is always loaded with whipped cream, by the way. And you have a better body than I do so I don't know what you are worried about, crazy."

After Gerard orders the pancakes and Mr. Dorsey heads off, Gerard leans across the table and says, "Did you ever do anything with whipped cream with Noah?"

"You need to stop!"

"Oh my good lord, you totally did! Was it like the scene from *Varsity Blues*? Oh please tell me. I am in a dry spell right now. I need all the details, honey."

And right then, almost as if the universe summoned him to Dorsey's, Noah walks in. Wearing a backwards hat, a grey hoodie that has New York Knicks printed on the front, jeans that fit him so tightly I can see every curve of his muscular legs and ass. He looks as good as ever and if that wasn't already unfair, that scruff he has acquired is the cherry on top of all of it. He was always clean-shaven in high school. I remember him being so happy when his facial hair started to grow out faster.

I feel every eyeball on me right now. Sweat is covering my body again and I pretend to focus on the menu, even though we already ordered. I cannot be caught staring slack-jawed at Noah right now. I hate being the center of attention and now I feel like I am under a microscope, with everyone taking notes about any little move I do or words I say. Any reaction when it comes to Noah is crucial to this town. We were their sweethearts. We were the ones who were supposed to be together forever. If it wasn't for that one phone call, we might have been.

"Oh girl, he is totally looking at you." Clearly, Gerard has no problem having his jaw reaching the floor and looking at Noah like he is about to devour him instead of the cinnamon bun pancakes he just ordered.

I pour three half-and-halfs and an excessive amount of sugar into my coffee. "That's great. Can we please talk about Christmas Eve and anything else we need to order?"

"We are not talking about work right now. We are at breakfast. We need a break from all things work. Except for Noah, of course. We will never stop talking about him. He is just too yummy. He looks like a fricken lost puppy dog right now. The way he is looking at you. Ugh this is devastating that you are not giving him the time of day. What a shame."

"Excuse me, I am not doing it to be mean. I just don't know what to say to him right now. I made a huge scene in front of the whole town the other day and I am a little embarrassed, to be honest. I will talk to him when I am ready." I am too chicken to look up from my coffee cup. If I do, I know I will fall to pieces. The bell dings above the door.

"Okay, the coast is clear. He is gone. Unfortunately," Gerard pouts.

"We will see him at the inn. Don't worry your pretty little mind. You can gawk at him all you want later." I sip my coffee.

"Girl, you are the one who should be worried. That man is going to sweep you off your feet and you aren't going to see it coming because you are too engulfed in the work. Try to enjoy life once in a while."

"I will enjoy life when the inn is up and running. Better yet, when it's profitable. Besides, Noah is probably over me by now, G. It's been seven years."

Dorsey returns to our table with our breakfast and then he places something else I didn't order next to my plate—a hot chocolate with whipped cream and cinnamon on top.

"Oh, thanks for the hot chocolate, Dorsey. You must have read my mind. I was just about to order one after I finished my coffee."

"Oh it wasn't me, sweetheart. This is all Noah."

My heart swells and Gerard raises his eyebrow as he drinks his own coffee, giving me a knowing look and a non-verbal *I told you so.*

"Yeah, that's a man who is so over you," Gerard says sarcastically.

AFTER BREAKFAST, Gerard and I decide to walk around the square which is decorated with beautiful green garlands, twinkling lights and large red bows. Our town always has a vintage Christmas look. It smells like snow and firewood at every turn. Frost outlines the shops' windows and a few years ago they installed speakers in each corner of the square, playing Christmas music on a constant loop. Warmth fills my body as I sip my hot chocolate with extra whipped cream and cinnamon. Everything is perfect this morning, with the one exception of Gerard yapping in my ear about how good Noah looks.

"Seriously girl, did he look this hot back in the day because, my word." Gerard fans himself dramatically. "I would've superglued myself to that man and never let him out of my sight. Remind me, why didn't it work out the first time?"

I exhale. It is a memory that has been keeping me up at night and not helping my chronic insomnia. Ever since I found out my mom had cancer, I haven't slept more than four hours at night. A constant loop of possible cures, my to-do lists, questions to ask the doctors at my mom's appointments and moments that could have changed the course of my life – specifically moments with Noah that I wish I could change – inhibited my sleep and it hasn't gotten better. My body must be used to it, though, because I've learned to function on limited sleep.

"He looks better." I answer the first part of Gerard's question at least. *So much better.* That's what sucks the most. It would be so much easier if he got less attractive over the years. He didn't let himself go at all. In fact, it is the exact opposite. I swear I could see his muscles through that damn sweatshirt. And the hat was overkill. I decide to answer the second part of

G's interrogation. I exhale and look down at my dark brown boots, "And...it's complicated."

"So un-complicate it."

If only Gerard knew how much I want that to be the case. If he only knew about the nights I cried myself to sleep because of regret and guilt and grief. If only he knew how complicated it all really is. And just when I can't get any more annoyed, I see a big, red *Sold* sign plastered over the *For Sale* sign outside of the old house I've been dreaming about since I was a little girl. Old Mrs. Johnson's house. I would dog-sit for her when I was older as a small side job and she was the nicest lady. Ever since she passed away a few years ago, the house has been sitting there, part of a horrendous estate battle between her children, who all moved out of this town the minute they graduated from Hollybury High. They couldn't wait to get out of here. And here I am, wanting to put down the deepest roots. I love traveling as much as the next person, but I always want a place to call home. A place that feels warm and comfortable and safe. Those were vibes I always felt in Mrs. Johnson's home.

I envisioned myself buying it from her and renovating it just enough to bring my style to the house without compromising the historical and architectural integrity. Much like I did to the Evergreen Inn. So, when the house finally went on the market about a month ago, my head ran wild with all the possible ways I could scrounge up the money to buy this house. Mrs. Johnson's kids clearly wanted to get rid of it because they priced it low. I also know for a fact that the house needs a lot of work, and many buyers are turned off by a house that would need to be completely gutted. So I had a good chance and basically everyone in town knows how much I love this house.

Who the hell bought this so quickly? I don't think there was even an open house for it. But I've also been distracted by all things Evergreen that I did not notice much else.

I see the only realtor in town, Sheryl Baker, come out of the house, locking up behind her. I nearly slip on ice as I quickly advance on poor Sheryl.

"Excuse me, Miss Sheryl, when did this house sell?"

"The new owner just closed on it about an hour ago. It was a cash offer so it was a pretty quick transaction and the sellers were motivated to sell."

Damn. That was fast. "Um, is it someone new in town who bought it? Or is it a Hollybury resident?"

"Now, dear, I can't disclose that information."

I reach out and touch her forearm. "Please, Sheryl."

"All I am going to say is that he is an investor from New York."

I nod. Of course this rich New Yorker would come in and turn something as beautiful as this old historic home into something modern and chic and completely null of character. My worst nightmare.

Sheryl briefly squeezes my hand. "I'm sorry, dear. I have to drop off these keys to the new owner. I know how much you wanted this house, Evie. The kids just couldn't resist this offer. It was a good one."

"I understand. Thank you, Miss Sheryl. Have a good day."

Sheryl walks down the beautiful path leading to the

sidewalk and makes her way towards her little office in the square.

I turn my head toward my dream house and take it all in. I am not sure how long the exterior is going to look like this. I am locking these visuals away in my treasure box inside my brain and throwing away the key.

Gerard walks up behind me, "You okay, E?"

I wipe off tears trickling down my cheek and turn to him. "Yeah. I will be. I think I'm gonna head home and shower. Want to meet back at the inn in an hour?"

Gerard interlocks his arm with mine and smiles. "Sounds good to me, queen. I'll bring the hot chocolate. Extra cinnamon and whipped cream for you." He winks at me and that small gesture reminds me of how blessed I really am with friends like Gerard. He is someone I can count on to not only give it to me straight but also show me unconditional love. He is the brother I never had and that's what I have to focus on. The dreams and blessings that are in my life right now instead of the dreams and blessings that once were.

Still, there is a small part of me that wishes I could talk to the new owner and convince them not to completely destroy the beauty this home has to offer. I wish I knew who it was.

6

Evie

The next day, Gerard and I head to the local Christmas tree farm. Being in the undecorated inn was making me queasy and I needed a change of scenery – and, if I am being honest with myself, I needed to create some space between me and Noah. I thought him being confined to the kitchen would stifle the butterflies fluttering around in my stomach. Out of sight, out of mind, right? I guess that theory is thrown out the window when your hot ex-boyfriend is busy cooking the most delicious foods and the scents of those dishes are filling every nook and cranny of the building.

Now this is what I needed. The smell of fresh Christmas trees. "I love the smell of Christmas trees. Don't you, Gerard?"

Between leaving my car and the entrance to the Christmas tree farm, Gerard has managed to bundle himself up so much that the only skin exposed is his face. "This whole town smells like this farm...so I guess. I am freezing. How are you just in that small coat and little beanie? You are a special kind of crazy to love this weather."

"What's not to love?"

"Everything."

I roll my eyes. "Okay, Scrooge. Might as well add a 'Bah Humbug' to the end of that sentence." The snow crunches underneath my boots. "Okay, we are on a mission. We are looking for the *perfect* tree, Gerard. This is for the main living room and I want it to be magical."

Gerard rubs his hands together and blows into them. I am convinced that he has a thousand layers of gloves on. "I get it, girl. No Charlie Brown Christmas tree vibes. More Clark Griswold. I understand the vision. Are we going for a theme with the tree?"

"We have to keep it classic. I was thinking white lights with rose gold, gold and silver ornaments. Pretty velvet bows hanging from the tree branches. And of course a star on the top."

"Sounds fabulous." He gestures toward one of the hundreds of trees on this lot. "How about this one?"

I turn and look. It is a nice tree, but not exactly as full as I envisioned. "Mmmm, that is close but I think I want it to be a little fuller than that. But great height!"

We keep walking and see a stand with hot chocolate. This day is looking up. "Hey, G, do you want some hot chocolate?"

"Oh none for me, girl. I am going to keep walking around seeing if I can find this elusive tree for you."

"Okay, I will come and find you when I am done."

I approach the stand and notice that Jeremy Sullivan, one of my former classmates who was also on the football team with Noah, is running the stand. A huge smile spreads across his face as I come nearer. "Hey Evie! It's so nice to see you!"

I tuck my hair behind my ear and give a smile back. "Hey Jeremy. Things are going well. Kind of crazy with getting the bed and breakfast ready to open."

"Yeah, I heard that you and your parents bought the old inn and have been renovating it. I think it's great. Bring some new life into this old town. Do you want some?" He gestures to the large carafe of hot chocolate.

Tingles travel across my body as I fully take him in. I don't remember him being so tall. His blonde, wavy hair is peeking out underneath his black beanie and his brown eyes are gleaming in the bright sunlight. I snap out of whatever temporary trance I am in. "Yes please, thank you!"

He pours some hot chocolate in a to-go cup and asks, "Marshmallows?" Not my first choice, but I doubt he has what I usually put on my hot chocolate on hand. This is a small Christmas tree farm, after all, with no refrigerator in sight.

"Sure."

He brings out a bag of mini marshmallows. "Take as many as you want."

"Thanks." I smile. I start pouring from the bag and some marshmallows fall to the ground. Shit. I bend down to pick them up.

"Here, let me help you." I look up to see Noah, who is wearing a dark blue beanie and a gray hoodie underneath a tan jacket. Forget about the tingles I just felt for Jeremy. My body is on fire right now. And the butterflies resume their usual fluttering. I did not think that after seven years, Noah could have the same effect on me as he did when we were teenagers. I was clearly wrong.

"What are you doing here? I thought you were going to be busy in the kitchen all day." It comes out harsher than I intend. Noah's presence just throws me so off-balance, right when I was finally finding some stable ground. It's really a cruel joke from the universe.

Noah tosses the marshmallows into a nearby trash can and clears his throat. "I needed to take a break and get some fresh air." His eyebrows pinch together as he places his hands in his jacket pockets. "I overheard your parents say that you went to go find a tree. Figured you might need some help getting it back."

I open my mouth to insist that I am fine and can handle it myself when Jeremy pipes in, "That's a service that we could provide for her if she needed it."

Noah's jaw clenches as he glares at Jeremy. Seriously, if looks could kill.

"Noah...you remember Jeremy, right?" I say in a sing-songy,

yet shaky voice. I cannot read how this interaction is going to go. Assessing Noah's glare, I am expecting the worst.

Noah's features soften, but he still doesn't showcase my favorite smile. A smile that makes me weak in the knees no matter how many times I have seen it. He reaches out his bare, veiny hand. "Yeah, of course, Jeremy Sullivan. Good to see you." Then I see Noah's classic charm show up when the crinkles around his eyes appear.

There's my Noah.

Jeremy's hand collides with Noah's. "I heard through the grapevine that you were back in Hollybury and I couldn't believe it, man. I thought you would never come back. Not after all the success you have achieved."

"Yeah, there was just an opportunity I couldn't pass up." Noah's eyes shift to me for a split second, then jet back to Jeremy. "I wouldn't pass up."

My stomach flips as I grab my hot chocolate covered in a mountain of marshmallows. I gesture over my shoulder. "I better try and find Gerard. Knowing him, he got lost in the maze of all of these trees. He has a terrible sense of direction." I start to walk away but remember I didn't pay. I turn quickly and a few more marshmallows fall from the mound. *Shit!* I reach into my pocket to grab some cash. "I forgot to pay you for the hot chocolate, Jer."

Jeremy waves me off. "No, Evie, don't worry. It's on the house." He winks at me and almost immediately I sense the furrowed brow has returned to Noah's perfect face. All signs of a friendly ceasefire are gone. Apparently he's in a fighting mood today.

I stuff the money back in my pocket. "Really? Thanks. And sorry about spilling half a bag of marshmallows on the ground."

He smirks at me. "No problem. Let me know when you find the perfect tree."

"Will do." I raise my small paper cup and start walking toward the sea of trees.

"I'll join you," Noah says spritely as he catches up with me. The heat from the hot chocolate penetrates my gloves, but I also feel some warmth from the man walking right to me. Strands of small, white Christmas lights zig-zag above our heads and the smallest of flurries start to fall from the powder-white sky.

"So." Noah's scruffy voice breaks through the jovial Christmas carols playing on the one large speaker by the entrance.

I take a sip of my hot chocolate and immediately burn my tongue. To distract myself from the searing pain, I retort, "So?"

"Since when do you like your hot chocolate with marshmallows? I thought you were a Redi-Whip-only-with-an-ungodly-amount-of-cinnamon-sprinkled-on-top kind of girl."

Something tugs at my heart a little for him remembering that about me. I keep a straight face even though my insides are twirling about like a ballerina doing pirouettes. "For a while now," I lie. It's not the best hot chocolate. Noah's is better.

"I see." He pauses. "So, how long have you and Sullivan been a thing?" he asks nonchalantly while perusing the evergreens around us.

My heart skips because of how ridiculous it is that Noah should think this. Off of a wink and smirk? Is he serious? If he only knew that I have not thought about dating since he left. I got so caught up in my mom's diagnosis, treatments, school and opening this bed and breakfast that I really did not have time to date. I was also trying to heal my shattered heart after our breakup that might as well have been on national news, the way the gossip travels around town.

I blow on my beverage and pretend to look at a tree. "We aren't."

"Hmmm." He puts his hands in the pocket of his hoodie. "You know he had a crush on you in high school, right?"

I whip my head toward him and almost shriek, "What?! No he didn't. There is no way."

"Way." He shakes a branch of one of the trees and sparkly snowflakes fall to the ground.

"That's ridiculous. First of all, Jeremy dated like half of the cheerleading squad. And second," I pause, my heart sinking in my chest, "I was with you."

"That's exactly why he never did anything. He knew I would pummel him if he even looked in your direction. You were off-limits."

I can't shake the look of death he gave Jeremy back at the hot chocolate stand. "And now?"

We stop in the middle of the winding walkway. I look up at Noah, who is looking down at me like he is about to do things to me that he hasn't done to me in years. Something tells me that Noah has gotten better at more than just cooking while we have been apart. Jealousy now courses through me as I think of all the women he has been in bed with since me. I shouldn't be jealous. It is ridiculous. But it brings me a little comfort that Noah might be a little jealous of Jeremy right now.

The snowflakes are getting larger and fall on Noah's eyelashes and scruff. They slowly melt away as a smirk causes his dimples to appear. "Now what?"

I study his face. "Am I off-limits?"

His jaw tenses again. A strand of hair flies across my nose, and he reaches for it and tucks it behind my ear. His finger grazes my jawline softly, making my heart pound hard within my chest. He whispers, "Always, Evie."

"Girl I think I found the perf–" Gerard bulldozes in and shatters the snowglobe Noah and I just occupied. Noah retreats and sticks his hands back in his coat pockets and I raise my eyebrows and drink my cooled-off hot chocolate. I guzzle nearly half of it before Gerard speaks again, "-fect tree." Gerard scans me and Noah and has a perceptive look in his eyes. I am praying to all the gods that Gerard doesn't say anything Gerard-like. "Oh, I didn't realize I was interr–"

"You aren't interrupting anything, G." My voice squeaks in my protest. Noah retreats and rubs his jaw with the same hand that was just on my skin. I keep whatever focus I have on Gerard's stunned face. "You said you found the one! Show me."

Ten minutes later, Jeremy, Gerard and Noah strap the tree to my dad's truck that I borrowed for this little venture. It's is like watching a twisted version of The Three Musketeers completing a mission. Gerard gets in the passenger seat and starts the truck so it can warm up.

Jeremy taps the side of the truck and walks toward me.

I reach for my cash once again in my coat pocket, "Jer, thank you so much for all your help today! Your family's lot always has the best trees. Every year."

He holds up a hand and shakes his head. "Your money isn't good here, Evie."

I scoff, "Jer, please let me pay you for the tree. You already gave me hot chocolate for free."

"Nope. I am not going to accept it."

I let out a small laugh and glimpse a broody Noah standing within earshot of our conversation. That's why what comes out of Jeremy Sullivan's mouth next surprises me. "So, Evie, do you want to go to dinner sometime?"

Did he really just ask that with Noah being so close? Apparently, in Noah's eyes I am still off-limits but in truth, I haven't been his in seven years. *Always, Evie.* I nervously play with my gloves. I don't know how to answer this question. Noah is all I've ever known, but I need to at least try to get over him.

"Hey, you don't have to answer right now." Jeremy eyes Noah, who slams the door to his old Chevy truck and revs up the engine. "How about I text you later? And no pressure. I understand if you aren't ready."

"Sounds good."

Jeremy opens my door and I climb in.

"And thanks again for the tree. And the hot chocolate."

He closes the door. "Anytime, Evie Hawkins. I'll text you later."

"Bye." I wave at Jeremy as he walks away. I direct my attention to the steering wheel and picking out the perfect Christmas playlist to play on our drive. Even though we are ten minutes away, it's still important to have the right music on. I hear the screeching of Noah's tires as he drives off toward the inn.

Ella Fitzgerald's *Sleigh Ride* comes through the speakers. My favorite. I cannot wait to get back to the bed and breakfast, put on my Santa hat, blast Christmas music and start decorating the inn. It's going to look like Santa's workshop after I pull out all the decor.

I keep my eyes on the road but I can't help but look over for a second at Gerard, who has a shit-eating grin on his face.

"What?"He holds up his hands in surrender. "I didn't say anything."

"Say that to your face, G. I know what you are thinking."

"Really, friend? Do tell."

"That I am stupid not to accept Noah back into my life. That I shouldn't go on a date with Jeremy Sullivan because that would complicate things."

"Hmm. Yes to the first. I mean, have you seen that man? My goodness. But no to the second."

"You think it's a good idea to go out with Jer?" I blast the heater and put my right hand up against the vent.

"I think that it's good to complicate things once in a while. See where hearts truly lie. True feelings and conversations happen when things get stirred up. Stir them up, girl. And have fun while doing it."

7

Noah

I walk into the dimly lit pub and remove my coat. I blow hot air into my hands to defrost them from the frigid air outside. An enthusiastic, dark curly-haired woman waves wildly at me. "Over here, Noah!" A feeling of warmth and familiarity travels across my body and I know that this place is really my home. Although I haven't seen Allie and Kevin in over seven years, it's really like no time has passed.

I approach the table, jacket slung over my right forearm. Allie jumps out of the booth and practically tackles me. "Oh my gosh, Noah! It has been way too long." After her suffocating bear hug – a hug that Allie is notoriously known for – she releases me, then hits me as hard as she can in the chest. "Unacceptable. Seven years is unacceptable."

I bring her back in for another hug and say, "I know it is, Al. I am sorry it took me so long to come back here. Hollybury is home." I turn to Kevin, who has been my best friend since kindergarten. There is a small twinge of guilt that settles in my stomach. Kevin is not a person who holds grudges or makes you feel bad for the choices you make. He's the type of friend that I don't have to talk to on a daily basis, but when we are together, it's like we have not skipped a beat. I think everyone needs to have a friend like that. He's really like the brother I never had.

Kevin steps toward me for a hug. "Come here, big guy. Look at you. I can't believe you bulked up, buddy. You'd think since you didn't go to college for football, you'd let yourself go."

I slide into the booth, "Even more reason to work out. I did not have the luxury of a scheduled practice or training every day. I had to find it within myself not to let up." I hate how much I took for granted the built-in workouts I had every day. Luckily, my athletic nature kicks into gear no matter what. Plus, working out gives me the opportunity to let out any frustrations that have lingered since I left Hollybury.

"Well tonight we are celebrating your return home, bro. The first round is on me."

"Do my eyes deceive me? Noah Pearson?" Royce Walker, owner of Cherry Willow, finally comes over to our table with a wide smile, arms outstretched, ready for a hug. I'm happy Royce is still here and that Cherry Willow is doing so well. This man is like another father figure to me. Although I never met my dad, my mom had a village of people who stepped in and helped raise me. Not only did I have my grandpa, I also had Evie's dad, Royce and my football coach, Coach Staten, to guide me and mold me into the man I am today.

"Royce. How have you been?" I meet him halfway. He slaps my back a few times before letting me go. His white chef's coat is laden with sauces and other food particles. I scan his face and see the same man who I learned how to run a kitchen and a restaurant from. He gave Carmy Berzatto from *The Bear* a run for his money some days. He was so passionate about what he does for a living, he would get so caught up in the present circumstances and lose it on us if things were not perfect. I thrive on structure and order, so his personality was exactly what I needed in high school and definitely prepared me for culinary school. Now looking at him though, I see that there is a softness in his eyes. His eyes crinkle heavily on the sides as he speaks, "Rumor has it you are now the executive chef at Miss Evie's new bed and breakfast. Have they decided on a name yet? I know that's been a topic of discussion at the monthly town meetings, right guys?" Royce looks over at Allie and Kevin for their approval of his statement. They nod vigorously in response.

"Um, yeah. They did. It's the Evergreen Inn. And the rumors are true. Well, sort of. Evie has me working there on a trial basis. She says she will make a final decision after the soft opening on Christmas Eve." I shrug and raise my eyebrows. "I'll see how that goes."

"Oh, she's putting you through the ringer, huh? I've always

liked her." He pats me on the back. "What are you having tonight, Pearson?"

"I'll have a Blue Moon."

"Same for us, too, Royce. Thank you," Allie says.

"Be right back with those drinks, then I've gotta go make my rounds. Our new waitress in training should be over here to take your order soon. Take it easy on her. It's literally her first day on the job. Make sure you say bye before you leave, yeah? See you two lovebirds later." He points to my best friends, who start giggling like they are back in high school.

"How is it that after all this time, you both still nauseate me with your cuteness?" I give them crap, but that's only because I know they can take it. It also helps that they are just as aware of their nauseating cuteness.

"C'mon, look at this face." Allie squeezes Kevin's cheeks so he looks like a fish. "It's impossible to not love that face." Then Kevin grabs Allie's chin and brings her in for a kiss that would probably be more appropriate in an intimate setting. That's the thing with these two – they never cared what the world thought about their love.

Royce comes back with our round of beers and chuckles, already immune to Kevin and Allie's antics and lack of embarrassment of their public display of affection. I chug about half of my beer and after what seems like ten minutes, Allie and Kevin finally come up for air.

Kevin looks at the table. "Oh shit, when did these get here?"

"While you both were sucking face in front of the entire restaurant." I chuckle. "Seriously. Nauseating."

"Oh, stop. You and Evie were just as bad," Kevin says.

Allie's eyes get wide and she kicks Kevin under the table. "Ow, babe. What the—?"

Allie nods over to me, places her hand on her chin and mouths, "Sorry, Noah."

"Crap. And the award for the brainless asshole goes to..." Kevin points to himself.

I missed our friendly banter and teasing, but that still doesn't stop my insides from twisting. I fucking miss kissing Evie like that. "Nah, you're good, man."

In true Allie form, she tries to make everything right and distract from any awkwardness in any conversation or situation. "So, you need to tell us everything about culinary school. Was it intense? What is your favorite food you learned how to make? Oh, I saw that you traveled a bunch! What country had the best food? Tell me all the culinary secrets so I can learn to be a better cook for this one." Allie points at Kevin.

"You're already an amazing cook, honey. It was just that one time that you burned the soup. And the grilled cheese and the..."

"Okay, I think you just proved my point, Kev." Allie scrunches her face.

I cock an eyebrow. "You burned soup?"

"Yes, Judgy McJudgerson. I burned soup. I forgot to stir it 'frequently' as the recipe called for. Not all of us can be a world-renowned chef."

"To be fair, I don't think you have to be a world-renowned chef to not burn soup, Allie," I tease.

"See!" Kevin throws up his hands. "That's what I have been saying."

Allie and Kevin start their own side conversation about the soup debacle and meanwhile I am in my own head about Evie and her unwillingness to follow a recipe's directions. There is only one thing that Evie is an expert at making and that's her grandmother's cinnamon shortbread cookies. She never allowed me to help while she made those. Then, almost like she is summoned by my thoughts of her, Evie walks in covered in her bright teal winter coat and my whole world hits the pause button. Her red wool scarf is wrapped around her neck. Her face is radiant and glowing and everything that made me fall in love with her.

My heart starts racing as she moves past the hostess. Is this a setup? Did Allie and Kevin invite Evie to this dinner also and not tell me about it? They would.

That theory is thrown out the fucking window when Evie turns her head to someone behind her and who is it...none other than Jeremy Sullivan. Evie is out on a date with Jeremy fucking Sullivan? I heard him ask her out back at the Christmas tree lot. I just didn't think she would say yes to him. Not because she can't date anyone else. It's that I don't want her to date anyone else. I am selfish as hell. Especially when it comes to Evie Hawkins.

Allie and Kevin's voices are drowned out by my thoughts about the woman I never stopped loving on a fucking date with Jeremy. I know we were buddies in high school, but seeing him sitting across from Evie, making her laugh the way I used to. My heart tugs. I want to know what the hell Jeremy said that is making her laugh that way. My eyes start to wander up and down her body. Her hair looks almost a deep golden brown in the dim lighting and the shortest dress in the world must've inched up slightly when she sat in the booth because her toned legs are on full display.

Evie must feel me glaring in their direction because she quickly steals a glance at me and knocks over the rolled-up silverware the waitress just put on the table. The metal utensils hit the floor and the entire restaurant's attention is suddenly on my girl. Jeremy comes to her rescue and picks up the scattered silverware. She is profusely apologizing. As she scoots in the booth, her dress rides up her thigh and I have the urge to go over there to cover her up with her coat so no one can see her exposed skin but me. *What the hell is she doing wearing such a short fucking dress in the dead of winter in Connecticut?*

A sharp pain hits my shin. "Ow, what the fuck?" I turn toward Kevin.

"Dude, we've been calling your name for the past two minutes. You good?"

It takes all my self-control to avoid resuming my staredown with Evie and Jeremy. I gulp down the rest of my beer. "Why wouldn't I be?"

Allie elbows Kevin in the ribs and nods over to the booth across the restaurant. His demeanor shifts. "Damn, I am about to put my foot in my mouth. I keep messing up tonight. Sorry bro."

"Nothing to be sorry about. She's single. She can do whatever she wants." Saying those words leaves a sour taste in my mouth. I never thought I would refer to Evie Hawkins as single. For so long, she was mine. I need to change the subject as fast as I can so I don't charge over to Evie and Jeremy's table and most likely ruin everyone's evening. "Tell me about what's been going on with you two."

I learn that Allie and Kevin are trying to start a family. The way their faces light up allows me temporary relief from the hell of being in the same vicinity as the love of my life and her sub-par date. Kevin is doing well in medical school, aiming to become a family doctor. People thought he was just a dense jock, but he was always the smart one in our small friend group. I know he is going to be very successful because he can diffuse any stressful situation and he has the best bedside manner. When I injured my knee, he was always by my side, doing massive amounts of research and writing down all the questions he was curious about for me to ask my own doctors. He was one of those people who didn't have to try very hard to ace tests–he just retained information so easily. Allie, meanwhile, is crushing it as a dental hygienist and she also got her certification to be a Pilates instructor so she could start teaching at the fancy new studio. It makes me happy that my friends are doing so well and are so happy in Hollybury.

Allie is in the middle of telling a horror story of a client biting her while she was cleaning their teeth when movement from across the restaurant triggers my attention. Evie scoots out of the booth, adjusting her dress down her legs with each scoot. She heads toward the bathroom and I know this is my opportunity.

"Hey guys, I'm running to the restroom real quick. Be right back." Allie and Kevin aren't even phased, which is typical since they are lost in each other's eyes ninety-nine percent of the time.

I finish off my beer – at this point, I have lost count of the number I've consumed tonight.

I know this restaurant like the back of my hand and instead of taking a left to head to the restroom, I stay right and hide next to the entrance of the kitchen. I nod to the confused waiters coming out with trays of food and drinks. I am seconds away from barging into the ladies room to talk with Evie but the door swings open and she steps out. I discreetly and smoothly grab Evie by her arm and pull her into the kitchen.

The hustle and bustle. The loud clangs of dishes in the sink. The sizzle coming from the frying pans. The yelling and code words. Everything that makes a kitchen run as smooth as can be – it is not for the faint of heart. But I love the pace of the kitchen and how, like football, everyone in a kitchen has a job. Something they are responsible for. If one person isn't on their A-game, the rhythm is thrown off and success usually slips from your fingers. It opens the door for mistakes. And a lot of times, there aren't second, third or fourth downs to recover from your screw ups. For a moment, I miss it. Working in the inn is so quiet, but I'd give up all the hustle and bustle for her.

This restaurant is the reason I wanted to become a chef in the first place. When I worked here in high school, I received a lot of informal on-the-job training and it really sparked my love for cooking and wanting to run a restaurant someday.

The blueprint of this place hasn't changed. I nod and wave at the cooks that have been a part of this institution since its inception. The homecoming in Hollybury has been nothing but welcoming...well, with one exception. Clutching Evie's arm, I weave my way through the work stations and reach the back of the kitchen to my destination: the pantry. Save for the freezer and refrigerator, this is the only space in the kitchen that has a door so we can talk privately. I close the pantry door behind me and that's when I realize that Evie is trying (and failing) to get my attention by hitting my forearm and repeating my name.

"What the hell are you doing?" Her eyes are ablaze and I know she is pissed and thrown off-guard. But it is worth it. My body is aching that she is not wearing that dress for me because what I wouldn't give to rip it off her body right now. *Focus, Noah.*

"You must be cold," I say with a straight face.

"What?" The crease between her eyebrows deepens and her deep green-blue eyes are almost black with fury.

I match her fury and cross my arms. "You are aware it's the middle of winter, right? Why the hell are you wearing that dress?"

Evie stands firmly in front of me and places her hands on her hips. *God she's still the hottest thing to walk this earth.* "Because I wanted to. I didn't know you became a fashion expert while you were away. Why did you drag me in here, Noah?"

"I wanted to talk with you, and since you insist on leaving me high and dry every chance you get at the inn and around town and won't return any of my texts or calls outside of working hours, I figured this is the only way."

"By kidnapping me outside of the ladies room?"

"Kidnapping is a strong word. And would you have been willing to talk with me otherwise? I weighed all the options and even though this is a risky route to take, I think it's worth it."

She crosses her arms. "And how do you figure that?"

"I got you to talk with me." I flicker a grin at her.

Color rises to her cheeks. Her eyelashes flutter before she speaks. "Speaking of calling and texting, how did you get my number?"

"Lydia gave it to me. I figured I need the contact information of my bosses. You know, in case I needed to call in sick. You are my employer after all, Evie." I step closer to her and her arms drop to her sides. She's wavering a little.

"That's true." She studies my face. "In that case, you are fired."

"Okay, then, I am fired." I step closer. I can smell her cherry chapstick and sweet vanilla perfume and it's just as intoxicating as the alcohol I have been drinking. She is wearing shimmery eyeshadow and her long eyelashes are skimming her eyebrows. "Enjoy explaining to your folks that the chef they were excited to get for their inn, an inn by the way they want to see become a success, especially for their only daughter, whose dream they are helping her achieve, is no longer the chef." She opens her mouth to snap back but then closes it quickly when it becomes clear that I am right. "Are you enjoying your date?"

She pauses and straightens up her back, trying to resist the inevitable heavy, heated air between us. I know my Evie. She is too stubborn to give in when she has fought so hard to get to the state she is in now. I want to respect that. She always deserves respect. The devilish side of me tells me to fuck it and take her back right now. But my good will is stronger than my devilish side.

She finally answers, "I *was*, until a psychopath grabbed me by my arm and held me hostage. And a drunk psychopath, no less." She starts to go around me but I step in front of her and place my hands on either side, locking her in. It brings back memories of when we would find all the secret places to make out or have sex, giggling and being so impassioned with each other and we would forget about the outside world. Nothing else mattered but us. We were two crazy teenagers in love. We had a plan, and then we fucked up that plan.

Evie avoids looking at me at all. I take a chance and breach the invisible wall Evie built the moment she saw me in the kitchen at the inn. "Look at me." I lift her chin–a gesture that had a high success rate with Evie back then, so much so that she deemed it the swooniest thing I could ever do. I am pulling out all the swoon. That's all I have left to pull.

Evie's eyelashes flutter. "I need to get back to my date, Noah." Her eyes are pleading with me, begging me to let her go. That look sobers me up and I let my hands fall to my sides. That look is my Achilles heel. She knows how to soften me in my toughest moments. I let her move past me and exit the pantry. I place my hands on my hips and hang my head down. It sets my teeth on edge to see her with another man. This whole scenario is throwing me for a loop and usually I pride myself on being a quick problem-solver. Evie is going to need concrete proof that I am not leaving this time.

8

Evie

Is there no other restaurant open in this town?

Out of all the places Noah, Kevin and Allie could have gone to meet up for dinner and drinks, why did it have to be this one? I mean other than Dorsey's Diner, it's my favorite spot to eat. I was already anxious about going out with Jeremy at all. I know that the whole town has eagle eyes on me to begin with, and the questions have been incessant ever since I finished college. *Are you dating anyone? How are you doing, sweetie?* And the worst one of all: *Have you talked to Noah lately?* Just what this town needs is more gossip and I am providing all the juicy secrets and officially publicly declaring I am moving on. Well, trying to move on at least.

My palms are sweaty and my heart is beating a mile a minute. I cannot believe Noah pulled me into the kitchen and schmoozed his way into my lovely evening with Jeremy. I have not felt this way in a while. Completely annoyed. And completely hot and bothered. It is disorienting.

"Are you okay? You seem really hot." Jeremy's eyes widen in horror. "I mean flustered. Not that you're not hot. I've always thought you were hot. I just always had to bite my tongue when it came to my feelings because of Noah. I never thought in a million years that I would have a chance with you. I'll go ahead and shut up now." He drinks some water and plays with the collar of his shirt, obviously completely nervous about being here with me. I don't blame him. Hollybury is the town you go to for not only the Christmas spirit, but for all the hot gossip. I know that our date is going to be the talk of the town. I don't know if anyone saw me and Noah go into the kitchen or not, but that would likely add to the scandal that Evie Hawkins is dating someone other than Noah Pearson.

Jeremy's flustered state is endearing. And I am extremely flattered. Back in high school, I honestly thought that Noah was the only one who thought I was hot. He did not let me doubt his love for me. Not once. My heart tugs a bit because deep down I know I messed that up. I ruined what we had because I was in a perpetual state of fear.

"I'm fine," is all I can muster. I don't know what else to say. I don't want to talk about Noah right now in front of Jeremy. I sip my French 75 to buy myself time in this weird personal hell I am trapped in. I want to be over Noah. That would make things easier on the job front. Then I can hire him without any complications. Without any strings, just in case he ultimately decides to return to New York City. I would not care anymore. I don't want to care anymore.

The rest of the dinner goes well enough. Jeremy isn't the worst to look at and he actually makes me laugh. A guy hasn't made me laugh in a long time. And I am not doing it to humor him. All my reactions to Jeremy have been completely genuine.

Jeremy can tell all the jokes in the world, but they are not enough to fully distract me from Noah's stare. It's like he is branding me with his stare. I feel like the entire restaurant is watching my every move with Jeremy because everyone remembers me and Noah together. We were attached at the hip and Noah was never shy with public displays of affection. I blush from the memories. Before I can gesture to the waiter, another French 75 appears before me. I cock and eyebrow and look at Jeremy, who looks equally as surprised as me. I turn my head to the right and see cocky-as-hell Noah raising his own beer and giving me a wink. Damn him. That wink is damn near irresistible.

Hell, it's all the way irresistible.

I poke around at my food. I usually never hesitate to eat. Food is my love language. But my appetite has been replaced for the night with nervous butterflies. I don't know who the butterflies are for and it's pissing me off. I need to redirect them to the man sitting across from me instead of the man shooting daggers at me. Well, maybe the daggers are for Jeremy. But still, I need to leave.

"Hey, did you want to get out of here?" I reach over and touch his hand. I want to relieve this man of my suffocating past clouding my ability to fully enjoy this date.

Jeremy stutters, "Uh-um, sure. Yeah, sounds good." He waves down our waitress for the check. I tap the side of the French 75 glass and quickly glance back over at Noah, whose eyes are fixated on me. For a second, I swear he doesn't look cocky anymore. He looks defeated, which is not a look I am used to seeing on Noah Pearson's face. The waitress steps in my eyeline, breaking the invisible string holding Noah and me together still. A string that I thought would wear and tear and eventually break apart with time. I have never been so wrong in my entire life.

THE CAR RIDE conversation is filled with random memories from high school and stories about the teachers at Hollybury High. We talk about our college experiences and catch up about our families. "How is your mom doing?" Jeremy asks, hitting the blinker and turning onto my street. "I see her around town and she seems pretty lively."

I tuck some hair behind my ear. "She is doing really great, actually. Scans have been coming back clean and her energy has skyrocketed since she stopped doing treatments. They really wore her down and there were moments where she wasn't my mom. The light that makes up Lydia Hawkins was diminished temporarily and I didn't realize how much I missed that part of her until it was gone. I used to get so annoyed with how positive she was all the time. Even in dark times. *Especially* in dark times, and I didn't understand it. But now, I see that her positivity is her superpower and is one of the things that helped save her over and over and continues to save her."

"Your mom is the happiest person I've ever had the pleasure of meeting. I'm glad her illness didn't ruin that part of her." I don't even realize we are parked in my driveway when I stop my apparent therapy session. To be fair, he did ask me the question.

He kills the engine and quickly hops out of the car, runs around the front, and before I can open my own door, he opens it for me.

"Thank you," I say. "For that and for dinner. It was very nice. And thanks for giving me a reason to dress up. It's rare. I am usually dressed in some sort of leggings and oversized sweatshirt."

"You're welcome. And you do look extra beautiful tonight. Have I already said that?"

"Yes, but I appreciate it." This dress is too short for this weather, but it's my favorite dress and it makes me feel powerful and sexy. Still, my legs are freezing. I'm surprised they have not turned blue yet. I should have worn tights.

Jeremy takes his eyes off me for a second while we approach my front door. "Wow. No decorations yet? Your house is the only one on the block that doesn't have any Christmas lights or inflatable Christmas characters. I thought you were the Queen of Christmas."

I fiddle with my keys and smirk. "I've been a little busy with renovating and working on opening up an old historic inn and all. Queen of Christmas. I like that title. Maybe I should wear a sash around town so no one forgets who I am."

"No one forgets who you are, Evie. You are pretty unforgettable."

My heart tugs, and suddenly I develop butterfingers and drop my keys. I bend down to pick them up and apparently so does Jeremy, because as I stand back up, I knock the bottom of his jaw with the top of my head.

"Shit. I am so sorry, Jeremy. Are you okay? I didn't mean to do that!" I rub the top of my head, knowing there will for sure be a bump developing soon.

He massages his jaw. "It's okay, Evie. I am the one who should have just let you pick up your own keys. I was trying to be overly chivalrous and it bit me in the ass."

I let out a small chuckle and reach out to rub his jawline. "Seriously, are you sure you're okay?" This is quickly becoming one of those moments in the movies where the two characters kiss on the doorstep. If I really want to move on from Noah, I need to at least try again and see if there are any sparks between me and Jeremy.

Jeremy must read my mind because he starts leaning in. The scene from *Hitch* immediately pops into my head. He is leaning in that ninety percent. He is leaving the final ten percent for me.

So I take that extra ten percent and kiss him.

His kiss is soft and gentle. His fingers weave into my hair and he pulls me closer. I place my hands on his chest and deepen the kiss. His hands move from my hair to my back and he lowers them until they are on the crux of my lower back.

Even though he is kissing me and touching me in all the right ways, I feel...nothing. Nothing is shaking me. Nothing is making me feel the sparks I want to feel. The sparks I *need* to feel.

This kiss is nothing compared to *his* kisses. *His* touch. Everything about Noah has ruined me forever. This is the same thing that has happened with every guy I've tried to date. I've tried to step over the threshold of a new love. A new relationship. I have been unsuccessful with each attempt. And this kiss with Jeremy is no exception.

I stop the kiss because I don't want to lead him on or give him the impression I want more than just a kiss. "I'm sorry. I can't do this. It's not you, I swear."

He removes his hands from my lower back and takes a step back. "*It's not you, it's me.* I figured as much." I suddenly feel super guilty. But then Jeremy holds onto my hands and says something that I am not expecting him to say but is nevertheless the truth. "I think it's the person who couldn't stop looking at you in that restaurant."

My lips part in surprise. He shakes his head and says, "I am the fool who thought I could override the hold Noah still has on your heart. But I'm not that guy. And that's totally okay, Evie. Just be honest with me. I can handle it. Noah has had your heart since the moment you two met. Anyone who tries to get in between you both is an idiot. You guys are Noah and Evie. You two are meant to be."

"Jer, I am so sorry. I really had a great time with you tonight.

I promise. But you deserve to be with someone who can give you your whole heart." I swallow hard because I am about to tell him one of my truths that I have never said out loud. "I gave Noah my whole heart years ago and I don't think I ever got it fully back."

Jeremy brings me in for a bear hug. It is no longer fueled by any type of sexual tension. It feels like a big brother hug. I squeeze back. "You are seriously an incredibly decent man."

He rests his probably bruised chin on my head. "Seems like that's always been my setback."

"It's not a problem. It's an amazing quality. The right woman will be so lucky to have you as their person."

"I'm just not your person."

I shake my head and slightly shrug.

"Understood and I respect that." He kisses the top of my hand like the decent man he is. Most guys in my past got angry and defensive when I would stop anything from happening further, which only solidified my feelings for Noah. He never pressured me into anything. Never forced me to do anything with him. He respected me in all ways and always put me first. Other guys didn't understand because they didn't know Noah. Maybe Jeremy understands because he was there. Him and Noah were good friends who recognized that the love we had for each other was real, even though we were just kids.

"Well," Jeremy says, "you better head inside. I am sure you are freezing your ass off." He hugs me one more time and steps down my stairs. Snow starts to fall and I watch as he approaches his car. I'm inserting my key into the lock when I hear, "Hey, Evie!"

My head whips around. "Yeah?"

"Noah is a good man. He loves the hell out of you. Let him."

He drives away in a flash and I finally unlock the door. The heat in my house feels amazing against my icicle-ridden legs. I unbutton my teal coat and out of habit reach for my red scarf, but there is nothing to grab onto. *Shit. I left my scarf in the booth.* In my quick getaway from the restaurant, I left my favorite accessory.

I hurriedly take my phone from my handbag and look up the number for the restaurant. I would go back and see for myself, but I don't want to run into Noah again tonight. I am not strong enough for that. *He loves the hell out of you. Let him.*

"Hello? Hello, is anyone there?"

I snap out of it. "Yes, hi. This is Evie. Evie Hawkins. I was just there and left maybe thirty minutes ago. I left my scarf there in the booth. It's red. Can you check if it's still there? Maybe someone turned it in and you all put it in the lost and found."

"Please hold. I'll go check."

My heart is pounding again, like it did in the restaurant. I pace my living room, hoping that no one took it. I love that scarf. It may seem trivial to others, but it's of sentimental value. That scarf holds memories that a new scarf can never replace.

"Ma'am, you still there?"

"Yes!" I almost scream, then clear my throat and say in a lower tone, "Yes. I am here."

"There was no scarf in the booth or in our lost and found. Someone must have grabbed it. I'm sorry. If it turns up, we'll let you know."

Sadness overtakes me and I do my best to sound like I am not on the brink of a breakdown. "Okay, thank you for checking. Have a good evening."

"You too, ma'am." The call ends and I plop onto my couch. My eyes start misting. I can't believe it's gone. At this moment, I am glad I have my own place so I don't get asked a thousand questions from my parents about the date or why I am on the verge of an emotional breakdown. I kick off my heels and drape the softest, warmest, fuzziest blanket I own over my thawing legs. Stupid idea to wear this dress. What the hell was I thinking? *That you were possibly going to get some tonight and you wanted to be prepared. And that your ex-boyfriend is in town and maybe you would run into him?* I wrap myself in the fluffy blanket and walk over to my kitchen. I fill my light blue tea kettle with water and place it on the burner. I reach for a packet of dark hot chocolate and toss it next to my giant Santa Claus mug that I use year-round. In the fridge, I find the large red can of whipped cream.

I spray a large amount of whipped cream in my mouth as I return to my couch. I find the remote and browse through the plethora of Christmas movies at my disposal. I avoid all the ones that have anything to do with second chances. I need to escape my current situation. Not invite it in even more. I settle on my favorite Nancy Meyers film, *The Holiday,* and press play.

I am in for another sleepless night. At least Jack Black and Jude Law can keep me company.

9

Noah

I check my watch and see I have already run over five miles around the track that surrounds the practice field at Hollybury High. I woke up this morning feeling the indisputable need to blow off some steam after my encounter with the new love birds in town. *Did they kiss? Did she invite him inside her house or did he drop her off at her doorstep? Did she sleep with him? Did he have his hands all over her body?* Irritation channels through me and propels me to work out harder than I have in a long time. My hair is dripping with sweat and there is a dull ache in my knee. I need to stop. I go over to the bleachers and do an exorbitant amount of push-ups and sit-ups until my body shakes and my arms and abs feel like mush. Then I throw on my old Hollybury Huskies gray hoodie to fight off the cold breeze hitting my sweaty skin.

I squirt water into my mouth and slowly make my way over to the regular football stadium. The dead grass crunches underneath my feet as I walk to centerfield. There is a faded maroon H with an equally faded ferocious-looking husky right in the middle of the field. The silver bleachers stand high against the brittle grass. I put my hands in my pockets and can see my breath in front of me. This is where it happened. I remember it so clearly.

It was a play we ran over and over and, in hindsight, maybe that's how they got past the offensive line. The opponent watched the tapes and took notes on our playbook. The cheers from the crowd ring in my ears and I am seventeen years old again, ready for my life to change. Ready to be recruited to play football for a division one university. I called the play and the leather contacted my taped fingertips. I looked over to my right and then, next thing I knew, I felt a sudden, sharp pain and a pop in my left knee. It was a blindside hit. I remember Evie running over from the sidelines, handing her camera to one of the cheerleaders and kneeling down next to me, panic and concern in her eyes. The athletic trainers tried to pull her away, but Evie fought back until some of my teammates actually removed her from my sight so that the medical staff could take care of me. I passed out from the blinding pain and woke up in the hospital with my leg already in a cast. I saw a sea of ash blonde hair on the hospital bed. I had a strong feeling she hadn't left my side since I was granted visitors. I remember my doctor saying the words I already knew: *"Son, your football career is over. I am so sorry."* Evie squeezed my hand so hard and tears streamed down her face. She knew how much I wanted this and that I had lost one of the most important things in my life. But all I could remember thinking is: *At least I haven't lost her.*

Little did I know, I would eventually lose her.

"As I live and breathe. The best quarterback I ever coached. Noah Pearson. How are you, son?" My old coach, Coach Staten, is standing next to me. "Are you just visiting, or back in town for good?"

He looks exactly the same, save for the gray hair developing above his ears. I give him a firm handshake. "Coach, it's nice to see you." He releases my hand and I tuck it away in my large pocket in my hoodie. "I'm back in town. I am the chef, well almost the chef, at Evie Hawkins' new inn. The Evergreen?"

"Ah yes. I'm so proud of that girl. She has worked her ass off trying to get that inn up and running with her folks. I've been meaning to stop by Lydia and Bill's. How's Lydia doing? It's unfortunate about her cancer diagnosis all those years ago." He looks off toward the yellow goal post, contemplating what happened to all of our lives. It seemed like everything started to change once I had my injury.

I clear my throat. "Yeah, she seems to be doing all right. In remission and as spunky as ever."

"And Evie?" My skin gets hot when he says Evie's name again. "Now that would have been a sight to see. You two together again. I could barely get you to focus when she was on the sidelines taking pictures."

I smirk and nod. "She's doing good. The inn is looking amazing. She brought her Evie magic to the table and it shows." I scuff my foot against the grass, creating a small divot.

"That's wonderful. I'm planning on coming to the soft opening on Christmas Eve. I got the invite a couple weeks ago."

I nod. "I think she invited the entire town."

"Sounds about right." Then he pats my shoulder. "How about you, son? Seems like culinary school treated you right. I've been seeing you in the news and on TV shows. I'm proud of you. You made something that most people would have used as an excuse to give up on all their dreams into something impactful and downright admirable. Seems like you found a silver lining and went with it. Most people only see the dark clouds. Never the silver linings."

Not everything turned into a silver lining. My relationship with Evie certainly didn't. "Some clouds stayed dark, Coach."

I must have a pained expression on my face because Coach winces and he continues, "Well, maybe that one dark cloud will light up a bit now that you are back in her life."

He caught on quickly. He knows how much Evie meant to me and he's astute to realize that has not changed. I sigh. "That's the hope."

He nods and crosses his arms. "I am glad to see your face again, Pearson. Since you are back in town, would you be interested in coming to some practices? Teaching these young men a thing or two about resiliency and maybe kicking their ass at some drills? Looks to me like you can keep up with them."

"I would be happy to, Coach. Just send me your practice schedule and I'll stop by when I can."

"I'd appreciate that, son. The season just ended, but if you are still in town, I will reach out. Now, I'll let you get back to it. Looks like you have a lot of things you need to sort out in your mind based on the amount of laps you ran and push-ups you did." He gives me a knowing look and laughs. The same one he used to give me when he knew I was full of shit or had a lot of things on my mind. Other than my grandad, he was the closest thing to a father that I knew.

"There's just one thing on my mind, Coach. It's the same thing that's been on my mind since I was in kindergarten."

"Sounds about right." He starts walking away. He waves a hand up in the air and shouts, "See you soon, Pearson."

I take in the worn-out football field one more time before turning on my heel, heading back to my truck and nearly finishing my giant bottle of water. After I slam the door shut, I glance over to the passenger seat. Evie's red scarf lays there. Fucking teasing me. Reminding me of her. I grabbed it the other night because I didn't want anyone else to steal it. I figured it was safe with me. I would have gone over to her house right after Kevin, Allie and I were done, but we stayed until the last call and I didn't want to wake her. Plus, I want to be in a clear mind when I see her next. I was too drunk to even remember my own name by the time my head hit the pillow.

10

Noah

"Bingo!!"

An hour after I left the football field, I decided to stop by to see my grandad, Walter, at the nursing home he moved into right before I left for New York. I wanted to make sure he was going to have company since I didn't know how often I would return home. The move to the nursing home wasn't because he physically needed care. It was because he needed company. Turns out, between my busy schedule at school, internships, jobs and travel, I didn't have a chance to come home and keep him company. Walter never held it against me, though. He also understood how hard it would be for me to come back, especially since Hollybury is a permanent reminder of one of the greatest losses of my life–my relationship with Evie. I did, however, call him every day and he finally learned how to use FaceTime. He knew I would come home if anything ever happened to him and he really needed me back. But he didn't want me to move back just for him. He respected that I needed to pursue my dreams. So much has been taken away from me without my control–he understood this was something I could control, and he let me live my life. I've always been grateful to him for that.

All that being said, I have visited him every day since I've been back. Even if it is for just ten minutes. Every minute counts.

Another "Bingo!" is shouted from across the room and I rub my forehead. My head is still ringing from my hangover. I thought my intense workout at the football field would negate the after-effects of a night spent trying to drink away the fact that the love of my life went home with another man. My jaw clenches. No amount of jingle bell rocks or rocking around the Christmas trees could lift my spirits. I am a regular Grinch at this point.

"So, how has your first few weeks been at Evie's new inn?" My grandad asks as he clears his Bingo card.

I let out a sigh, reflecting on the past couple weeks of hell. "I think this is going to be my own version of the twelve labors of Hercules. She comes in guns blazing. All business. No bullshit or any notion of flirting, despite my best efforts. Grandad, I even tried to distract her by making her favorite guilty pleasure snack: parmesan truffle fries."

My grandad makes a revolted face. "I'm not surprised those didn't work. Those are disgusting."

He still hasn't gotten on the truffle fries bandwagon. And not to brag, but I make the best damn parmesan truffle fries in the world. They have been her favorite ever since I made them for her during our junior year of high school. Our recent conversation runs circles through my head:

"Are you trying to get on my good side? Schmooze the boss. Are you trying to kiss my ass?"

"Whatever it takes to get in your good graces. I want to impress you with my talents since I am here on a trial basis. I know what you like."

As she bit into the fries, a look of pure satisfaction came across her face. I knew that she secretly wanted to scarf them down in less than five minutes but I also knew she would never admit that. She wouldn't do it in front of me because she doesn't want to let me in. She doesn't want to admit that I am in fact slowly making my way into her good graces.

My strategy is simple. Do the small things first. Show her that I remember the little things about her and know what makes her tick.

"Still giving you the cold shoulder, huh?" My grandad intently looks down at his bingo card and places a marker in the free space square.

"It's worse than that. There are moments where I think she is letting her guard down, but then her guard is back up when she is being too soft with me. When things start getting familiar and easy, she makes it difficult. I can't help but wonder if it was worth coming back." I finish off my coffee I picked up from Dorsey's before coming here.

Phyllis, a vibrant yet frail woman probably in her mid-nineties, chimes in, "Honey, for love, it's always worth it."

I give a subtle grin and scoot the bingo markers around the table. She's right. It is worth it. Evie is worth it. But there is still so much hurt from both of our ends that it's going to take some time to pick up all the fractured pieces we scattered everywhere when I left.

"Bingo!" Phyllis yells right in my ear. It's like nails on a fricken chalkboard. Between the small bingo balls circling in the bingo cage, the announcer who doesn't understand the concept of a microphone and is still yelling out the numbers, and "Bingo!" getting screamed at every turn, I don't think my massive headache is going away anytime soon.

Then out of nowhere, "You're a damned fool if you let that girl get away again."

Shock rolls through my body, sobering me up. Especially since that comment came from my own grandfather's mouth. To be fair, he has never been one to sugar-coat things.

I rub my temples and say plainly, "She doesn't want to be with me, Grandad. I messed up when I left for New York. I should have stayed behind and been with her. She is the most important person in my life and I should have stayed. I don't think I'll ever have a chance with her again."

"That's not the grandson I raised. I taught you how to be a gentleman, but I also taught you to have confidence within yourself to get what you want out of your life. Now, you may think that I didn't have a fantastic life living in this town, but the life I shared with your grandmother, who oddly reminds me of Evie, headstrong yet an absolute softie, humble while also being an absolute knockout..."

"Grandad..." Even though what he is saying is true, I can't help but almost vomit when he uses phrases like "knockout" when talking about Evie.

He chuckles then continues, "I am just stating the facts. Lord knows why Evie Hawkins ever glanced in your direction, but she has once before. I have a feeling that she will again. Now, go show her the kind of man you are, Noah. I didn't help raise a quitter."

11

Evie

It has been a couple of days since my flop date with Jeremy and I haven't gotten much sleep. I have been dragging in the mornings out of pure fatigue, but my only motivation is getting this inn up and running in time for our soft opening. Part of the reason I can't sleep is because I am so bummed about losing my red scarf. I remember the Christmas Noah gave it to me. He saved up his money from working at the restaurant to buy me a nice cashmere scarf. It was also the same Chrsitmas he said he was going to marry me one day. It wasn't a promise ring, but that scarf held all the promise of our future together. And I lost it.

I park behind Gerard, someone who is notoriously ten minutes early to any appointment or shift. I push open the door to the inn, awaiting some snarky comment from my best friend. The first thing I see are boxes of Christmas decorations already set up in the living room, next to the bare tree I have been meaning to decorate for a few days now. I know most of the boxes are filled with garlands wrapped in white twinkly lights that I plan to hang along every possible entryway and mantle possible, and of course wrap around the staircase. Other boxes are filled with an insane amount of ornaments and little festive knick-knacks I want to scatter throughout the inn. A rush of excitement courses through my body, providing an immediate dopamine hit that I have not received yet from my hot chocolate.

"You're alive!" Gerard exclaims at me when I walk into the inn thirty minutes late. "I have all the decorations out and ready for you to work your Christmas magic all around this inn. I expect it to look nothing less than a Hallmark movie thrown up in here. And thanks for texting me back last night. You promised to tell me all about this date. Don't spare any details." He comes around the front desk and takes a good look at me. "Ooof, you look rough. No sleep again?"

I unwrap my subpar plaid oversized scarf from around my neck and hang it on the coat rack. "First, thank you for getting the boxes out and ready. Second, I did not really sleep at all last night." I can feel a headache starting to creep up and I hope decorating will be the cure. I need it to be the cure for all of my problems as of late. The main problem being a certain hot chef ex-boyfriend who decided to bulldoze back into my life without so much as a warning.

"Oh wait, is it because you were up all night having sex with Jer-Bear?" Gerard wiggles his perfectly groomed eyebrows and has a silly smile.

The door slams behind me. "Morning," Noah gruffs as he walks past us. I didn't hear him open the door. Perfect timing, universe. It looks like he didn't get that much sleep the past couple of nights either. His hair is unkempt and his scruff appears to be a little fuller, meaning he didn't bother to shave this morning. He is also in a grumpy mood.

"Morning, Mr. Pearson." Those words roll off my tongue as smooth as a raft braving the rapids. Even though he requested not to call him Mr. Pearson, I cannot help but keep it professional between us. The spark between us is still there. I just don't know if I am ready to ignite it yet.

He barely acknowledges my response and goes into the kitchen.

"Someone woke up on the wrong side of the bed this morning. Sheesh," Gerard observes.

"I think he's upset at me." I hand Gerard his coffee that I picked up from Dorsey's and take a sip of my hot chocolate.

He cocks an eyebrow. "Why? Because you haven't taken him back yet?"

Maybe, but I am not ready to admit that yet. "He was at the restaurant where Jeremy took me on a date the other night."

Gerard's eyes widen. "Girl, tell me more. Give me the whole damn tea kettle."

I lean my elbows against the desk. "Everything was going fine and then I got up to go to the bathroom and after I was done, Noah hijacked me and took me into the kitchen and..."

"Ravished you. Oh my god, this is so much better than I ever thought possible. Is this why you haven't been getting much sleep? You were having sex with Noah! Look at you playing the field. First Jer-Bear and then Noah."

"That's not even remotely what happened. You are the worst at listening to stories or watching movies or TV shows. You always jump to crazy conclusions. Will you let me finish?" My body feels flushed from the thought of having sex with Noah again. Is Gerard's recap what I *really* wished happened that night?

"Ugh, boring. Okay, fine. Continue."

"He took me into the pantry in the kitchen and asked me how my date was going and why I was wearing such a short dress and..."

Gerard holds out his hand in front of my face. "Hold on. Why were you wearing such a short dress?" He cocks his eyebrow, apparently judging my choice in dress. "It's below thirty degrees every night here, Evie. You're insane." He gulps down some coffee.

"That dress makes me feel wanted and sexy and I wanted to get laid, okay?" Before I can reprimand him for interrupting my story yet again, a large crash comes from the kitchen. Gerard and I run into the kitchen and see Noah picking up broken pieces of what looks like the remains of a large ceramic mixing bowl.

"Are you okay?" I rush over to him. Noah doesn't respond to

me and his eyebrows are pulled together so harshly I am convinced the line that has developed will stay there permanently. I squat down and touch his bicep to get his attention. He's not even looking at me. "Noah, stop. We'll get a broom."

"Ah, shit!" Noah exclaims and then I see droplets of blood drip down his hand. Fuck.

"G, go get the first-aid kit." I tug on Noah's bulky arm and he's not budging, "Noah, get up and come with me to the sink. We need to clean this."

"I can get up on my own, Evie. You don't have to help me." He snaps and heads over to the sink. I meet him there. Blood and water mix as they go down the drain. His face hasn't changed. I thought pain would sink in at his point. Nope. It's almost like he is a statue and his face is carved into a permanent scowl.

Gerard jogs back into the kitchen with a white box and holds it out. "Here is the first-aid kit. You okay, handsome?"

"I'm fine." Noah's jaw clenches.

The phone rings at the front desk and Gerard finds this perfect opportunity to leave me alone with Mr. Grumpypants. I turn off the water, then open the kit to grab some gauze. "Here, we need to put pressure on the wound to stop—"

"The bleeding. Yeah, this isn't my first cut, Evie. I work with sharp knives every day." He quickly grabs the gauze and presses it against his hand.

"Okay, you don't have to be a dick about it." I slam the first-aid kit shut. "I guess I'll leave you to nurse yourself back to health."

I notice Noah's breathing becomes short and shallow and his body begins to tremble. "Noah? Are you okay?" He doesn't answer, and his breathing becomes even more erratic. I've seen this before–he's having a panic attack. He used to get them before a big game or a big test or when he was stressed about something in his life. These attacks presented more when he got older. I remember teachers would pull me out of classes or his coach would send someone to look for me in the stands so I could calm him down. I was the only one who knew how. One time it got so bad that he said he couldn't see anything in front of him. I don't know how severe this one is going to be. I set my annoyance and anger aside and help him. I stand in front of him and place my hands on the sides of his face. "Noah, look at me." He keeps his eyes tightly shut and shakes his head. "Noah, please look at me."

He opens his beautiful green eyes and all I see is pain. I don't want him to be in pain and I know that seeing me with another man hurt him. It's not like I planned for us to be at that restaurant together. I would never flaunt any new man in front of the man I thought I was going to spend forever with. His breathing is starting to slow down. "Be here with me rather than wherever you went just now. I'm here. You are safe. You are going to be okay. Breathe."

I rub my thumbs along his cheeks, press my forehead to his, and breathe with him. His head rests in one of my hands and his breathing becomes normal. His body finally stops shaking. "Breathe. Keep breathing." He does as he is told.

As the panic attack subsides, he says, "Thank you."

We lock eyes and that's when I notice the bags under his

eyes. Even though he is devastatingly handsome 24/7, I can tell he didn't sleep well and something is eating him up inside. "You're welcome. Are you all right?"

Instead of giving me a yes or no answer, he states, "Please tell me you didn't sleep with him. Please, Evie."

I pause out of sheer shock he would ask me that. I must take too long of a pause because he snaps out of it, clears his throat and says, "Never mind. Don't answer that. It's none of my business who you sleep with." He nods over to the wall-mounted rack he usually hangs his aprons on. "You left that at the restaurant. Figured you'd want it back."

He quickly grabs another gauze pad and walks out to the back porch for, I am assuming, fresh air and to get away from the girl who is still breaking his heart. I run my hand over my face, look over to the rack, and see my red scarf hanging there. Relief sets into my body and I feel like I could cry. I shut my eyes and press my palm to my head. Unfortunately this tired headache has now morphed into a stressful one.

Dammit, Noah Pearson. You make it impossible for me not to love you.

12

Noah

The crisp winter air hits my skin as the back door slams behind me. I didn't have to be such a dick to her. It's my own shit that I am projecting onto her and it's not fair. I cannot believe that I had another panic attack. It has been a while. Though the last time I had one, it was right before a segment on Good Morning America and I was alone in my dressing room hoping that no one would walk in and see me in that state. I've been able to hide it pretty well from the outside world. There are only a few people in my life that know I suffer through it.

Evie is the only one who can truly calm me down in record time. I manage fine by myself, but when she was the one who told me to breathe and held my face in her hands, it made everything better.

I take a good look under the gauze and the cut isn't as deep as I thought. I've definitely had worse cuts from knives in the past. It's a pretty clean cut, no ceramic shards got under my skin. I need to find some hydrogen peroxide and bandage it up so I can get back to work.

I step back into the kitchen and notice the floor is completely cleaned up and that Evie's red scarf is gone. There is a bright orange post-it note on the counter next to my knife set. I pick it up and see the words: *Thank you* scribbled in cursive. Now I feel like an even bigger dick.

I rinse my hand one more time and find a miniature bottle of hydrogen peroxide in the kit. I pour some over my open wound and wrap an ACE bandage over my hand. Voices emerge from the hallway that leads to the kitchen, and Lydia and Bill walk in.

"Have you seen the bookings lately, Bill? We are booked through June! I don't think Evie has had a chance to realize that."

"That's great, honey, but don't you think we should be slowing down? You seem a little tired lately. Evie and Gerard can handle most of the operations."

"No, I think being involved as much as possible is the best thing for me right now."

"But the doctor..." I open the fridge to start prepping some sample food for today and it unintentionally cuts off their conversation.

"Noah. I'm sorry we just barged in."

"You are never barging in, Lydia. This is technically your inn. You can barge in whenever you want." I muster up a smile and pull out a cutting board and a knife from my knife case.

"But this is your domain and I never want you to feel like we are an imposition." She comes over and gives me a side hug. And just when I am about to tell her how she is never a burden, she catches sight of my wrapped hand. "Noah, what happened?"

"It was stupid. I got distracted and the damn ceramic mixing bowl slipped from my fingers. Rookie mistake."

She investigates my hand. "Is it deep?"

"I've had worse."

"My gosh, Lydia, give the man some breathing room. This is probably an occupational hazard of being a chef."

I laugh out of relief that I don't have to reassure Bill of anything. There are very few things in this world that phase Bill Hawkins. "Bill's right. I am used to these kinds of injuries."

"Doesn't stop a mother from worrying." Her eyes are the same as Evie's, just a little more wrinkles surround them. Except today – Bill is right, she does look extra tired. I should talk, though. If I looked in a mirror right now, I probably have the darkest circles around my own eyes.

Still, I can't shake the feeling that something is off about Lydia, she just doesn't want to tell me. Or anyone. She always wanted to protect us from anything she was dealing with. She never wanted to be a burden.

"You don't have to worry, Lydia. Is everything okay with you?"

"Ha, I am fine, hon. You definitely don't have to worry about me." She taps the side of my face with her cold, delicate hand.

I do worry about you is all I want to say to her. But I will leave it alone for now.

All of a sudden, Brenda Lee's voice echoes through the inn.

"Well, that's the cue for Evie's annual decorating extravaganza." Lydia goes to the cabinet to get a mug and reaches for the handle of the checkered tea kettle. She starts walking to the sink, but I stop her.

"Here, Lydia, I got it." I snatch the kettle from her grasp.

"Noah, I am very capable of heating up my own water."

"Just because you are capable, doesn't mean that someone else can't do it for you. Go relax in the living room. Go be with Evie. I got it. Plus I need to make up for all the times I couldn't make you green tea when I was gone."

She squeezes my arm and tears well up in her eyes. She does need to rest. I am sure Evie has handled the brunt of the renovations and business decisions, but Lydia's been through a lot and I want to help lower her stress as much as possible.

Once the tea is nice and steeped, I head to the living room to give Lydia her drink. When I open the swinging door that leads into the living room, I stop dead in my tracks. It's unrecognizable. The entire living room is a sea of green, red, silver and gold. The mantle is covered with large garland and gold bells hanging off the edge. The banister to the stairs is also covered in garland. How in the hell does she work this fast? I have literally been in the kitchen for at most twenty minutes.

I've always been convinced that Evie is a Christmas elf disguised as a human with how much she loves Christmas, but also the knack she has to turn any space into a magical, classy winter wonderland. It's like I got dropped right into the North Pole.

I glimpse Evie's Santa hat appear from behind the massive Douglas fir. She is belting out the lyrics to Darlene Love's *Winter Wonderland.* She steps in front of the tree with a bundle of lights. She sways her body side to side and it makes my insides melt. She hasn't changed. She may have more confidence and sass now, but deep down, she is still the girl I fell in love with. I don't think there will ever be a day that I am not falling for her. No matter how many walls she puts up. No matter how many years have passed. Evie still dances around the living room, blasting her favorite Chrtstmas music, sings at the top of her lungs and decorates for the holidays. She's still my girl.

I give Lydia her mug while my eyes do not leave Evie. I don't care if I look like a sappy, lovestruck teenager. It's the only look I know when it comes to Evie Hawkins. I lean against the wall and cross my arms and take in this completely uninhibited version of her. The happiest version of her.

At some point during my reverie, Lydia and Bill stand next to me. I say, "Let me guess...Evie has been listening to Christmas music since what? Mid-October?"

They steal a glance at each other, almost like they are surprised. Bill chimes in, "Yes...you remember that about her?"

I look at them, "Mr. and Mrs. Hawkins, I remember everything about your daughter."

13

Noah

A couple days later, still unable to get Evie dancing and singing out of my head, I confidently drive up to the inn and decide that today is the day I will muster up the courage to bring up our past and see if this relationship can possibly go anywhere past a working one. I desperately don't want to get stuck in a twisted, torturous limbo where I get to see the one person I want more than anything in this world, but can't do anything to actually get the girl. I walk up the creaky old stairs to the main door and smirk at the abundance of garland adorning the porch and any available beam or window frame possible. With Evie's permission, Bill and I handled the outdoor decorating while Evie performed wonders on the inside.

I don't have a key to the inn yet, part of my trial period conditions, so I knock on the door and wait for someone to answer.

"Noah, come on in. I am so sorry. I keep forgetting to give you a key so you can let yourself in," Lydia waves in and pats me on the back as I walk past her.

"No need, Lydia. I'll wait until my trial period is over. I want to respect Evie's terms. You would do this for any other candidate right?"

"Noah." She gives me a look indicating that she could detect the bullshit from a mile away. "You and I both know – well, let's face it, the whole town knows – that you aren't just any other candidate. Do you need me to talk Evie down a little bit?"

I shake my head. "No. I think she already felt blindsided with me being here in the first place. I want her to have control of this situation. I don't want her to feel like she can't find any stable ground on something she is leaping into with all her faith and ambition. She has wanted this for so long. I don't want to ruin anything for her."

"Trust me, you aren't ruining anything for her. I haven't seen this light in Evie's eyes in a long time. Honestly, your presence alone is good for the bed and breakfast." She gives me a sly smile. "We have a celebrity in our midst."

I hang up my jacket on the coat rack and chuckle. "I am hardly a celebrity."

"Stop being so humble, Noah. You made it, honey. I know that you didn't live your dream of being a pro football player, but that always made me nervous anyway with the possibility of concussions, and to be fully transparent, I winced every time you were tackled. It was like watching my own child out there getting a proper beatdown every Friday night. I was just happy that my only child was on the sidelines, safely taking photographs for the school newspaper."

Photographs. I run my hand through my hair and it's damp from the flurries descending from the gray skies. "I saw some of her photos in the darkroom the other night. I'm glad she is still pursuing that passion."

"Oh, yes. Not as of late, because we've been busy with all of this!" Her arms flail around animatedly. "But in whatever spare time she has, she'll go out for a few hours and take photos around town. It's amazing what she captures."

The phone rings. Lydia heads over to the front desk and before she answers, she says to me, "Her work is up on the walls, hon, if you want to see what she's been up to...Hello, Evergreen Inn, this is Lydia."

My heart leaps. It was one of my favorite things to do with Evie: watch her develop the photographs she took. The other night in the darkroom made me miss those moments with her even more. The way her face lit up when the photo turned out better than she expected. Seriously, the best fucking thing is her smile.

I am technically a little early, so I walk around the bed and breakfast and look at every photograph on the walls. Every single one of them are Evie's. All in black and white. All capturing little moments in time. She doesn't discriminate between capturing people or places. She is the best at capturing them all. Classic Evie.

Then there is a picture in the corner by the bookshelf in the main living area that stops me in my tracks. My heart is beating wildly for a completely different reason. Admiration morphs into anger real quick.

There in a matted black frame is a picture of the Institute of Culinary Education. In fucking New York. She always writes her signature and the date on the bottom right corner of every photograph she takes. Leaning in, I see the date on this photograph was two years ago. A flood of emotion courses through me. How could she have come to New York – to the exact place she knew I would be – and not see me? Not contact me? Not even try to connect?

Then, as if she was summoned by my Bat Signal of Rage, Evie walks through the front door and smiles warmly at her mom. Lydia just nods in return, since she is on the phone again and clicking the mouse to input something into the computer. It's a damn shame that Evie's smile is about to fade because of me...again.

I stride over to her as she takes off her red scarf and hangs it on the coat rack on top of her light teal winter coat. Before she can actively avoid me again, I say, "You were in New York?"

Evie's eyes widen. I can tell she forgot that photo is on display. Her eyes shoot over to Lydia, whose eyes are just as wide, and who shrugs sympathetically. I think she forgot, too.

Dammit Evie looks beautiful today, but nothing is new

there. She's always beautiful. Evie's perfect mouth opens and then her eyes flutter as she looks down, not saying a word.

I grab onto her hand and practically drag her over to the photograph. "What the fuck is this, Evie?" I slam my free hand against the wall, making the Christmas decor rattle. "You have some nerve telling me off in the square, in front of the entire town I might add. You're mad at me for not coming back when you know that you didn't want me to come back and also, I was busier than I have ever been in my life, so I didn't have much time to come home for a visit. And yet, you had the time to go to New York to take pictures and couldn't pick up the phone to fucking call me? How hard is it to even text someone?" I'm not holding back, but I don't care. I am hurt. We both burned our relationship to the ground. Tore up the pages of our love story and threw it in the damn fire. But dammit if I'm not going to try like hell to salvage any pages from the embers threatening our relationship again. We need to lay out all the burned pieces on the fucking table. It may be ugly, but I still care.

Evie's blonde hair frames her face and her eyes are filled with tears. She sniffles and says, "I...I didn't think you were ever going to see that photo."

"You didn't answer my question." The only sound I hear other than my heartbeat pounding in my ears is the fire crackling. Evie has not had time to go start blasting Christmas music throughout the whole bed and breakfast yet.

Lydia is the first one to break the silence: "I'm going to do some inventory in the back." She raises her eyebrows and purses her lips, directing her gaze onto Evie.

Once she leaves the room, I repeat, "You didn't answer my question, Evie."

She stands up straighter, trying to match my stature. I cross my arms because I am not about to lose this standoff. I always found it exceedingly sexy when she would try to do this when we were together. "I went to New York two years ago. I've always wanted to go...you know that. And as far as reaching out to you..." A tear escapes her eye. "I couldn't, Noah. I wasn't sure if you wanted to see me. I figured you had moved on and I just..."

"So you assumed I wouldn't want to see you?" I advance toward her, making her take a sharp intake and look down again. I lift her chin up, not letting her escape this conversation. "If you really think that, then you don't know me at all."

We stand there for seconds that feel like minutes. I keep pressing because my thoughts are getting the best of me: "Why do you have this photo hanging on the wall, Evie?" I need to know that she has been thinking about me just as much as I have been thinking about her.

She clears her throat and backs away from me, forcing me to release her chin, and suddenly the air is cold. She tucks her hair behind her ear and starts playing with her silver necklace, almost like it is out of habit. A comfort to her. I can't help but notice that the necklace looks familiar and then my stomach drops again. It can't be *the* necklace, can it? Does she wear it often? Maybe she does and I haven't noticed; maybe it's usually tucked away under her winter sweaters. Suddenly, I feel like the biggest asshole in the world. She kept it after all this time.

She notices that I am staring at her hand fiddling with the

silver chain with the half a heart on it and stops immediately. Another tear streams down her cheek as she walks past me toward the stairs. "Don't you have a menu to come up with or something? I want the menu to be ready so we can go over it in a few days. I need it to be perfect."

I put my hands on my hips and take a deep breath. She still wears her half of the necklace. She still cares about us.

14

Noah

Seven Years Ago

The summer flies by. Between attending doctor's appointments with Evie and her mom, moving my grandad into the new senior living facility, getting everything ready to move to New York, and working some shifts at the restaurant, Evie and I barely have time to talk, let alone spend much time together. I don't want to push her about New York but I have this heavy weight in my stomach that she isn't telling me something. She's holding back. She hasn't mentioned New York since the day on the football field. I've been in this weird place of wanting to give Evie her space but also be available when she needs me.

I feel her pulling away from me and that's never happened in our relationship. I hate it and I want to fix it now before we head off into our new lives.

The moment I knock on the Hawkins' front door, I can't shake this feeling that my life is forever going to change. My usual mode of entry is climbing up the tree and knocking on Evie's window, but out of respect for the fact that their only daughter is leaving the nest, I decide to take the traditional approach and enter through the front door.

My truck is packed to the brim with all of my belongings. I already said my goodbyes to my grandpa. I am chomping at the bit to start my life with my girl and I want to whisk her away from all the sadness that our last summer in Hollybury brought.

I knock on the door again and I am greeted by Bill, who has bags under his eyes. He has been carrying the brunt of all the housework and workload in general since the diagnosis. He's tired. It pains me to see the always-positive Hawkins family become so riddled with sadness and pain and grief. It was a plot twist we never saw coming. And I say *we* because the Hawkins are family to me.

"Noah." He sneaks in a small smile and hugs me. He pauses for a second and I let him. I don't let go of this man who I already consider a father. He is hurting, so I hug him back a little tighter. "Um, Evie is in her room and Lydia is sitting on the back porch drinking some tea."

"How is she?" I glance beyond Bill toward their back porch.

He gives me a light smile. "It's a good day. You came on a good day to say goodbye."

I grab the top of his shoulder. "Why don't you go rest for a bit, Mr. Hawkins? I got them."

He nods, relief taking over his body, and slowly and tiredly walks up the stairs, closing his bedroom door behind him. I pass through the kitchen to the French doors leading out to a beautiful wooden deck covered in potted plants and trees. Through it all, Lydia hasn't stopped gardening. I am sure it has been very therapeutic for her. Lydia is sitting on one of the cushioned wicker chairs with a mug full of tea. I wrap an arm around her shoulder. "Hey, Lydia. How are you doing today?"

She leans in and pats her left hand on my hand. "Oh, Noah dear. I am so happy to see you." I walk around and sit on the seat next to her. "I am having a good day today and glad it's nice out."

"Yeah it's a pretty good day. I think some storms are supposed to roll in later, though. I want to try and get out of town before it does. Hopefully it doesn't take us too long to pack up my truck with Evie's things."

Lydia looks at me with pained eyes and it's a foreign look from her. My gut takes a hit. This isn't the Lydia I have come to know and love. I am in pain for her and I just want to kick cancer's ass right now for taking away even a little of Lydia's glow. Because taking away Lydia's glow has dimmed the sunshine that is Evie. My girl is my sunshine.

She places her frail hand on my knee. "You know Evie loves you, right?"

I let out a small, incredulous laugh. "Yes, I do. And you know how much I love your daughter. She is my world, Lydia, and I promise I will take care of her. And that I will stay in touch. I'll write to you." I place my hand on hers.

"Would you? Oh Noah, that would make me so happy. How I miss getting happy mail. Lately it's been 'get well soon' cards and they've honestly made me more sad. I know that's not people's intention with sending those. It's just I am already living in so much sadness. My body is literally at war with itself and I just want to laugh and smile more. Bless Bill because he tries. He really does, but I even sense this shift with him. He is treating me differently and I really don't want him to. Same with Evie. She is walking on eggshells and my fearless girl has become so afraid. Afraid of living her life when that's all I want her to do."

I nod slowly, processing everything Lydia has to say. Savoring every intonation and inflection of her voice. I don't know if I'll ever hear it again. I am staying optimistic with her treatment and I have this gut feeling that she will get through this, but there's always a chance that this can go south.

"Well I am really going to miss you, Lydia."

She smiles and rubs my cheek. "I'm going to miss you too, sweetheart. You take care of yourself in that great big world. And remember to breathe when you get overwhelmed. I'm so proud of you, Noah. Both Bill and I are. I can bet that everyone in this town is rooting for you to go off and be great. I expect to see nothing less."

"Thanks, Lydia." I kiss the top of her hand and take in this moment with her. I don't know if I will ever get moments like these again with the woman who raised the girl that I love. There's a stillness in the air. It's both comforting and ominous. I can smell the rain heading toward us and that's my cue to stand up.

"She's upstairs." She sips her tea. "She's been waiting for you."

"How much has she packed? Her entire life? Is this going to take multiple trips back and forth from New York to fully move her in?" I joke.

Lydia looks confused and sad. I know that Evie moving away is a hard thing for both Lydia and Bill.

"I promise I will take care of your daughter."

She nods, still with a pained expression, and I kiss the top of her head. The soft, cool silk from her head scarf scratches the surface of my lips and suddenly I am stuck in the reality that she no longer has her blonde hair. There has been so much loss in this family. I just hope Evie is ready to grow and rebuild her happiness with me.

"Do you need anything before I go up to Evie's room? More tea? A blanket?"

"No, Noah. Just promise me you will keep in touch and take care of yourself, honey. And that you'll always love Evie."

That is not a tall order since I already love Evie with all of my being. "I will. I promise."

I skip steps up the stairs and before I knock on Evie's door, I hear low snores coming from her parent's room. Bill is completely knocked out. I can't even imagine how exhausted he must be feeling right now. I close his door, head across the hall and faintly knock on Evie's door. After a few moments of no response, I turn the knob and push open her bedroom door. "Evie?"

I walk in. There are a few boxes made up, but they aren't filled at all. Her room looks exactly the same as always.

Nothing is packed.

My heart drops.

Evie is on her bed, wrapped in a blanket and staring blankly at the floor. Her eyes are puffy and red. I sit next to her on her unmade bed, another clue that something is not okay. My girl isn't here right now and it breaks my heart.

I give her a side hug and kiss the side of her head. "Hey, baby girl. How are you doing today?"

She sniffles. "Not good." Still staring at the floor instead of at me.

I lift up her chin and turn her head towards me. "What's going on, Evie?"

She shakes her head and stays silent. I exhale and look at the empty boxes that are taunting me. I know she has been going through so much, but that still doesn't stop disappointment from filling every inch of my body. I really thought she would have something packed by now.

I stand and grab one of the boxes. "Do you need help packing up? I am excellent at packing. You should see my truck right now. It's like the ultimate game of Tetris." I place her camera bag, notebooks and pens in the box.

"Noah, stop," she blurts out and there is finally life in her body. This is the most animated I've seen her these past few months.

"Am I doing this wrong? Did you have a packing system in place that I am not aware of? Tell me how to help."

"Just stop!" she yells as she unpacks everything that I just packed and covers her face with her hands. She is getting angry and now I am, too.

"Stop what, Evie? Please tell me why you haven't packed," I say with a clipped tone.

"Because...I'm not going with you!"

My breath becomes shallow and every tool I know in the book for stopping a panic attack from starting is thrown out the window. Nothing could have prepared me for Evie to say those words. The floor crumbles beneath me and I feel like I am falling into a dark abyss I will never escape. I catch my breath just enough to say, "What do you mean you're not going with me?"

She approaches me and cradles my face, something that she does to keep me calm when I start to have one of my notorious panic attacks. The ones I would have before a big football game, before meeting a really important college scout, before submitting my application to culinary school. All of those vulnerable moments, she has been there for me and has gotten me through every single one of them.

Her eyes are filled to the brim with tears. "I have to be here with my mom right now. I can't just leave her all alone."

I grab her wrists and shake my head. "She won't be alone. She has your dad and, hell, she has this whole goddamn town to look after her and take care of her. Have you seen the amount of casseroles you have in your freezer? Jesus Christ, Evie. Don't fucking do this." I push her hands away and start pacing the room.

"Why are you so upset?"

"Because we have our whole lives to start living! We've waited so long to get out of this town and now this is our chance. New York is not that far away, Evie, and you know it." I am towering over her now. I am fucking hurt. How can she do this to me? To us?

She crosses her arms over her oversized blue flannel. Her blonde hair is in a messy bun and it hasn't been brushed in days. Her bunny slippers are peeking out underneath her long gray sweatpants. The outfit should have given me every clue that she isn't coming with me. This is her stay-at-home outfit. She isn't going anywhere. "It's too far for me right now. Are you seriously going to stand there and pretend that nothing has changed? Does my mom's cancer not even matter to you?"

Now I am pissed and hurt. I point a finger at her. "Don't. Don't you dare say that your mom's cancer doesn't matter to me. You know how much your mom means to me. But I know that your mom wants the best for you and for you to live your fucking life. She wants you to be happy. I thought that going to New York with me and starting our lives together would make you happy."

Tears are flowing down her rosy cheeks and she keeps her arms crossed. "I guess it doesn't anymore. I can't leave, Noah." She backs away from me. "I think it would be easier for us to end this. A clean break. Before anyone gets hurt."

"Well it's too fucking late for that." I place my hands behind my head into the surrender cobra stance because that's what it feels like I am doing. Surrendering to us being over. I don't accept it. I close the gap between us and cradle her face this time, pressing my forehead to hers. "Please. Please, Evie, don't do this. I love you so damn much. Don't break us."

Her hands rest on top of my shoulders and I feel her head shake from side to side. "I love you, too, Noah. And that's why I have to let you go." Her forehead leaves mine and she looks up at me. "We broke the moment I got that phone call on the football field."

I am gutted because some part of me knows this is the truth. I just naively thought we could recover and piece together what was broken.

"Look," Evie says. "I won't hold you up anymore – just go. I'll be fine and I want you to go and show the world how special you are."

"Well, maybe we can try and do long distance for a little bit and I will come back to visit every chance I get. Or maybe I'll just stay here and go to the same college as you and…"

"No!" She shakes her head vigorously. "You are not going to make your life small for me, Noah Pearson. The world deserves to know you. I am not going to be selfish and keep you all to myself."

"My life is never small with you, Evie. I am *not* leaving." I kiss her tenderly, hoping that this life is a damn fairytale and this one kiss can break the terrible spell that has been cast over our lives. Her lips are warm and soft and she tastes like cherries. I will sear that into my brain until the day I leave this earth. She pulls away far too soon.

"Yes, you *are* leaving. You are meant for so much more than this town. I don't want to do anything halfway. I don't want you to visit. Don't even call or text me, Noah. We need a clean break. It will just be easier that way." She swallows hard and looks at me dead in the eyes. With a straight face, she says the phrase I never wanted to hear come out of her mouth ever: "I need you to go." She pushes against my chest and even though the gap between us is just a few inches, it may as well be the size of the fucking ocean.

My jaw clenches. "This is what you really want?"

She looks down at her silly bunny slippers and nods. "Yes." I swear I hear her voice crack. She is trying to be brave. This time I don't know if it's for her or for her mom. It doesn't matter. She has made her decision and if there's one thing I know about Evie – and I know a lot of things about her – it's that once she makes a decision, she sticks to it like superglue.

I just never thought I would be the exception.

"Goodbye, Evie." I say without looking back because I know if I do, I won't ever leave this room. She wants me to leave. I will always give her what she wants. Even if that means I'm not in the picture.

I hear the faintest, "Goodbye, Noah" as I walk out of her room and force myself not to slam the door.

My vision is blurred as I barrel my way down the stairs and out the door to my packed-up pick up truck that suddenly seems like a cruel joke. I get into the driver's seat and slam the metal truck door so hard it shakes the entire vehicle. I hit the steering wheel repeatedly with the palms of my hands hard, letting as much frustration and hurt exit my body. "Dammit!" I yell. I press my forehead onto my hands that are gripping the top of the steering wheel.

I hate that the universe gave my girl's mom cancer. I hate that Evie cannot see the light that our love provided for both of us. Our love wasn't strong enough for this type of fault that shifted the foundation of our relationship and obliterated our lives. My eyes shift to the two to-go cups from Dorsey's Diner. One is coffee. The other is hot chocolate, Evie's version. I never thought a coffee cup could hold so much mocking power. But I stand corrected.

I stand corrected about a lot of things today.

Don't go back. She doesn't want you anymore. Don't go back.

Fuck this. I am not leaving without her.

I grab the hot chocolate and stride back up onto her porch. Just when I am about to knock, I glimpse through the window and see Evie and her mom snuggled on the couch. Her mom's chin is resting on the top of Evie's head and her arm is wrapped around her only daughter. My heart plummets because I realize this is what Evie needs, time with her mom. More than a new life in New York. More than me. She needs time because it isn't guaranteed. My desire for Evie to be mine is snuffed out by the sight of Evie needing her mom more. I can't be selfish. I am asking her for too much right now. Time was taken away from me when my parents died thirteen years ago. I can't take this away from Evie and her mom.

I set the cup down on the porch and run back to the truck. I turn on the ignition and roll down the windows. I take one last look at Evie's house and drive off. And for the first time in a long time, I don't know what my future looks like.

15

Evie

Still clutching onto my necklace, I head down to the basement to escape Noah's wrath. I completely forgot that I hung up that photo of that trip I took to New York. My mom convinced me to go once she was officially in remission and it was my first solo trip outside of Connecticut. I just remember feeling a mix of emotions, ranging from completely enamored and elated I was there to an insufferable sadness and heaviness, knowing that was supposed to be my life with Noah. I strolled around until I found the culinary school Noah got accepted to. I desperately wanted to see him, but I was scared of what I might find. A Noah I didn't recognize. A Noah who did move on and was dating someone who wouldn't break his heart.

He's right to be angry with me. I did give him so much crap about not reaching out. But, if he had, would I have really been ready for him to reach out? All the guilt I thought I'd eradicated from my heart came rushing back when Noah slammed his hand against the wall. The stairs to the basement creak. I see my mom in my peripheral vision, but I continue to look aimlessly in an unlabeled box.

"You really shouldn't be so hard on Noah."

I scoff, still in defense mode, "Well, you are my mom, you should be on my side with this."

"I am always on your side, Evie."

"Then why are you down here defending Noah?" I rummage through the unmarked box and find some Christmas hand towels I can actually use as back stock for the bathrooms. I tuck them under my arm and continue my search for nothing in particular. My mom's cold hand touches mine.

"Why are you really upset, Evie? Is it because your father and I hired Noah without telling you? Or is it because you are hurt that he is back now and he actually respected your wishes and didn't come back and visit?"

"Both." I look down at my twiddling thumbs. "Maybe more of the latter." I start mindlessly folding the towels over and over again.

My mom takes my hand and says, "C'mon. Drop those

towels. We are going to the house really quick. There is something you need to see."

<hr>

TEN MINUTES LATER, I sit on my parents' couch as my mom opens the hallway closet and reaches up to grab a small box.

"Mom, do you need my help?"

"My goodness, Evie. I think I can handle this. I am not as delicate as you think, sweetheart." She closes the door with her hip and heads over to the living room. She hands the box to me and sits in the arm chair.

I hold the box out in front of me, afraid of the contents. "What is this?"

"Just open it and see."

I set the box on my lap, open the top, and see a thick stack of letters. As I sift through them, I notice that all of these letters are addressed to my mom. There are probably over a hundred of them. "Mom, I don't understand what this has to do with me and Noah. Do you have a secret admirer that I know nothing about?" Then I finally look at the return address and it is a New York City address. And then I see the familiar penmanship matched with the name at the top: N. Pearson.

He wrote to my mom? All these years? There is a sudden twinge of disappointment that the letters aren't addressed to me.

"Noah wrote you letters?" *Why not me?* I shake my head in disbelief. "I don't understand."

"Yes. They started showing up about a month or two after

he left for New York. He wanted to check in on how I was doing with the chemo and radiation. Sometimes he asked for advice. He wanted to make sure that everything was okay and I was recovering." My mom comes over and sits next to me. She rubs my back like she does any time I need to feel supported. "Before he left the house that day, he promised that he would write to me. At first, I didn't really believe he would follow through. I figured he would be so busy with school and whatever else life had to offer him that he wouldn't find the time to actually sit and write me letters. But he kept his promise, Evie."

Yup, that has Noah written all over it.

"Just like he did what you wanted him to do. He went to New York without you. I know that must have killed him, sweetie."

Tears involuntarily fall down my cheek. As if she can read my mind, my mom adds, "Just as much as it killed you."

I mindlessly flip through the box. This is evidence that he never truly left me. He never truly left Hollybury behind.

"Evie, I kept this from you because I wasn't sure what your reaction was going to be and plus, Noah wanted to respect your wishes. He could've easily cut us out of his life, but he didn't. And I think you know why. It's the same reason you haven't taken off that necklace." My mom points to the silver chain hanging down near my heart.

Dammit she's right.

She pats my hand, which is still clutching one of the envelopes and without a word, she gets up and heads toward the kitchen, leaving me with more questions than answers. More curiosity than knowledge and understanding. I am aching to find out everything he told her, everything he asked her about, every thought that went into writing these letters. I shakily turn the envelope and run my finger along the torn opening.

"Go ahead and read one!" my mom yells from the kitchen.

I jump in my seat, nearly toppling the box of letters off the couch. "Geez, Mom, you seriously have to stop doing that."

"Doing what?" she yells back innocently.

"Reading my mind."

"I'm your mother. I know you better than anyone else. Plus, I think it will start to heal all the pieces of you that are broken when it comes to Noah. Do you want tea?"

Classic Mom. Saying the most profound thing and the most normal thing all in the same breath. "Sure."

I pull out the letter and slowly open the top flap. I note that the letter is dated shortly before I took my own trip to New York. Funny how the universe led me to open this particular letter.

Dear Lydia,

I am so happy to hear you are feeling better. It's such a relief that the treatment is working for you. I know that you are ready to get up and do everything for everyone else, but please promise me that you will continue to rest and limit as much stress as possible. I am praying for you every day and hope to see the word remission on a letter from you.

School is kicking my ass. I thought football was hard. It has nothing on culinary school. I feel like I am in the military with the amount of scrutiny and perfection that is expected of me. I know the professors are tough for a reason—they want me to learn and be the best I can be. They remind me of someone else I know ;). I kind of miss the Lydia Hawkins version of a drill sergeant. Tough but nurturing all at once.

New York is everything I thought it would be and more. I am finally learning my way around without looking at directions on my phone constantly. Still, I find myself hesitating doing all the touristy things like going to the top of the Empire State Building, taking a carriage in Central Park, or even trying the famous Magnolia cupcakes. I know that I am holding off on all those things because Evie is the person I wanted to do all those things with.

I know in my first letter I wanted to focus the conversation around you and me, but I'm sorry, Lydia, I have to ask about Evie. How is she? Is she in school? Is she still taking beautiful photographs? I hope she is doing all of those things. There have been so many times I wanted to follow her again on social media to see what she's been up to, but knowing Evie, her socials wouldn't help me discover any of that. She would rarely post anyway. I am just going crazy wondering about her but I also don't want to come back to Hollybury if she doesn't want to see me. I talk to my grandfather every day and know that he is well taken care of there. I feel bad for not being back in a while but I don't know if I can go back right now anyway. I don't think my heart can take it if she is dating someone else. She has every right to. It's just that my heart is already shattered, I'd rather not crush the pieces further.

You don't have to answer any of those questions. Just know that I think about Evie every second of every day.

I will never stop loving your daughter.

Until next time.

Love,
Noah

16

Noah

The town hall is done up floor-to-ceiling with Christmas decor. Garlands hang on every exposed beam, with twinkling lights embedded in each garland strand. Large evergreens stand at every corner of the room and Christmas music blasts from overhead speakers they apparently installed at some point while I was gone. This town definitely learned to be technologically savvy while I was away.

I walk slowly around the room and nod to townspeople

waving at me saying, "Nice to see you again." But really, there is only one face I want to see today.

Kevin and Allie approach me, holding hands. "Ah, Noah, you came! I am so happy we reminded you of this at dinner."

I must have been so far gone from drinking the other night that I don't even remember them mentioning this event. I play along, though. "Yeah, good thing you did. But honestly, I don't know if I can ever forget this contest. I swear any time I'd pass by a gingerbread house in New York, it would transport me to this very room. Looks like they've stepped up their decorating game though."

"That's all Evie." My heart swells. "She has been on the decorating committee for the town, especially Christmas, for the past five years or so? I think her mom forced her to do something other than school and caretaking. She loves to decorate for the holidays."

"Yeah, she always has." I smile as I remember the other day when she was shaking her cute little ass to *Rocking Around the Christmas Tree* while decorating the tree in the common living room.

I am on the lookout for my fiery blonde, hopefully wearing a beanie. That's one of my many favorite looks of hers and my heart is aching to see it.

"She's not here yet," Allie pipes in.

I try to play it off cool. "Who is not here yet?"

"Dude," Kevin chimes in. "That lost-puppy-dog look hasn't left your face since the other night. It's not a good look for you, bro. Do you think you can bullshit a couple of bullshitters? I don't think so. You are looking for Evie."

Both Kevin and Allie give me accusatory looks.

I give in. "Okay, fine. I am looking for Evie. Is she coming? I really need to talk with her."

"Don't you work with her every day? Aw bro, is she giving you the silent treatment?"

"Pretty much. And when we do talk, it's all about work. And we didn't leave things the best the other day. I kind of got upset with her and I have been feeling crappy about it." I rise to my tip toes to look around the crowd. Where is she? If she was in charge of decorating, I am sure she would want to be here to see how it all looks during the event.

"You are going to pull a muscle doing that, Noah." Allie glances behind her shoulder. "I'm sure she'll be here soon. She never misses this. And she really outdid herself this year. It's very old-timey Christmas."

No, it's very Evie. Rows of tables are covered with white linens, glittery pinecones, holly, and gingerbread house making kits, all provided by Mr. Dorsey, of course. He never misses an opportunity to sponsor an event. Contestants have a half-hour to build the best gingerbread house. It has to be structurally sound and neatly decorated. The contest has been this way for as long as I can remember.

Mr. Dorsey taps the microphone. "Welcome, everyone, to our annual Gingerbread House Making Contest sponsored by yours truly."

The crowd claps. Looking over to the barn doors that open to the great room, I see long ash blonde waves. My heart leaps and my body is possessed by my want for Evie.

I tune out Mr. Dorsey, lean over to Kevin and Allie, and whisper, "I'll be right back."

I waltz up to Miss Lizzie, the co-host of this whole event. She is the mastermind behind all the pairings.

"Miss Lizzie. You look extra beautiful today in that festive Christmas sweater."

"Oh, you are such a charmer. But you can't fool me, Noah. I know where your heart lies. And she is standing right over there." Miss Lizzie gestures toward Evie, whose blonde hair is down underneath a black beanie, curls flowing down her bright red sweater. The small amount of blue in her eyes is popping under her dark, thick eyelashes. She has a travel cup in her hands which I am assuming is filled with piping hot cocoa and a large black digital camera hangs from her neck. She must have also volunteered to take the photos of the competition. She wears so many hats around here that I wonder, when does this woman sleep?

Our eyes meet for a second and I swear my whole world is made.

I rub my jaw. "You don't miss a beat do you?" I say to Miss Lizzie.

"It's easy when the beat is as loud as a heavy metal rock band. What do you need, handsome?"

"You are still the one who draws the name at random, right?"

"Yes."

"Well, I was wondering if you can maybe skew the randomness of the pairings and put me with Evie?" I hand over a small paper with my name on it.

Miss Lizzie smiles deviously. "Of course, honey. She is supposed to be the one taking pictures of the event, but I have an idea to take care of that." She throws me a wink.

I knew she would be down for a scheme. Especially when it comes to love and relationships. Meddling is her superpower. "How can I ever repay you?"

"You can cook me a fabulous meal before you jet off back to New York."

I smile and nod. "Done. And to be clear, I am not going back. I'm staying right here, Miss Lizzie. I never should have left in the first place."

Miss Lizzie pats me on the forearm before making her way to the small stage in the town hall.

"Well, well, well, if it isn't Noah Pearson. I heard you were back in town. This town hasn't been the same since you left." A short lively brunette with a fuzzy white beanie walks up to me. I can already tell she has an agenda. I know how to read people pretty well and Blair Winters is no different.

"Blair Winters. Nice to see you again." She stops short of running into my arm. I move over an inch to create some distance between me and her. She was always persistent, asking me every time she saw me if I was still dating Evie. The answer was always the same. Always. "And I don't know, the town seems pretty much the same to me. Hasn't changed in seven years."

"You left a pretty big hole in this town. I know a lot of us were left with broken hearts." She closes whatever space I created a few seconds ago. My jaw clenches. My heart was broken too. Still is.

Blair has never been one for liking silence. "Are you participating in this competition?" She cocks an eyebrow and runs her fingers against my forearm. Everything about her touch feels wrong to me. I glance over to where Evie is and we briefly make eye contact. Those eyes still leave me breathless. Anytime I see that shade of blue, I think of Evie and I swear every moment we had together flashes in my mind like a fucking montage. She blushes, abruptly looks away, and starts some kind of bullshit conversation with fucking Jeremy.

It's killing me to know if anything happened between her and Jeremy the other night and the soreness in my body is evidence that even hard-core exercise couldn't exorcise those thoughts ruling my mind. My blood is boiling at the thought that Jeremy would so much as hold Evie's hand. I fear what I might do if I find out that they did anything else. I'm selfish as hell when it comes to Evie. I hear her captivating laugh from across the room as she chuckles at something Jeremy just said. Is he a comedian now? Apparently me not paying attention to her doesn't deter Blair from grazing my fucking forearm is a salacious manner.

"Yeah I am." I finally answer her question and hope that my clipped tone stops this conversation in its tracks.

"What a coincidence, so am I. Well, maybe we'll be partners." She scans my entire body. "Here's hoping."

"Maybe. We'll just have to see." Then I hear the most beautiful name over the microphone: "Evie Hawkins." Evie lowers her camera and looks surprised and confused. "Ah, yes, Miss Evie Hawkins. Let's give Evie a round of applause for her wonderful decorations!"

The crowd cheers for Evie as she puts on the fakest smile I've ever seen in my life. She is in full-blown panic mode right now as she makes her way to where Miss Lizzie is standing.

"Tell the crowd who Evie is paired with this year, Miss Lizzie," Mr. Dorsey continues over the loud chatter in the room.

In her best shocked state, Miss Lizzie says, "Noah Pearson." I swear between Evie and Miss Lizzie they deserve an Academy Award for the worst fake performances of all time.

A hush comes over the crowd and Evie stops dead in her tracks, her eyes widened out of horror instead of excitement that I secretly hoped for. All eyes are on us and our next move. Possibly waiting for a rematch of what happened at the gazebo.

Dorsey saves us when he says, "And the final pairing is Jeremy and Blair. Okay, that's all the contestant pairings everyone. You have five minutes until we start!" He raises his eyebrows in our direction as he steps down from the stage.

Evie resumes striding toward Miss Lizzie. I need to step in and rescue Miss Lizzie from Evie's wrath.

"Um, Miss Lizzie? I think there has been some mistake. I'm going to be taking pictures of the event. I am not competing this year." She raises her camera in case anyone is brave enough to dispute her.

"Well, you are now. Give me your camera. I'll take the photos. My job is already done anyway. I have all the time in the world." Miss Lizzie holds out her hand under the red poncho she is wearing.

Miss Lizzie is my girl.

"But..." Evie starts to protest.

"Evie Hawkins." Miss Lizzie puts on her stern voice. A

rarity. "Give me your camera. I think I can handle clicking a button."

Evie is about to contest but smartly decides against it because with Miss Lizzie, it's moot to try. She lifts the camera over her head and gingerly hands it to Miss Lizzie, who shoos us away with her hand. "Go on, you two. The contest is about to begin. Go. Strategize. Have fun. Talk." She begins to walk away, but not before throwing me another wink.

I place my hands in my jeans pockets and rock back and forth. "So, interesting turn of events, huh?"

Evie stares at me suspiciously. I feel like I won the lottery with her looking at me at all.

I snort. "What?"

"What was that look between you two?" She crosses her arms across her bright red cable knit sweater. It matches her beautiful red lips. Evie rarely wears lipstick and now all I want to do is push her up against a wall and ruin it.

"There was no look," I play it off nonchalantly.

Evie rolls her eyes and huffs, "Whatever you say. I know Miss Lizzie. I also know she has a soft spot for you. She'll do anything you say."

"She has a soft spot for everyone. You more than anyone. She is your godmother, after all. Here, looks like this work station is empty." I point to an empty station. She nods and we scope out the supplies. Seems standard except for one thing: there is a small white envelope.

Dorsey gets up on stage, "So before we start, we decided to add in a little twist this year to make it interesting. At each station, you will find a small white envelope and inside is a Christmas movie that you have to emulate through the construction and decoration of your gingerbread house. Now, Miss Lizzie and I have seen all of these classic films multiple times so there is going to be some harsher judging this year. Good luck, everyone! Let the best team win! Your thirty minutes starts now!"

Run Run Rudolph booms over the loud speakers, so loud I can't hear myself think. Great. This is not an optimal environment for me to talk to Evie about the other night, or just talk to her in general.

Evie grabs the envelope and rips it open like it's a present on Christmas Day. I forgot how fricken competitive she can be. Her eyes skim over the text on the white card.

"What movie did we get?"

"*It's A Wonderful Life.* I swear the universe hates me."

"Why do you say that?" I place the bottom of the gingerbread house in the center of the table.

She takes another piece of gingerbread and holds it up on the side of our foundation. "Because I really loved the house over on Main Street, I think partly because it reminded me of the ratty old house in *It's A Wonderful Life.*"

I get the icing into a piping bag, staying silent.

"Do you remember I had a dream of buying it from old Mrs. Johnson and renovating it?"

"How can I forget?" My heart is pulsing so hard against my chest. Evie has her walls down with me. I can listen to her talk forever.

"Well, it's off the market."

I nod and press my lips together. This dark cloud hovers over Evie and I don't like it.

"Maybe it's for the best. You know, I bet you the old wood floors are rotted and the foundation is shot. You don't want to have to deal with that, Evie. And you have the inn now so you can really focus on transforming that place into something wonderful. And from my assessment, you already have."

Her eyes meet mine and the power she has over me is unnerving. I am not above destroying our work station and making out with her on this table in front of the entire town. I was not joking about ruining that lipstick.

She looks down and clears her throat. "Are you planning on wasting all of our icing?"

I follow her gaze and look down. I was pressing against the icing in the bag so hard that it was leaking from the small opening. There is icing everywhere except where we need it. "Shit."

Evie laughs and her entire face lights up. And then she cocks an eyebrow. "And you call yourself a classically trained chef? You sure you can handle the icing? This needs to look neat."

"I think I can handle it. I'm really good with my hands." I wink at her.

Evie's cheeks turn very pink as she moves her hair behind her shoulder and glances at my hands.

I smirk. "Comes with the job. Like you said, I am classically trained."

She grabs the icing bag from me. "Will you stop?"

"Stop what?"

"Distracting me."

"Apologies. Didn't realize I was distracting you." I flash her a smile and roll up my sleeves.

She clocks my exposed forearms, her weakness. "Well you are. With all your innuendos and..." She waves her hands animatedly towards my body. "All this."

"Who said anything about innuendos? I was just speaking the truth. I'm a chef. If I'm not good with my hands, there is a serious problem. I was also the star quarterback. Being good with my hands comes with the territory of both those things. You need to get your head out of the gutter, Evie. This is a family event."

Evie turns even more red and she cutely tries to deflect. "Geez, you're like my own personal ghost of Christmas past."

"But I'm like a hot ghost of Christmas past though, right?"

She shrugs and purses her red lips. "I don't know. With all that scruff, you're looking a little old, Pearson. You have total Marley vibes."

I rub my jawline. "Ouch. So you hate the scruff look, huh?"

"I never said I hated it." There's that blush again. She intricately lines another wall to the foundation. Damn, I forgot how good she is with icing. Focused Evie is also my favorite. I love the little crease that develops between her eyebrows. It's a little different than the crease that is present when she is upset.

I go up behind her and frame her in with my arms. "Don't forget to line the inside, too."

Her hands get shaky and I can sense her breathing shift. She looks over her shoulder at me. "How can I forget? You taught me that."

My stomach twists. It's like no time has passed between us. We are suddenly those teenagers competing in our town's closest thing to the Hunger Games. We were champions every year.

Evie's eyes flutter and she brings us back to reality. "Let's get the roof on and make sure it stays up."

"You got it, boss."

"So, which version of the house should we do? I was thinking the one that Mary actually fixed up into a cozy home. I always loved the idea of her transforming a house that people did not think twice about. She also took matters into her own hands and made her dream into a reality. Plus, it screams Christmas."

"You have the lead on this one, Evie. I agree."

She smirks as she continues icing. I look around the room and spot Jeremy peering over at us, clearly zeroing in on Evie. There is a slight scowl on his face. I know he is pissed he didn't get paired with Evie. He was probably hoping for date number two.

"Twenty minutes everyone!" Dorsey calls out, as if there isn't a giant timer above his head that we can all see and keep track of the time ourselves.

I clear my throat and start doing some reinforcement icing along each seam. "So, how has your dating life been?"

She furrows her eyebrows up at me. "Fine."

"That bad, huh?" I tease, while simultaneously feeling a rush of relief set into every fiber of my being.

She stretches out her shoulders and places more icing in the bag. "No, it's just...You know what? It's none of your business.

My dating life is none of your business. It's not like I am asking you about all the women you have been with since you left town."

I want her to keep prodding. *Prod until you reach the truth, Evie.* "Ask me. I'm an open book."

She takes a deep breath and hurt flickers across her face. "Let's just focus on this. I can't let anyone else win this again. It's already been hard enough watching other people win. I haven't done this since..."

Her voice trails off and knots form in my stomach when I realize why. "Since I left?"

She squeezes the icing bag and slowly creates a border on the rooftop. "Yeah, I just didn't have the desire to do it anymore. But I still wanted to come and be part of the magic of the season. That's when I decided I would be the unofficial photographer and decorator. I needed to be around the joy. It helped me see other people smiling and having fun. It was a magic portal that took away all the trouble and grief and... heartache I was feeling."

"Heartache over your mom getting cancer...or me?" If she won't prod, I will. I want to get to the hard truths. I want to face our demons. Rid us of everything that tore us apart.

She continues decorating the house and without skipping a beat says flatly, "Both."

The last fifteen minutes fly by, but we finish the drafty old Bailey house right as the timer goes off. It really does look like the house, complete with windows and the turret in front. Evie had a great idea to use our extra gingerbread pieces to construct the turret. It was an essential part of the structure, so naturally we had to include it. We even dusted white sprinkles over the house and the ground to make it look like snow.

"Good job, team." I hold my hand up for a high-five.

Evie's hand collides with mine. Her touch ignites every single spark in my body. I want so desperately to interlace my fingers with hers and pull her towards me until she is nestled comfortably in her favorite nook. I stop short. *Baby steps. I got her to smile and let go a little today. Don't push her.*

Our house is the last to be inspected. Mr. Dorsey and Miss Lizzie have been brutal to basically everyone's houses. I am low-key nervous of their critique, which is comical since I have been critiqued by the most intimidating food critics in the world. They don't even take two seconds to look at our house when Mr. Dorsey declares, "Well, I think we have our winners! This is just magnificent, you two. The champions are back."

He goes up to the stage to announce our win and the crowd cheers. Evie smiles and tucks her hair behind her ear. She claps excitedly, and Allison and Kevin come over and give us both hugs. Just like old times. Warmth spreads across my chest. This is what I've been missing. Community.

"Now, scoot in together, you two," Miss Lizzie gestures towards us. "Kevin and Allie, move out of the way. Y'all's house was terrible."

"Okay, tell me how to make *The Polar Express* work! There isn't a set house in the film!" Kevin almost shouts. Evie, Allie and I all start giggling like teenagers at Kevin's reaction.

"Regardless, you could've done a little better. Now move out of the photo. Noah and Evie, move in closer to each other. Come on." She pushes Evie toward me until she hits the side of my arm. Evie drops her hands in front of her and I do the same. Miss Lizzie looks through the lens of the camera and makes a face. "Jesus, you two look like you are about to take a mug shot. This won't do. Noah, place your newly sculpted arm around Evie's shoulder, sweetie. At least pretend you are happy to see each other again."

I feel myself turning red and I look down at Evie, who is now the color of her lips. I scoff to make light of the situation. "Um, excuse me? 'Newly sculpted'? Did you forget I was a number-one prospect for division one football, Miss Lizzie?"

"Those arms were nothing like the arms you have now, honey. Now hush and do what I say." Miss Lizzie looks through the lens again and waits for me to do as I am told. I wrap my arm around Evie's shoulder and pull her a little closer. She still smells like cherry and vanilla. For a split second, we are back at Hollybury High, taking the cutest couple photograph for the yearbook. Evie's rigidity softens the longer I hold her against me.

"Smile."

We do and Miss Lizzie finally snaps our picture. She looks at the picture before handing over Evie's camera. "Perfect. Oh! I almost forgot, I have your prize right here."

She hands Evie another white envelope. Evie tears open the envelope and reads, "An intimate dinner for two at Enzo's Italian Restaurant." She shakes her head and presses her fingers against the bridge of her nose. "You have got to be kidding me."

"I am not kidding you at all, darling." She pats Evie's hands and turns to walk away, her red poncho swaying with each step. "Oh, by the way, it's void after Christmas Eve, so I would get to using that." Miss Lizzie gives me a final wink before she exits the Town Hall.

Evie presses the envelope and voucher against my chest. "Here, maybe you can use this with Blair. You two seemed to be getting cozy earlier. I'm sure she would love an intimate dinner with *the* Noah Pearson."

I grasp the voucher before it falls to the ground. "Evie..."

She secures her beanie and throws the strap of her camera around one of her shoulders, pulling her hair out from under the black strap. "See you later at the inn, Noah."

17

Evie

I am plopped on the couch at the inn, looking through the photos that Miss Lizzie took to see if any of them are usable. She actually did a decent job. They are mainly candids, which is what I was going for. The only problem? About two-thirds of them are of me and Noah.

The worst thing about it is that we actually look happy. The way he is looking at me in these pictures is making me melt.

How is it possible that he got more good-looking with age? I want to kick myself for saying that he looked like old-man

Marley from *A Christmas Carol* when it couldn't be more opposite. I wince at the memory because what I really wanted to say was, "You look like the new Superman except so much hotter." The scruff that lines his jawline and the tattoos...those tattoos are something I never thought I needed until I saw them on Noah Pearson. Miss Lizzie captured the moment when Noah is behind me, trapping me between him and the table, a position I actually wouldn't mind if it wasn't for being in public and the fact that we aren't together anymore. I look a little flushed but maybe it is because he is so handsome it hurts to look at him sometimes. That's how I felt about him for years and that sentiment hasn't changed. It's only been amplified. His deep green eyes always have a way of seeing into the depths of my soul.

"What are you looking at?" Gerard peeks over my shoulder. I fumble my camera and catch it before it falls on the floor. Thank goodness for my cat-like reflexes.

"What the hell, G? I thought you were going to cut some more firewood! We need to make sure that we have an adequate amount. It's supposed to snow pretty bad in a couple of days."

"First of all, good morning to you. Here is your piping hot vanilla latte. Honestly I'm surprised that you requested a latte. Going for the hard stuff this morning...we will get into the reason later, which I am assuming has everything to do with the photos of Hottie McChef." I grab my coffee from his hand. "Second, it's fucking Antarctica outside and I am not about to go out there and freeze my ass off. I'm sure we can find a suitable person for this job. What about your new beau Jer-Bear?"

"He's not my new beau and don't call him Jer-Bear."

"Interesting. So what is he to you if not your new beau?"

"A sweet man who went on a date with me and had so much compassion and grace for me after I turned him down the other night."

"Excuse me, you did what now?"

I sip my coffee. "I just wasn't feeling it the other night. It felt...wrong."

"Like wrong as in 'he was trying to force himself on you' wrong? I will slap a bitch."

I snort. "No, not like that. It started with a kiss goodnight on the porch which turned into a make-out session. He had all the right moves but it just didn't feel right." I shrug. "Maybe I wasn't ready."

"Or maybe he isn't Hottie McChef."

I shoot him a look. I am not going to give Gerard the satisfaction that his observation is spot-on. "Or maybe I don't need a man anymore. I've been pretty good at keeping myself satisfied."

"Oh girl, a vibrator can't do what the man in those pictures can do. Trust me. Let me see those photos again."

I reluctantly hand over my camera. Gerard skips through the photos of everyone else, then pauses and makes all kinds of silly faces. "What?"

"Whatever do you mean?" He hands my camera back to me.

"What are those faces for?"

"Call me crazy..."

"We are already there, so continue." I click through the photos mindlessly.

"As I was saying before being so rudely interrupted by your snarkiness, it seems to me that he brings out your glow. I have never seen you this way. In all the years I have known you. You've never glowed. It's a nice look on you." He bumps into me in a loving way. "I don't want you to be afraid of loving a man who clearly is still in love with you. No one has ever looked at me like that man looks at you."

I don't know what to say. There is so much history between me and Noah that it is going to take time to divulge every detail to Gerard. We were so busy in college, letting go and having fun with each other, that I didn't really get into the tome that is the history of me and Noah. It all seemed so heavy. I didn't want to go there.

Gerard squeezes my shoulders and points to the small screen on my camera. "That one is my favorite."

It's the same photo I paused on earlier and suddenly I have this primal need to get back in between Noah's bulky arms. To feel the warmth that radiated off every inch of his body. To be in his bubble. It used to be my favorite place and I didn't realize how much I missed that bubble.

"Just give me a little bit. I am going to pour some more coffee. That one cup was not enough. I need more caffeine if I am going to do any sort of manual labor. You better hope I don't injure myself."

I turn off my camera and set it on the coffee table. I poke the crackling fire and add another log. I yell over my shoulder, "You know, G, I told you I can chop the firewood but you insisted that you could do it. Something about you being the man and all. So I don't feel sorry for you one bit." I place the fireplace screen in front of the large flames and straighten the stockings and garland hanging on the mantle. "You are such a drama queen."

That comment doesn't elicit any kind of reaction from my best friend. Anytime I call him a drama queen he is quick to deny it—even though it is completely true. He has this ability to turn any small situation into something grander than it has to be. But I guess that is part of his fabulousness. If Hollybury had its own spin-off of Real Housewives, Gerard would be the star.

I push open the door to the kitchen and Gerard is standing by the coffee machine and staring out the window above the sink. I approach him and say, "Paging Mr. Drama Queen." Gerard clearly does not register that I am standing next to him, and I realize that coffee is overflowing from his full mug, thus getting all over the counters. His mouth is parted and obviously whatever he is staring at outside must be more important than prepping the bed and breakfast for a massive winter storm. I frantically rip a paper towel off the roll and the stand falls into the sink.

"G! You are making a huge mess. Um, hello, what the heck are you staring at?"

"Him." Gerard exhales and I decide to look outside to see what – or rather, who – has him so distracted.

A fire ignites in my body when I register the sight before me. There in a tight white henley shirt and snug-fit jeans is Noah, chopping firewood. His strong, rhythmic movements match my heartbeat as I watch him. His sleeves are rolled up, exposing his veiny, tattooed forearms. It seems like every single muscle on that man is engaged in each swing, and with as hard he is hitting the wood, I honestly think he is going to break the axe.

Thud. Thud. Thud.

A vibration travels through every inch of my body each time the axe meets the wood. Despite it being a whole forty degrees outside, droplets of sweat are falling down his face and small tendrils of hair are dangling above his stern, thick eyebrows. Between the sweat and what I am assuming is an obvious misjudgment of shirt size, it looks like that white shirt is painted on his body. I can see every ridge of his chest and abs and it leaves me breathless.

Teenager Noah is long gone. He has been replaced by Man Noah...Sexy Noah...Tattooed Noah...This is a new and improved Noah Pearson. I thought I knew every inch of that man's body. I was clearly wrong.

Gerard clears his throat. "Girl, you know that you are going to puncture that bottom lip of yours if you don't stop biting down on it."

I snap out of whatever spell Noah's muscles just put me under and relax my mouth. Gerard just wiggles his eyebrows. "I was just getting whipped cream off my lip...nothing else."

"Sure, nothing else made you look like you were about to pounce on your smokeshow of an ex-boyfriend. If that's your story."

"It is." I look out the window again and Noah lifts up his shirt to wipe off his sweaty face. And that's when I see his abs. They should be on exhibit at a museum. They are too beautiful and unreal. He looks through the window right at me. His eyes are intense and soft all at once. Then he gives me a wicked grin and winks at me. Fucking winks. I have told him on multiple occasions how hot and bothered that makes me. It's unsettling and throws me off-kilter. So naturally, I drop to the ground, hoping this is all a weird dream and that I fell asleep on the couch and not the reality of what it is–that I was checking out my ex-boyfriend.

Gerard bursts into laughter. "Girl, who are you trying to fool? I don't know what you are waiting for. Go out there and climb Noah like the big bulky tree that he is. You are still down bad for this man. It's all over that cute little red face. Don't deny it."

I touch my cheeks and they are indeed on fire. It makes me blush more. "It's not that. It's just hot in here from the heater and fire. Plus, I dropped something on the floor. I had to pick it up."

"There is one fatal flaw in that defense."

"What, are you a lawyer now?"

"I have been watching *The Lincoln Lawyer* on repeat because, hello. Have you seen the guy that plays Mickey Haller?" Gerard fans himself for a brief moment, then helps me on my feet. "Don't deflect, Evie. The only hot thing that made you all hot and bothered is walking in from the backyard now."

Right then, the back door squeaks open, and Noah steps in. He is fricken glistening with sweat. He proceeds to take the flannel shirt that I am assuming he wore over that skin-tight henley and wipes off his face. He scrunches his eyebrows together when he notices a coffee-stained paper towel still in my hand and clocks the counter, still partly covered in the coffee flood that occurred minutes ago. "What happened here?"

I lean against the sink. "Gerard spilled coffee."

"I can see that. I guess the question I should have asked is, 'Why did he spill the coffee?' " He comes closer to me and that's when his familiar woodsy masculine scent muddles my thoughts. My knees become shaky. It's like my body glitches around Noah. Like I can't think straight. The steady level-headedness I have developed over the years is obliterated in his presence. There is a constant ebb and flow of memories of us and the reality of us. It's super disorienting. I focus hard on looking at only his eyes because if I look anywhere else, my knees would truly buckle and I'd be on the floor in seconds.

I clear my throat and shrug. "Just got distracted, I guess."

In my peripheral vision, I see Gerard leaning against the counter, sipping his coffee and smirking, clearly enjoying the show Noah and I are giving him. All he needs is popcorn and he is set. I shoot him an annoyed look before my attention is right back to the musky, muscle-y man who is now inches from me.

"You know I always thought you were cute when you would play it cool."

Gerard starts choking on his coffee. I leer at him.

"Why would I be playing it cool? There's no need to play anything cool. Even if there was anything I'd have to be cool about, it is just my natural state of being. Cool as a cucumber."

Cool as a cucumber? I mentally slap my hand to my face. I immediately get on the defensive. "Why are you standing so close to me? Did you need something, Mr. Pearson?" *Keep things professional. Because that's all this will ever be. A business arrangement.*

He points to the sink, "I need to wash my hands. And you are kind of blocking the sink, Ms. Hawkins."

I move across the way and lean on the island as Noah runs his large, rough hands under the water. The way the sunlight is hitting his chiseled features is too much to handle. There's a dazzling haze around him, like he is a vision or a mirage that I mustered up in my head. I still cannot believe he is back. It's strange. I wanted him to be back for so long. I don't know when I began to block out that desire. It was probably masked in the midst of all the other coping mechanisms I leaned on while my mom was sick and I was trying to continue on with life.

"I was outside chopping some firewood for a while. Figured you needed to stock up before the big storm coming in next week." He dries his hands on the kitchen towel and starts ogling me like I was just doing to him. Scanning me from head to toe, trying to figure out his next move or next thing to say. I know that I have been very standoffish with him since he has been back. It's crazy what fear can do to someone.

I shift my weight to my other foot, making a feeble attempt to shift the stifling energy in the room. "Thank you for chopping the wood."

"You're welcome." His eyes never leave mine. I swear he can hear my heart beating like a kick drum. "Well," he continues, "I'll bring that wood in and stack it for you."

"No, that's not necessary, Noah. Gerard here can do it."

Gerard scoffs as if it's completely out of the ordinary that I would suggest such a thing even though he was the one responsible for the heavy lifting before Noah came back. I leer at him again. He is enjoying this interaction way too much.

Gerard is about to rebuke my statement, when Noah grabs the to-go coffee cup I abandoned on the counter and hands it to me. Our fingers brush for a second and my breath hitches as my body tingles. I look up at him, his deep green eyes searching mine, waiting for a sign that it is okay that he is completely breaking open everything I fought so hard to close. Our past is now muddled with our present. The air between us gets heavy. Maybe Gerard isn't too far off-base about me and Noah.

Maybe that photo wasn't deceptive.

Maybe that photo said everything.

"I insist." Noah throws the towel onto the counter and heads back out to the backyard. I exhale and shake my head before snatching another paper towel and absorbing the now-lukewarm liquid covering the counter.

"How do you not fall to your knees and worship him? I know I want to."

"You say that about any hot guy who crosses your path."

"Ah, so you admit that he is hot?"

I never said he wasn't.

18

Evie

It has been a few days since the wood-chopping incident and luckily Noah and I have been so busy with our own tasks, nothing awkward has happened between us. We do have to finalize the menu for the soft opening at some point in the near future. There have been occasional interactions, mainly him bringing me an extra cup of hot chocolate or food that he whipped up. The flavors are always nothing short of fantastic. I was stupid to think I could truly enforce a trial period for a man who makes the most incredible food that I've ever consumed.

Today, thankfully, I have another distraction from Noah. I have to go pick up some vintage decor from a nearby town and I need to use my dad's truck.

Unfortunately, my dad is in the kitchen shooting the shit with Noah. It's not lost on me that my dad has missed having someone to talk about football with. Other than somewhat understanding the quarterback position, I know nothing about football. I take a deep breath and swing the kitchen door open. Sure enough, my dad is leaning against the island with probably his third cup of coffee while they are discussing the outcomes of the Thanksgiving games. The only things I am interested in on Thanksgiving are the food and the parade. "Hey, Dad! Clay called earlier and said he has some inventory at his antique shop that is perfect for me. Can I use the truck to drive to New Hartford?" I breeze past Noah toward the fridge and grab a water bottle.

My dad scratches the back of his head. "Not today, Evie. Remember, Mom has her check-up appointment."

The fridge door shuts harder than I mean it to. "Shoot. I'll just call Clay and tell him to hold those items for me until the truck is available." Out of the corner of my eye, I see Noah wiping down the counters. Even when he does something as mundane as wiping down counters, he makes my knees weak. I thought my body became used to not being around him. It's now reminding me every second I am near Noah that it's clearly not immune. Then a solution pops into my head: "Actually, Dad, let me text Jeremy! He has a truck and he can drive me over there."

I'm about to pull out my phone and text Jeremy when I hear Noah say, "I'll drive you."

I start to protest but Dad steps in. "Oh, that's a great idea." He walks over to Noah and pats him on the shoulder. Noah is smirking as he unties his apron and places it on the golden hook he insisted I install. "It's solved then! Oh, and Noah, bring my daughter back in one piece. Safe and sound."

"You got it, Bill." Noah gives him a little salute, something he used to do back when we were dating.

I sigh and gesture to the door. This is the first time we will be truly alone for an extended period of time since Noah came back to town. I can't stay mute the entire trip. Can I?

I walk out of the kitchen and head to the reception desk, where Gerard looks a little out of breath and is organizing the drawers for the thousandth time. I know he was eavesdropping on the conversation in the kitchen and hustled back here when he heard us coming toward the swinging door. I wrap my coat around me, take out my beanie I stuffed in my coat pocket, and place it on my head. "Okay, I'll be back. You're in charge, G." Gerard gives me a sly look. I mouth, "Behave."

"You have a fantastic day, Gerard," Noah says while putting his own coat on. And then he fricken winks at Gerard. Winks. I think Gerard is going to fall to the ground from sheer bliss. Once I shut the door, I feel my phone vibrate:

> You need to get over yourself and just bang him already.

> Nobody says bang anymore. It's not happening.

> That wink was lethal, girl. If you don't,
> I will.

I click the side of my phone. I am not entertaining Gerard's suggestions. Noah strides in front of me and opens the passenger door. The faded red paint color of the 1960s Chevy pickup looks exactly the same. As if no time has passed. But that's a lie.

"I can open my own door, Noah."

"Oh, I am well aware that you can open your own door. Doesn't mean that I can't do it for you. Grandad taught me better than that."

I climb into the weathered seat.

As he is shutting the door, he says, "You know that." I do know. All at once, I remember the very first time he picked me up for a date and I attempted to get into this truck and he said, "Don't you dare, Evie. When you are with me, you will never open your own door."

Noah props himself in the driver's seat and turns on the engine. He blasts the heater. Even though this truck was made in the sixties, Noah has maintained it very well. He adjusts the radio until he finds a station that is strictly Christmas music. My core starts to heat up slightly from the comfortability of it all. From the utter familiarity and the memories that this car holds. Memories where I am on top of him, mouths crashing together wildly, hands running through each other's hair. Being completely in the moment with no regard of what was going on outside the truck.

My cheeks flush. I adjust my beanie and sit on my hands,

trying to keep them warm. Noah chuckles softly. I glance over at him and I see his dangerously sexy dimples appear underneath his scruff, which he never had in high school, and which I secretly love.

I finally break the silence. "What?"

"Nothing." His dimples deepen as his smile widens.

"Tell that to the smirk that's spread across your face. Tell me what you are thinking."

"You first. You're the one who was blushing out of nowhere." His eyes are sparkling like he already knows the answer, which he probably does since he was involved in the very graphic memory that popped into my head that I actively tried to push away for the past seven years. He could always read me way too well. Other than my parents, he is the only one who could.

"I just can't believe you still have this truck, that's all."

"Really? You're not thinking about that night after we made the football playoffs and we went out to the middle of nowhere and...celebrated in ways that your parents and my grandfather would disapprove of?"

"Maybe." I'm not ready to fully admit to him that he's had a hold on me since day one. I am grappling with the new reality that he is actively back in my life again while simultaneously confronting our old reality of being inseparable.

I wasn't expecting the love of my life to come back to me. It's what I dreamt about for years. And yet, I am struggling to let him in. He was gone for so long that I learned to live without him. I let go a long time ago of the dream that he would come back and stay. And now that the dream seems possible again... I don't trust it.

Noah drives by the old house that I wanted to get my hands on once I started making profit from the bed and breakfast. Seeing the SOLD sign plastered to the For Sale sign makes my stomach twist with disappointment. I cross my arms and look back out the wide windshield, watching small flurries fly off the tree branches, then circle around and land on the glass.

Noah cuts through all the noise swirling around in my head. "I wonder who bought it."

I tighten my grip on my arms. "Probably some rich New Yorker wanting to come in and get rid of all the charm that house has to offer."

He clears his throat and turns on the blinker. "You're still cute when you pout."

"I'm not pouting." I stand my ground, knowing full well that I am.

"You are pouting. But it's endearing as hell. Always has been."

My pout softens and I study him. His veiny hand grips the steering wheel and he looks completely at ease. It's not as if he just called me "cute" and made my insides twist around and my face get hot once again.

I play with my necklace. For years, it has brought me comfort and I always had this silly notion that maybe Noah kept his half. I remember giving him the other half in high school. I remember Noah teasing me about it, but I got it engraved on the back with our names. I wore the side that said *Noah* and I gave him the one that said *Evie*. I will never forget the words he said to me: "You are more than a best friend to me. You expect me to wear this?" All I could say in response was, "You don't have to wear it, but I always will." At that moment, I put the necklace on and said, "There. Now you will always be close to my heart."

"Now you will always be close to my heart." Noah's deep voice pierces through my trip down memory lane. He looks over at me. "I remember, Evie."

We stare at each other for far too long, because we hear a horn blast and Noah slams on his brakes. I don't know when we got into town. Between Noah making me flustered, my memories coming to the surface, and Noah's recital of the very words I told him almost eight years ago, I have never been so distracted from my surroundings. He almost ran the red light, so naturally people are trying to get our attention. His hand presses against my chest, sending a shock wave through me because, to be honest, I haven't been touched like that in a very long time. I know that he only threw out his arm instinctually, to protect me from ramming into the dashboard, but I really do not want his hand to leave my body. Every single time he has touched me since being back, it sends tingles across my skin. I feel like I am going to burst. I missed his touch. I missed him.

"Shit." Noah smiles and waves to the angry cars crossing in front of the truck and mouths, "Sorry." Then he clocks that his hand is still on my boob and says, "Shit. Sorry," again and retracts his hand like he just got scolded. I can't help but laugh because this is classic Noah. Always so respectful.

"I thought you were going to get me there safely. You promised my dad to get me to my destination in one piece," I say jokingly. "Don't worry, this will be our little secret."

The light turns green and I see a dangerous smirk cross his face. "There are plenty of secrets this truck has kept for us, Evie. I think this old girl has room for at least one more." He winks at me. "I will always protect you. I promised you I always would."

My face flushes again. I swear this man has always had that effect on me. It goes to show that time doesn't necessarily heal everything or change anything. Not for us.

"There's Clay's store there to the right." I point forward toward a small shop nestled in the town square. Noah pulls into a spot right in front of the store and before I unbuckle myself, he is halfway around the truck, opening my door for me. Without asking and like he did in high school, he grabs my hand to help me down. I don't want to protest. Partly because I missed this type of chivalry. Partly because I do need help getting down. I am barely scratching the surface of 5'3" and Noah is a whole foot taller than me. He doesn't have these issues, but he is always attuned to what people around him need. At least he has always been attuned to me. That's one of the things I love about him.

Loved about him.

"Thanks." I look up at his green eyes. I scan his features. He is definitely older, but his eyes haven't changed one bit. They still glitter with kindness and mischief all at once. I hear a bell ring and see a figure come out of the old turquoise door of Clay's store.

"Hey Evie! Glad you came by! I have some things that I think you might like for the bed and breakfast."

I finally divert my eyes from Noah's and I am convinced that I hear a low growl coming from him. I move past him and say hi to Clay. Noah slams the heavy metal door and walks up to the entrance of the store.

We step into the store, following an excited Clay toward the back. "When we got these pieces in, I was telling my sisters that Evie needs to see them! She's going to love them!"

"Thanks for thinking of me. Show me the way."

Noah clears his throat. "Hey man, my name is Noah." He outstretches his hand.

Clay looks up at Noah, who has a solid five inches on him. Clearly not picking up on the protectiveness and, dare I say, jealousy in Noah's demeanor, Clay approaches Noah with a hug instead of a handshake and it makes me smile from ear to ear. I am *so* going to tease him about this later.

"Noah Pearson! I know who you are. It's so nice to finally meet you. My sisters love you and your appearances on all those cooking shows. I swear they have been addicted to the *Food Network* ever since you joined the lineup. And Evie has told me just a smidge about you." He scrunches his face and puts his hands in his pockets, "You two used to date a while ago, right? Evie is my favorite customer."

"Right. It's nice to meet you, Clay. Can you show us the merchandise that Evie will be so in love with? I promised to have her back soon."

I shoot Noah a pissed-off look. Why is he being so rude to Clay? Clay is literally the nicest person. Not to mention the goofiest person I've ever met. And so completely not a threat.

"Oh yeah!" Clay bumps my shoulder playfully. "I promise these are perfect for the bed and breakfast. And of course if there is anything else in the store that you want, let me know."

I follow him excitedly. I need a few more decor items to make the bed and breakfast feel more cozy, and Clay's pieces never disappoint. My excitement is dampened slightly by Noah's shitty demeanor.

"Ta-da!" Clay points me in the direction of some beautiful artwork, a side table I could use in the common living room, a couple of small accent chairs, and other small items. "Feel free to peruse for as long as you want. Hey, Noah, nice to meet you, man. Seriously, a pleasure."

Noah gives a smug smile. "Same to you, Clay."

I don't have time to process everything that just happened. I want to enjoy my time shopping around. I decide to get all the pieces Clay set aside for me and some other items as well. I lose track of Noah. Clay's store is always stocked from floor-to-ceiling and wall-to-wall with so many treasures, I am sure Noah got lost in the chaos.

I am about to hand Clay my card to pay, but out of the blue Noah lays down his black Amex card on the desk and next to that, he places a Leica M6. "This too."

My heart skips a beat. This camera is beautiful and every time I visit Clay's store, I have wanted it. Its gorgeous walnut veneer and glossy black finish caught my eye months ago. I have been so busy budgeting for the inn, I hardly shop for myself anymore. How did he know?

Clay raises his eyebrows, smiles and says, "Sure thing, boss." He swipes Noah's card and gives it back to him.

"Noah," I exhale.

He looks directly at Clay, "Does this still work, Clay?"

"Yes! I fully restored it before placing it on my shelves. That way whoever bought it could use it if they wanted to. Or it could be a decorative piece. It's really up to the buyer."

Noah slides his card back into his wallet. "Thank you so much for your help today, Clay. You made Evie very happy."

"No, thank you for coming in. And I think it's safe to say that you have made her happy too! Right, Evie?"

Still flabbergasted that Noah just bought me this gorgeous, limited edition, operational camera, I say, "Yes. Thank you, Clay. I'll see you at the soft opening, right?"

"Wouldn't miss it. Now, you all better head out. It looks like a storm might be coming in. Don't want you to get stuck in it. Do you need help loading everything in the truck, Noah?"

"Sure man, thanks." Noah lifts one of the accent chairs and heads to the doorway. "You coming, Evie?"

Somehow I am frozen. Unable to move my feet. Unable to process all the emotions coming to the surface. It's everything all at once. Can I really accept this? I look down at the beautiful black camera in my hands. My thumb runs over the cool metal and flashbacks of me on the sidelines of his football games emerge in my brain. Those were some of my favorite photos. Capturing him in moments of pure happiness while he was doing something he loved. He has always been so unapologetically himself. This thoughtful gesture–him buying me this vintage camera that he knew I would love–is so on-brand for him. I don't know how I can ever repay him, but if he is the same Noah Pearson I loved once, he wouldn't even allow me to repay him if I could. I clutch onto this precious gift and exit Clay's shop, wondering what else Noah might have up his sleeve.

WE PULL into the driveway to the bed and breakfast. Noah orders me to stay in the truck while he unloads everything inside. The whole ride home, I carefully held my new camera, admiring its every angle and feeling this burst of excitement and inspiration I haven't felt in a while. I have been so busy with renovating and getting the bed and breakfast up and running, I don't have all the time in the world to take photographs. The gingerbread contest was the first opportunity in a while.

By the good grace of the universe, it doesn't start sleeting until Noah is done getting the last piece of furniture from the bed of his truck into the building. He runs back out to me, hair wet and falling over his piercing green eyes, open coat and flannel shirt wet from the frozen rain. He looks so irresistibly handsome. His scruff is a nice new touch to his look. He didn't have it back then. As if he can't get any hotter. He makes me breathless.

The sky is quickly turning dark from the storm clouds. And the only light illuminating anything is the front porch chandelier. Noah slides back into the driver's seat and slams the heavy door behind him. "Damn, that sleet is really coming down. It seems like your parents went home right after the appointment. Looks like Gerard has left, too. At least I don't see his car. Did you want to make your way to your car? I locked up. Here, let me find an umbrella. I have it somewhere." He reaches down under my feet and aimlessly moves his arm back and forth, attempting to find this elusive umbrella.

I set my camera on the dashboard and touch his forearm.

"Noah." His name barely escapes my lips as his body tenses under my touch.

He slowly perks up, hair still dripping. His eyes scan my face. I am certain he can hear my pulse throbbing and I suck in a breath from the shock that has flooded my entire body. His hand that was mindlessly searching for the umbrella slowly traces up my leg until it reaches the side of my hip. His face is still slightly lower than mine and his lips are parted. The porch light hits his face just right and his eyes turn to emeralds. Droplets fall from his hair and land on my hand that is still holding onto his forearm...correction, digging my nails into his forearm.

He lingers about an inch in front of my face and I have lost the ability to breathe normally. The sleet is hitting the windshield hard, intensifying the air between us. I am unable to care that we are broken up. Unable to care how terrified I am that he is this close to me. All I can think about is how much I miss his lips on mine and how much I want to twist my fingers in his wet hair.

My self-control is being tested and I fear that I may fail.

"Evie..." he whispers.

My mouth is suddenly dry. *Words, Evie. Say words.* "Yeah?"

His thumb traces my hip, making me quiver. I close my eyes and give in to whatever is about to happen because clearly my body wants it. I want anything that Noah cares to offer me on a silver platter.

A bright set of headlights causes us to pull away from each other and shield our eyes. It's Gerard's car. He was here after all. He must have parked in the back. Maybe he was in the basement and didn't hear Noah come in to drop off all the treasures I found today. Gerard waves at us when he passes the truck and I quickly retrieve my keys from my purse and tuck the beautiful camera in my coat to protect it from the elements. I unlock my door and push it open.

"Evie, wait."

I don't give Noah a chance to say anything about what just happened. All I know is I need air. I slam the door and run to my car. By the universe's good graces, I don't slip and fall on my ass in the midst of the crazy sleet. I drop with a thud into my driver's seat and shut the door quickly. The leather padding on my door is covered in droplets of sleet, which are slowly melting away and creating their own little trails as they fall towards my door handle. The droplets falling from Noah's wet hair are all I can see. I shake my head and then ease back into the head rest. I am not sure what just happened in that truck. I just know that one second my body was in full-blown overdrive with desire and the next, my body short-circuited and brought me back to reality. Those eyes. They are the greatest reminders of all the things that made me fall for Noah. And now my last memory of Noah leaving in his truck from my parents' living room window is officially replaced by this memory of Noah. All I see when I close my eyes are his eyes, looking at me, assessing me.

The headlights from Noah's truck slowly disappear and that's my cue to head home, too. I press my cold hands onto my face and they provide a relief my overheated skin needed.

What just happened between us?

19

Evie

I cannot stop tossing and turning. My insomnia has gotten so bad. I can't stop thinking about all the things I have to do in the morning at the inn, including baking cookies for the senior center like I do every year. I throw my cozy sheets off me and jump out of bed, pull on some comfy clothes and head to my kitchen. I look in my pantry and fridge and realize I need to desperately go grocery shopping. I do know of one place I can go to that is fully stocked. I snatch my keys from the small bowl on my entryway table and head to the inn.

I turn into the driveway of the inn and notice a light is on inside. "Ugh, Gerard forgot to turn off the lights again," I mumble to myself. He is the worst with that.

I adjust the wreath so the large red bow is centered and unlock the door. I hear a sound coming from the kitchen as I close the door behind me. My breathing gets heavy and anxiety sets in. There is no other car outside. My heart starts to beat really fast and I grab an umbrella from the coat rack. I need some line of defense. Another thing on my infinite to-do list: install a security system.

I tiptoe down the hallway toward the kitchen and as I approach the swinging door, I hear a deep voice singing *White Christmas*. I push the swinging door open and my heart beats faster as I see Noah with a kitchen towel over his shoulder, sprinkling spices into a steaming saucepan on the stove. It smells like everything I love about the season–cinnamon, nutmeg, and frasier fur. Noah looks so in his element, my insides twist with happiness because I know he is always the happiest when he is in the kitchen. No matter how successful he was on the football field, it was nothing compared to how he felt when he was prepping a meal.

My grip on the umbrella handle softens when I gaze at Noah. He is wearing a tight white short sleeve shirt, revealing the intricate sleeves of tattoos along his arms, and dark gray sweat pants. He is wearing an old Hollybury Husky hat backwards and some hair is peeping out underneath near his ears. He looks so different when he is not in his chef's coat. He looks like my Noah again.

My heart skips a beat when he continues to sing aloud to

one of my favorite Christmas songs. He has his air pods in his ear and I know he couldn't hear me even if I belted out his name. I can't help but smile and enjoy the free concert I didn't know I was going to receive at this early hour of the day. Even though I was expecting to be alone in this historic inn, I am kind of glad that I'm not.

I stealthily approach and tap Noah on his shoulder. He swings around so fast that he elbows me right in the cheekbone.

"Ow! Noah. It's me." I rub my cheekbone, knowing that I bruise like a peach. This is just great. A few weeks before our grand opening and I look like I got into a boxing match with Rocky Balboa.

Noah registers that it's me, frantically turns off the gas stove, and turns toward me with concern in his eyes. "Shit, Evie. I thought I was alone. You scared the hell out of me. I am so sorry, baby gir–" He immediately stops his train of thought. *Baby girl.* He always used to call me that. He clears his throat, throws his air pods on the counter and inspects where his elbow made contact, squinting like he's the one in pain. "Let me get you some ice." He goes into the freezer, grabs an ice pack, and wraps it in the towel draped over his shoulder. "Here." He presses it gently against my face.

"Thanks." Out of all the scenarios that raced through my head on what our next interaction would be, this wasn't one of them. Being in such close proximity to Noah makes my heart race, makes me dizzy. The other night in his truck was no exception. I slide my fingers under his to grab hold of the ice pack. They are warm and rough and exactly how I remember them. "I got it."

He peels his hand away slowly, as if wondering if that is the right move or if he should tell me to stop pushing him away because that is exactly what I am doing. Keeping him at arms-length. I don't want to get hurt again.

Still, the heaviness between us is unbearable. It needs to be lifted immediately. "So, is this karma for hitting you in the darkroom?" I joke.

His entire face lights up. Oh how I love how the crinkles in the outer corners of his eyes are getting deeper. "Um, I guess so. Although I am pretty happy with my karma right about now." His eyes shift to my other hand, which is still holding onto the umbrella. He cocks an eyebrow. "What's with the umbrella?"

"I was planning on using it on whatever nut job broke into my inn."

"First the tongs. Now the umbrella. I like that you are prepared enough to use whatever is around you to defend yourself. Scrappy."

"I've had to learn to think on my feet. You never know what curveballs life is going to throw at you." And just like that, the air gets heavy again.

"Well, I'm glad you can take care of yourself. I spent all of those years worrying about you and turns out, I didn't need to." He was worried about me? "Why are you here in the middle of the night, Evie?" He turns toward the stove again and turns on the burner under the sauce pan.

"I could ask you the same thing," I deflect, but I am also genuinely curious.

"You first." His voice is deep and slightly scratchy and completely heats my insides.

"I couldn't sleep." I do not want to tell him about my breakup/cancer-induced insomnia that developed seven years ago and never went away. "I was thinking about my checklist of tasks that need to be completed by Christmas Eve and then I remembered I forgot to bake cookies for the senior home. I didn't have enough ingredients at my house and I knew this kitchen was fully stocked so I decided to come here." I head to the pantry and get flour, baking powder, anise, salt, margarine, and sugar. I set everything on the island, then open the fridge and get out one egg.

"You still bring them your famous cinnamon sugar shortbread cookies?"

I take out a large cream mixing bowl and set it next to all the ingredients. "Famous? That's high praise from an acclaimed chef."

He comes closer to me and presses a palm on the counter. His presence almost makes me pour the whole bottle of cinnamon in the bowl. "I'm still me, Evie."

His scent is invigorating and familiar. I start measuring the ingredients to hopefully distract my body from completely crumbling from Noah's presence. "And to answer your question, yes. I bring them every year. They are Walter's favorite, after all. I aim to please. I need to be in Walter's good graces."

"You are always in grandad's good graces, trust me." Noah hands me the measuring spoon. "I think he loves you more than he loves me."

"That is not true. He adores you, Noah." I mix all the

ingredients together. "Now, do you want to know a little secret?"

"I'm the best at keeping secrets." The box of letters comes to the forefront of my mind. I'm not ready to talk about that, though.

"The original recipe for these cookies does not call for cinnamon."

He gasps. "You little rebel."

I wiggle my shoulders out of pride. "I think it adds a little extra something and it balances out the strong flavor of the anise, don't you think?" When Noah doesn't answer me, I look up at him and he is just staring at me with soft eyes and a goofy smile. "Why are you looking at me like that?" Then I get insecure and wipe the top of my nose, then my forehead. "Do I have something on my face?"

Noah chuckles and brushes his fingers along my forehead and nose. "Now you do. Hold still." He concentrates on the areas of my face that are covered in flour. "I just... missed you like this. Hair in a messy bun, in sweatpants. Not so buttoned-up and professional. Smiling at what I have to say and not fleeing in the other direction. The Evie that I used to know."

My heart aches because I know exactly how he feels. This is the Noah I fell in love with and it's scaring me. I convinced myself that he would change over the years. I am very wrong. "What are you making over there? It smells good."

"I am making some homemade horchata so I can make horchata eggnog. Thought I'd try it out for the party."

My stomach curls and I open my mouth to veto this very awful and disgusting idea.

He holds up his hand to stop me. "Now, I know that you hate eggnog. You had a bad experience when you were younger blah blah blah..."

"Not bad. Traumatic." I pretend to gag, remembering the very bad experience as a child when my cousin decided to switch out my regular milk with eggnog when I wasn't looking. When I took a drink of it, I thought the milk went bad and ran immediately to the bathroom to throw it up. I have not touched eggnog since.

Noah proceeds to turn off the burner, give the rice one last stir, and removes the cinnamon sticks. "Even so, I promise you that you will love this eggnog." He sets it aside to cool. "Maybe you should give eggnog a second chance, Evie."

For some reason, I feel like he is not just talking about the eggnog getting a second chance in my life. Like the eggnog, Noah leaving town left a sour taste in my mouth, even though I was the one who told him to leave. I was the one who ruined everything. Him staying away just made everything worse.

We continue our work in loaded silence, with only instrumental Christmas jazz blasting from the speaker on my phone to keep us company. About thirty minutes pass by and Noah and I have found a nice rhythm in the kitchen. I roll my last fresh batch of cookies in the cinnamon sugar mixture as Noah places the freshly made horchata in the refrigerator to cool. He walks over to the counter. "These smell so good, Evie."

I smile, swipe a cookie off the cooling rack, and hold it up to him. "Do you want to try one? Make sure I didn't screw it up?"

I place the cookie in the palm of his hand and he takes a

bite. His eyebrows raise. "Wow. These are so delicious. They are literally melting in my mouth."

"It's all that butter. Is the anise too much? I am always scared of that and I don't want to gross out anyo–"

Noah shoves a cookie in my mouth before I can self-sabotage any further. Turns out, he wasn't lying. These are my best ones yet.

He stands in front of me and crosses his arms, awaiting my assessment. I nod. "Okay, you were right. They are delicious."

"Told you." He reaches into one of the cabinets and pulls out two small glasses. He grabs milk out of the fridge and before he pours any into the glasses, he pauses. "Do you still like to drink milk with your cookies, like a five-year-old?"

"As a matter of fact, I do."

"Me too." He smiles and pours milk for both of us.

He places some cookies on a napkin and brings me my glass. "Do you want to watch a Christmas movie out in the living room? See how magical your Christmas tree looks all lit up?"

Oh, he's good. He knows that I am a sucker for a Christmas movie, especially watching one with the Christmas tree as the only other light source in the room. Simply magical.

When I don't answer right away, Noah backtracks. "I mean, if you don't want to or you are too tired, I totally understand. It is two in the morn–"

It's my turn to stuff a cookie in his mouth. "Noah. I am not tired. Let's go watch a movie." I grab the napkin of cookies out of his hand and take my glass of milk over to the living room. I sink onto the couch as Noah turns on the Christmas tree. I get the remote from the coffee table and turn on the TV. "What do you want to watch?"

Noah sits next to me. "Why are you even asking me that question? Since when does anyone else have a say in what Christmas movie to watch with you? You turn into a feral creature if anyone suggests anything other than what you want to watch."

"I do not."

Noah snorts and throws a blanket over us. There is maybe a foot between us but I can still feel his body heat and the energetic pull he continues to have on me. I desperately want to crawl into the little nook against his shoulder and chest like I used to, but I actively stop my body from moving from its spot.

"Maybe it's good to embrace change," I say. "Try something new." I hand him the remote.

He slowly takes it from me. "You sure? What if you hate my selection?"

"I won't. I trust you."

Noah browses the Christmas movie options and finally settles on *White Christmas*.

I widen my eyes at him. "Really, Noah? You hate musicals."

"Hate is a strong word. I am not the biggest fan of musicals, but I know you love them." He settles into his seat. "Besides, this one is growing on me a bit."

I FEEL the light hit my face and my body is extra warm. I slowly open my eyes and realize that I must have fallen asleep on the couch at the inn. The last thing I remember is watching Bob and Phil meet Betty and Judy.

That was the best night of sleep I have gotten in a while.

My head is resting on something hard and warm and comforting. Something that is definitely not the cushions of the couch.

Noah's chest. His arm is wrapped around my shoulder blades and his hand is resting on my lower back. His other hand is behind his head. He looks so peaceful and handsome in this morning light. I softly tap his chest and whisper, "Noah." His breathing changes and I can feel his heart race under my hand. My own breathing becomes erratic as he opens his eyes and I see my favorite shade of green in the world. I rest my chin on my hand. "We fell asleep on the couch."

He sleepily grunts. "This is probably the comfiest couch in the world."

"I don't mess around when it comes to comfy furniture. You should feel the mattresses." I immediately press my lips together when I hear how that sounded.

Noah picks up what I apparently put down. "Should I now?"

Then I hear a key in the lock and Gerard opens the front door. My body doesn't react fast enough. I nearly fall off the couch, but Noah's hand grips my arm to keep me on top of him. I feel the very hard ridges of his chest and abdomen and my stomach fills with flutters. Our noses are almost touching and my body is electrified.

"Evie? Is that you on the couch?" Gerard calls.

I pop up my head and smile as if I'm not on top of my ex-boyfriend. I try to push Noah down onto the couch in hopes that Gerard stays exactly where he is and he never has to know that Noah and I slept on this couch together.

Unfortunately, I am not as strong as Noah Pearson. He props up on his elbows, and says spritely, "Good morning, Gerard."

Gerard's face lights up and his eyes widen. *Here we go.* "Well, good morning to you, too. Let me guess, you are about to say 'This isn't what it looks like' right?"

"This isn't what it looks like," I chime in, trying to convince him that it is in fact not what it looks like.

"No, no – it's exactly what it looks like, and more, if you can imagine." Noah winks at Gerard, egging on this fantasy rolling around in Gerard's head about me and Noah. I am the odd woman out.

Gerard claps his hands excitedly. "Knew it!"

"That's not what happ— okay, you know what? I don't have to deal with whatever nonsense you both are creating right now. I need to go home and shower and get ready for the day. I'll clean up the mess later, Noah." I push completely off him and his face falls in disappointment. What did he expect? For me to completely fall for him again just because we spent one night together? Sure, it felt so nice to talk with him and watch movies like we used to do. And fall asleep on top of him like I used to. But things are different now. Besides, I really don't know how long he is actually going to stay. I'm scared and nowhere near ready to face all the demons of our breakup and what we missed in each other's lives.

Noah grunts as he sits all the way up on the couch. "Don't

worry about it, Evie. I got it. I'll have the cookies all packaged up for you to take over to the nursing home." He folds the large blanket and strews it on the back of the couch. His eyebrows press together and his jaw tightens as he fixes the pillows.

"Thanks." I throw on my coat and scarf and jiggle my keys before heading out the door. "I'll be back, G."

I open my mouth to say bye to Noah but the only image I am greeted with is his strong, muscular back heading to the kitchen. I know he was just playing along with Gerard to get a rise out of me, but I can't help but think that he actually wanted it to be true.

Outside, I close my car door and sit there in silence as my car defrosts. Everything that was once cold in my heart is warming back up. I don't want to admit that it's all because of Noah.

20

Evie

"Can we go over the menu again? We are a week out from our soft opening on Christmas Eve and I'm freaking out." I prop my elbows on the cold marble countertop and cover my face. "I'm sorry, this is just really important to me and you know people are going to talk if things don't go well. I'll be the talk of the town...but in a bad way."

Noah sits on a bar stool across the island and mimics my lean into the counter. "Evie, you don't have to say you're sorry. This is important to you. I want this to work out, too. That's why I took the job in the first place. My reputation is at stake, too, by the way. Let's run through everything again."

Noah starts going over the menu once more, but my thoughts are muting him. Is that the only reason he took this job? Selfishly, I wanted him to say that the only reason he took the job was because of me. I don't know why I feel that way, but here I am feeling those feelings. Feelings I never thought I'd feel again with this man standing behind the island that separates us.

"Are you okay with everything? Evie?"

I snap out of my haze. And everything becomes clear. He is looking at me like he used to when he was concerned about me. Those cute wrinkles on his forehead and between his dark, thick eyebrows. They have definitely gotten deeper over the years. I need to walk away before I let these feelings take over and I do something stupid like kiss that stupidly handsome mouth of his.

Then my name escapes his mouth again. "Evie."

"Yeah, everything sounds great. Thanks again for running it by me." I jump off the bar stool and grab my house keys from the counter. "Um, I need to go. Just remembered I have an early meeting with that one guy about that thing."

I wrap my red scarf around my neck and throw on my trusty teal coat. I barrel down the hallway towards the front door, swing it open, and almost walk out into a blizzard. I halt in the doorway. Damn it's fucking cold. Shit...the snowstorm came sooner than expected and is a lot worse than predicted.

Next to me, the door closes, Noah's strong veiny hand pressed hard against the wood. "You're not going anywhere in this weather," he nearly growls as his hand glides down and locks the deadbolt. I can feel his body almost flush with mine. The familiar butterflies fill my stomach. I whip around, hoping they'll diminish because I need them to.

I attempt to put up a front. "Noah, I literally live right down the block. I can handle a little snow."

"Yeah, well I can't handle losing you to the elements by way of turning into a human popsicle. Settle in, Evie. Looks like we are stuck here for the night." His gaze lingers on me for a moment before he sighs and walks over to the fireplace to add more wood.

I try to protest further because I cannot be trapped here with my high school sweetheart who just waltzed back into my life and completely upended everything that I fought so hard to build since he left. Seven years of trying to forget. Seven years of trying not to be in love with him anymore.

Attempt number two: incoming. "But," I try. "I am starving and I have a perfectly good box of mac and cheese waiting in my pantry for me to make at home."

"How dare you even say 'boxed' anything in front of me." He shoves the fire poker in its holder and strides back over to me.

"But..."

Noah grabs my shoulders and looks intently at me, sending warmth throughout my body. "Evie, stop trying to make up excuses to leave. Luckily for you, I kind of know how to cook." I smirk a little. "There it is." His hands leave my shoulders.

"There what is?"

"Your cute little smirk. I missed making you smirk like that."

The warmth comes back to my cheeks. I remove my coat and hang it on the rack. "So, chef, what do you plan on making since we are stuck here and I need to eat dinner or else I am going to get h–"

"Hangry, yeah I know. Don't worry about dinner. I've got it covered."

I tuck my hair behind my ears. "Okay, I can be your sous chef. What do you need me to do?"

"You can just sit down, put on a Christmas movie, and relax. You've been working too hard lately, Evie. You deserve to relax." He walks into the kitchen. "I'll bring it out to you when it's ready."

I AM in the middle of my millionth rewatch of *The Holiday* when Noah walks into the room with a large pasta bowl in one hand and a glass of white wine in another.

"Took you long enough," I jokingly say as he approaches and hands me the glass.

"I had to make sure it was perfect." He places the bowl on the coffee table. "It is your favorite, after all: homemade fettuccine alfredo with pan-fried chicken and an ungodly amount of parmesan cheese on top. You're lucky you aren't lactose intolerant."

My insides are molten. "You made my favorite meal?"

"Of course I did, Evie. I figured if we were going to be stuck in this bed and breakfast, I can at least feed you your favorite meal. I know it's not Christmas Eve yet, which is when you usually have this, or I don't know. I am assuming you still love to have this dish on Christmas Eve, but we are going to be a little busy with the opening and all." Noah plops a pillow on the floor and sits at one end of the coffee table. He shrugs. "Or I don't know, maybe I assumed wrong when I thought this was still your fav..."

I reach over and grab the top of his hand. "It *is* still my favorite. Thank you. And thank you for remembering such a small detail about me."

"No detail about you is small to me, Evie. You've always lit up every room you walk into. You're a hard person to forget." He drinks his wine and twists pasta with his fork.

I clear my throat and blink back tears. "Well thank you. So are you." I push my hair behind my ear and adjust in my seat on the couch. I finally take a bite of the pasta and it is unmistakingly the best pasta I've ever tasted. Noah has gotten better since the last time he made this for me on Christmas Eve. Trust me, I've tried to make homemade pasta and it never lived up to his.

"By that euphoric look, I'd say that you like it?"

I stuff my face even more and nod.

He laughs. "Good. And that wine pairs perfectly with it. When I traveled in Italy, it was the best Pinot Grigio I tasted. I brought some back with me, hoping that by some miracle I'd get to do this for you again and share that piece of my experience with you."

I continue nodding, because I don't know what to say. I wish I could have gone with him to Italy. I wish I could have gone with him anywhere. That ship has sailed, though. It left the dock when my mom got sick and he got accepted to culinary school.

We continue to eat in silence. The fire crackles in the background, giving us a soundtrack to the most emotionally loaded dinner I've ever experienced. Before I know it, the pasta in both of our bowls is gone and now there is no buffer.

It's just us.

"Do you want more?" he offers.

I shake my head. "No, I'll save some room for dessert. There are extra cookies from the batch I made for the nursing home. I'll have some of those in a bit." I start to get up, but Noah beats me to it.

"Stay right there. You probably warmed up that spot on the couch perfectly. I don't want you to get cold." He grabs my bowl before I can protest and takes it to the kitchen. Considerate Noah. He always had the ability to read my mind before I could even say anything. I've never met another man like him. I've tried to look for someone else. Someone to fill the empty space that Noah left behind. Clearly I have been unsuccessful.

He walks back into the living room with the rest of the wine. "Do you want more of this?"

I hold out my glass. "Sure."

He fills his glass as well and sits back down on the floor.

I run my finger along the rim of the glass and decide this is as good of a time as ever to talk about the last seven years. "So... did you also learn how to make pasta like that in Italy?"

His eyebrows scrunch together again and he clears his throat. "Um, yeah. Some older ladies taught me in a town called Gragnano."

I smile, imagining these old ladies fawning over Noah learning how to make the best pasta in the world. "I'm sure they loved sharing their recipes with you. Did you tell them that you are a world-renowned chef?"

Noah's dimples deepen beneath his scruff. "Yes, they knew I was a chef. I would not say world-renowned..."

"Please, Noah. You are way too modest. You've been on the covers of magazines. Been a guest on cooking shows. Shall I go on?"

"Those accolades mean nothing to me, Evie. You know that."

"You've always sucked at receiving compliments and awards for your accomplishments. Remember when you got Athlete of the Year and you insisted that you share the honor with the other nominees? Even though you were the most talented person up on that stage, you still took the spotlight off yourself. I never understood that."

"Like I said, that stuff doesn't mean anything to me." He takes another drink. "I just wanted one person to share any accomplishments with, and I stupidly made a choice seven years ago to leave her behind."

Here we go. To be fair, I started us down this road. I just didn't expect him to say that to me. Not after all these years. I blink fast to push the inevitable tears back. "It's fine, Noah. You actually listened to what I wanted and I shouldn't blame you for that or be mad at you for that. It was probably for the best that you went on your own to New York. Look at all you have accomplished."

"But that's just it, Evie. I wanted you to go with me so bad and you were so adamant about staying for your mom. We were just kids and we could've had everything we've ever wanted with each other. But we chose for each other without truly considering if that's what the other person really wanted."

"I just thought you would come back and visit at least once. But maybe that was too much to expect. Maybe that wasn't fair for me to put those expectations on you when I knew you would have this posh new life. Why would you want to come back here?"

"You're right, I didn't. I thought it would be easier if I followed your wishes. You wanted me to leave. Evie, when you told me you weren't coming with me, it was the worst moment of my entire life. It was wrong of me to assume that you would come with me despite everything that was happening with your mom. I was so engulfed in the plan we made for ourselves. As much as it killed me, I didn't want to pressure you to follow me anywhere. You love this place. I was also stubborn and scared because of the distance. But I never truly *wanted* to leave you, Evie."

My body tingles and my heart beats faster. I truly thought he would move on. I thought he did move on, especially after seeing him with that girl five years ago. A lump develops in my throat as I try to think of the right words to say, "Noah..."

"And I guess deep down," Noah continues, "I was also afraid of uprooting you from home and then not being a success. What if I was a massive failure like what happened with football? I had all of these colleges lined up for me to play and my football career was over the moment my ACL tore. I didn't want you to regret coming with me to New York, especially if things didn't work out as planned. I got scared and I was angry so I pushed you away as you were pushing me away. I should've fought for you more, Evie."

"But you didn't, and that is my fault. I shouldn't have pushed you away, Noah. I am so sorry." Tears are escaping now. "I should've gone with you. There were nights that I would stay up and think about what if you came back and asked me to go with you? Noah, I would've gone with you in a heartbeat. I would've followed you anywhere. And as for you possibly being a failure, none of that mattered to me. I believed in you that much. I was so blinded by my mom getting sick and losing her, I didn't stop to think how much this impacted you as well." I exhale. "And since we are laying out our truths here, I didn't completely back out of NYU. I just deferred for a year. I could've gone to New York."

"Why didn't you?" Hurt covers Noah's face when he realizes we could have started our lives together. It would have only been delayed for a year.

"Because, Noah, I didn't want to bother you in your posh new life away from this small town...I was heartbroken. And that's why I retracted my deferment into their program and finished school here."

Noah presses his palms to his forehead and shakes his head. His body softens after a few moments. He exhales then says, "Look, I loved New York, Evie. It was one of the best experiences of my life. Through my culinary degree, I was able to travel and learn about different cuisine from across the world. But there was always a part of me that couldn't let myself fully enjoy it or be proud of it because I knew you weren't proud of me."

"You really think I wasn't proud of you?" I stand up and walk toward the Christmas tree. I cross my arms and finally turn to the only man that I ever gave my heart to. "Noah, there is a box under my bed with all the magazine covers you have been on. With the newspaper clippings from the Hollybury Gazette telling your hometown what a star you have become. I mean, it was bound to happen eventually. It was either going to be as a football player or as a chef. I saved every Instagram post that featured you. I was so proud of you. I still am. I knew you were meant for greatness, Noah. I guess that's why I am still confused about you moving back here. You have the world at your fingertips. Why move back to Hollybury? This measly little job at an inn is nothing compared to Michelin-star restaurants."

Without a word, Noah stands up from the ground and meets me at the tree. He takes my face in his hands and wipes the tears from my cheeks. "I thought it would be obvious why I moved back." He lifts my chin. "Look at me, Evie." I finally let myself look into his familiar and safe eyes, equally filled with tears. "I didn't move back for the job...I moved back for you."

The words I've longed to hear finally reach my ears and my heart leaps. I knew in my gut that he moved back for me, but I never wanted to assume anything. We assumed too many things when we were young. We assumed we would never make it. We assumed we couldn't get through the long distance. We assumed that someone's dreams had to stop in order for the other's dream to come true.

I assumed I could live without him. And boy, was I wrong.

I've never been so happy to be wrong.

The Christmas playlist starts over and Noah lets go of my chin, walks over to my phone, and hits the pause button. He strides over to the record player stand and sifts through the basket full of old vinyls I collected through the years. Surprisingly, they are not all Christmas related.

He selects one and places it on the record player. The needle glides over the black ridges as Noah comes back to me. He slides one hand around the small of my back and presses me against him, while the other hand cups my hand with no indication of letting go anytime soon. We have not been this close to each other intentionally since the car ride back from the vintage shop, where I practically wanted to climb him like a tree. This feels different.

The warmth from his body is so comforting. I missed it so incredibly much it hurts. I press my cheek against his sculpted chest as I hear The Righteous Brothers' voices fill the room.

I can't help but start laughing. This is so on-brand for Noah, but I always like to tease him about his old-man tendencies. It's one of my favorite things about him. "I see that your eighty-year-old man persona is still going strong. *Unchained Melody* is a good one."

"Hey, my grandfather taught me well. He is the one who taught me how to woo women."

"Well, Walter definitely rubbed off on you."

He squeezes my hand and pulls me closer with the other, making our bodies nearly one. "Hopefully in the best ways, right?"

I smile. "In all the best ways." I take in everything about

Noah. His fresh masculine scent is unchanged. His smile is the smile I knew all those years ago. He is the same Noah, but in so many ways he is different. There are layers of him that I know nothing about.

But now, I am so ready to find out. I want to know every detail about him.

Before I do, I know I need to confess one last thing. Clean slate. No secrets or assumptions. "I have another confession to make..."

He looks down at me. "And what's that?"

I take a deep breath, knowing how hurt he was when he found out about me being in New York City and not telling him. Still, I forge ahead with a gulp. "I went to one of those events that were celebrating you and your newfound success in New York."

I can feel his body tense. "Are you serious? Why didn't you tell me? Or come up to me at the event?" His voice is laced with disappointment. At least that's a step up from anger. I feel relief as his hand slowly trails up and down my back, as though he is telling me it's okay to keep revealing all my truths.

Tears start to form. I could always tell all my truths to Noah. He is the type of person who holds space for anything and everything. "I was there and I was so proud of you and everything you accomplished, Noah. I didn't want to distract you from all the people there who admired you." I pause, knowing I am about to reveal the real truth. "And actually, I was about to go up to you and surprise you and take the chance that you would be happy to see me and maybe, just maybe, we could get our second chance – but there was a girl who gave you a kiss on your cheek and I just thought..."

Noah exhales and lifts my chin up again. "Evie." The tears finally roll down my cheeks. I can see his perfect green eyes through the blurry film of tears trying to disrupt my vision. "She was just one of my classmates...nothing ever happened. She wasn't anyone to me." His hand gets tangled in my hair and he gives me a small kiss on the forehead. "You were never a distraction for me, Evie. You were the love of my life. You light up my world and guide me. You've lit up my world since I saw you in kindergarten."

Nothing ever happened. Those three words repeat over and over in my head like the most glorious broken record. There are three other little words I so desperately want to say to Noah. Three words that we used to say to each other on a daily basis. But they are loaded differently now. Loaded with the notion that we aren't teenagers anymore. Loaded with all the mess adulthood brings. The complexities. The complications. The fear of letting love back in.

There are not a lot of second chances in life, and I was already blessed with the second chance of my mom being in remission. I don't know how many second chances you are allotted in one lifetime. Do I have room for one more? I don't want to hold out hope if there is nothing on the other side waiting for me. This all may be temporary. Noah may decide to go back to his big, exciting life in New York and live out the rest of his days as the hottest chef known to man and have his buffet of women to choose from. Or – and this is a big, no huge or – he may stay...for good. Can I even let myself dream of that?

Even through all the doubt, I still whisper what I want to say, without actually uttering those three little words to him: "Noah."

His lips return to my forehead as he gives me the lightest kiss. "I know, Evie." Those three words will do for now. There is one more thing I need to bring up because it's too important not to. I lean my head against his chest, finally allowing myself to let go and succumb to the comfort that Noah provides me. "You wrote my mom letters." I state it because I am not about to play dumb or coy or any of that bullshit. He knows me better than that.

He pulls me closer and I can feel his lips against the top of my head. "I promised her I would." Not denying it. Not trying to change the subject. Just honest and true. I squeeze my eyes shut and let out tears I didn't know I was holding in fall.

We continue to dance by the Christmas tree and for a moment, I feel like I am in a dream. Noah is here. Dancing with me in front of a cozy fire. In the inn that I renovated and poured my heart and soul into. I guess now it's time to renovate my heart.

My hands run along his muscular torso and I start to play with the buttons on his shirt, so tempted to start unbuttoning them. I want to revisit what I have been deprived of these past seven years.

His hand clenches my hair tighter and he forces me to look up at him. "Can I finally kiss you?"

21

Evie

"*Can I finally kiss you?*"

"Yes," I exhale softly.

I expect Noah to jump in and smash his lips onto mine. But that's not what happens at all. He kisses my jaw softly and then presses his lips against my neck, making my skin tingle with excitement and anticipation. Something about the way he touches me and lays his kisses on my body feels like home somehow. Each kiss is a puzzle piece falling back into its rightful place.

His mouth finally claims mine and I get lost in the all-too-consuming kiss I've been waiting for since I walked into that kitchen a few weeks ago. Actually, no – that I've been waiting for since I watched his truck drive away seven long years ago. His tongue grazes mine and my body goes into overdrive, my skin buzzing with knee-weakening pleasure. My fingers dig into his broad shoulders and he groans at how my body is reacting to his touch. I want his hands all over me. I want him to take me in every possible way. I am sick of holding back because we are scared of what could happen. I want to live in the now because here in this moment with him is the closest thing to heaven.

Noah breaks our kiss. "Fuck, Evie, I'd go back to that moment when I drove away. I'd go back and throw you over my shoulder and bring you with me. I think about that all the time." He lowers my sweater to expose my bare shoulder and leaves a trail of kisses, each igniting small sparks in my soul.

I raise an eyebrow playfully and get my lips as close as I can to his without touching them. "Well, throw me over your shoulder now, Noah. Show me how much you missed me because dammit, I've missed you so fucking much."

I squeal as he throws me over his bulky shoulder and my heart starts thundering. He practically takes the stairs two at a time and opens the door to the largest suite we have. He carefully lowers me onto the soft, warm, cream quilt. I rise onto my knees and he holds onto my jaw with both hands. I tug the sides of his shirt for stability because right now, I am barely able to stay upright. I forgot how intoxicating he is just by being him. He crushes his lips against mine and just like that, I'm a puddle.

I graze my hands underneath his shirt, and his abs tighten

from my touch. I take my sweet time finding all the different pathways I can go along his body. Some paths I remember and some are brand-new terrain I am so excited to discover. He must feel the same about me because his knuckles brush against the bare skin of my torso, while the other hand is still secured against my jaw. I start laughing against his mouth, which makes him smile but does not make his lips move from mine. My reaction is part me being extremely ticklish and part my complete disbelief that this man is back in my life and he is right here in front of me. Touching me. Kissing me. Romancing the hell out of me.

He strips my sweater off and throws it on the ground, leaving me in a very lacey black balconette bra that leaves very little to the imagination. Noah takes a sharp breath. "Damn," he whispers and advances on top of me, lifting me toward the headboard with ease. He props himself up on his forearms and I finally get a good look at his tattoos. I never thought of myself as a girl who loves tattoos on a guy, but I am loving them on Noah. I suddenly want to know the story behind all of them. I want to get filled in on all his life that I missed. His veiny arms flex with each movement of his body so as not to crush me with his body weight. It's silly that I thought he was in shape when he played football. I was clearly wrong.

His fingers find the hem of my jeans and he teases me by tracing along my sensitive skin. My hips hike up to meet his hips and I notice how hard he is. My core heats up at the feeling and my need for him is only intensified. His rough fingers clutch onto my jeans hem and he quickly unfastens them with such ease he should win an Olympic medal, all the while he is putting me under a spell with his devouring kiss. He doesn't move from his position on top of me as he slides my pants down and throws them to the floor next to my discarded sweater. One of his large hands interlocks with mine and presses it to the soft white pillowcase next to my head, while his other hand slowly but firmly caresses my thigh as he inches closer toward my matching black lace thong.

Before he reaches where I desperately want him to go, he pauses all movement, including our earth-shattering kiss. I need him to kiss me like I need oxygen. Noah studies my face intently as he brushes my hair back and tucks it behind my ear. "Are you still mine, baby girl? I need you and your love more than you know. Please tell me that you are still mine."

Baby girl. My heart aches from hearing that again. It's his turn to need some reassurance. Reassurance that this is what I want.

I run my fingers through his hair. His neck falls heavy with my comforting touch and his breath tickles the side of my very sensitive neck, causing goosebumps to cover my body. "Noah. I've never stopped being yours."

And the look he gives me after I say those words. Oh, the look. It's full of desire and promises and pain and relief all at once. It's breathtaking. He's breathtaking. Always has been. My pulse quickens when his mouth is on mine again. There's an undeniable hunger there, and I am here for him to savor every part of me because I want to do the same to him.

Just when I am about to rip off his shirt, he props himself up and grabs it from each side, smoothly lifting it over his head.

And then I hear my pulse ringing in my ears when I see what is hanging from a delicate, long chain around his neck.

"Is that...?" I reach for the silver charm glistening against his chiseled chest. I inspect the half heart with my name engraved on it.

He flashes his infamous boyish grin, exposing his sexy dimples, that makes me and every woman on the face of the earth weak-kneed. "Yeah, it is. I've never taken it off."

All these years. He kept it. No, not only kept it. *Wore* it. Every day.

I say jokingly, but also addressing the massive elephant in the room, "So, what have all the women you've slept with said about you wearing a necklace with my name on it?" I twiddle with the charm. Who knew that a small piece of sterling silver could hold so much weight?

He grabs my hand to calm my anxious thoughts. "I wouldn't know."

"What?" I ask incredulously, almost laughing at the ridiculous notion that Noah has not slept with any other woman in seven years.

"I haven't slept with anyone else, Evie."

That reality hits me like a ton of bricks. *How is that possible?* I must have offered my thoughts up on a silver platter because the next words out of his mouth are: "No one was you."

And there my heart goes again, beating a thousand beats per minute. I am thrown back in time to the way I felt when we first started dating, not understanding why he was dating me, someone who nerded out over the latest episode of *Fixer Upper* or *Extreme Home Makeover* and all things photography, instead of wearing the right shade of lip gloss and raising pom-poms in the air.

He holds onto my hand tighter and presses it against his chest. His pulse quickens, like it used to when he had his anxiety attacks, but his face does not show it. It gets softer, more vulnerable. "Have you...I mean, of course you have...I mean, look at you...it's obvious you've been with..."

I press my hands against his chest. It's my turn to calm him. "No."

He cradles my face in his hands, and lifts my face so that I am looking directly into his eyes. "No?"

"No. I haven't slept with anyone else. I mean, trust me, I tried to get over you so bad. It's not like I didn't go on dates or kiss guys but...I could never bring myself to allow anyone to get that close to me. For anyone to see that side of me. I always wanted you to be the only one."

I grab his necklace and pull him down on top of me. I want to feel every inch, every curve of his muscles, the heat of his body against mine. I hook my leg around his back and pull him closer to me. His hand swoops under my lower back and lifts me toward him so our bodies have no space between them.

I whimper as I feel Noah's shoulder muscles oscillate under his taut skin. His tongue licks my collarbone and I arch helplessly against him even more. I dig my nails into his back and glide down until I reach his jeans. "These are a little unnecessary. It's not really fair that I am in my underwear and you still have pants on."

"Patience, Evie." He gives me small kisses on my forehead. The tip of my nose. My cheeks. My lips. "I want to take my sweet time with you. I've waited way too long to rush this." He nibbles on my ear and whispers, "I promise they will come off. But I want to make you come first, if that's okay."

His hand skims my belly, making my entire body buzz and he finally reaches the hem of my panties. His fingers slide under the lace and then slide into my wet pussy. I gasp and move my hips with the same rhythm he establishes with his giant fingers. I am dizzy from the pleasure he's creating. *He still knows me so well.* Knows what makes me tick. Knows how to love me.

The truth is I never wanted anyone to touch me the way Noah touches me. I know deep down that no one would ever compare and I had no interest in finding out.

His thumb rubs my clit while his fingers move in and out of me, causing my back to arch. I don't want this to stop. The only thing better than this is for Noah to actually be inside of me. My heart flutters in excitement at the thought and I get even wetter. I'm so close. "Noah," I pant.

"Look at my girl. Almost coming for me. You're even more beautiful than I remember right before you come. I know what will help get you there. If memory serves me correctly..." Suddenly, he pulls his fingers out and positions his head in between my legs. His eyes are devilish and dark. "But first, these need to come off. They are in my way."

My body goes into full-blown overdrive when I feel Noah's fingers wrap around my panties and pull them down slowly. I lift one leg up. Then the other. He grabs my thighs and pulls me closer to the edge of the large king bed. My toes curl the moment his tongue licks my pussy. He spreads my legs even further apart as he anchors them to the bed. I am pinned and I have no desire for him to stop. This is so much better than I remember. He is so much better than I remember.

I am right on the edge. My fingers clench onto the soft sheets. Every movement he makes with his tongue and his fingers are magic and all my nerve endings are on fire. Fierce pleasure rolls through my body and he rides out my orgasm with me, his tongue matching each lift of my hips against his face.

"That's my girl. God, you are fucking gorgeous when you come." He releases my thighs from their temporary hold and I can't help but want him to pin me down in all kinds of ways. "I can't wait to do that again." He licks me again and makes my body jolt. "And again." He kisses my inner thighs. "And again." He kisses my belly. "And again." He pulls down my bra and sucks on my nipple for a moment, again sending an electric current down to my toes. He finally kisses my lips, then looks up and out the window behind the bed. "By the looks of it, I don't think the snow is letting up any time soon. Lucky me."

I look up and behind me. The curtains are not drawn. I was too busy getting carried by this hulk of a man to notice how hard the snow is still coming down. Thankfully it's late at night and the entire town is closed down due to this snowstorm. No one would be able to see our fun little sexcapade.

I tease him by saying, "Wow, your stamina has really gone up quite a few notches since the last time we did this." I wink at him while moving some hair from falling into his eyes. If he looks this undone, I can't imagine how undone I look.

He traces my jawline and says with total confidence, "You have no idea. You underestimate how much I am willing to guarantee you can't walk tomorrow, Evie."

My jaw drops to the floor as Noah begins to unbuckle his jeans and strips down to his underwear. I scan his body in its perfect glory. I have the feminine urge to trace my fingertips along the beautiful lines of his tattoos, along each ridge of his abs and arms. I have no shame in ogling him. I have been deprived for almost a decade. Cut a girl some slack.

And just when he is about to get completely naked, he mutters in disappointment and frustration, "Fuck."

"What?" A boulder the size of Texas weighs down my stomach.

He reaches his hand behind his neck and rubs it, showcasing his biceps. I think it's safe to say our working relationship is shot, especially since I apparently cannot stop checking this man out. Literally any movement he does from now on is going to elicit the strongest reaction from my body. I have to actively focus on the next words that come out of his mouth. "I don't have a condom."

"Oh." The boulder dissipates. I scoot toward him and prop myself up on my knees. My head is right underneath his chin. I don't break eye contact with him for a second as I sweep my fingers across the elastic waistband. "So?"

His abs tense and he inhales sharply. "Evie, are you sure?" The sweet, considerate side of Noah hasn't changed, even if his dirty mouth is a new development that I am a hundred percent on-board for.

"I am more than sure. I am on the pill." I smirk and lick the center of his abs, all along his treasure trail while squeezing his sculpted ass. How is it possible to be this hot?

"Jesus Christ. Evie." He grabs a fistful of my hair and tugs on it.

I look up at him and bite my bottom lip. "Do I seem sure to you, Noah?" I grab his huge, hard dick and start stroking. He shifts his weight and lets out a low growl. "I think I've waited long enough for you to be inside of me, don't you think?" Both my hands pull down on his waistband and Noah finally steps out of his underwear.

His eyes turn a deep shade of green as his pupils widen. He expertly unclasps my bra with his free hand before pinning himself on top of me again. He spreads my legs wider without hesitation and he teases me by placing the very tip of his dick against my pussy. The swirls of anticipation take over my stomach. Noah then slowly eases into me, stretching me in the best way. I have to breathe through each inch pushing inside of me. I forgot how huge he really is. Noah kisses me the whole time, slowly, deeply matching each thrust.

Every I love you. Every smile. Every laugh. Every ridiculous fight. Every piece of our relationship comes to the surface at this moment. I can't control the tears streaming down my face. This is how it's supposed to be. This is a once-in-a-lifetime love. He came back to me. A tear must have rolled onto Noah's hand that is pressed next to my head because he slows down almost to a complete stop and says, "Are you okay, baby girl?"

"Better than okay. I'm just so happy." His thumb wipes the rest of the tears from my cheek and he continues to move his hips in a way that makes my breath hitch.

"Me too, baby girl. I finally got you back. There is nothing else I ever want more than you, Evie."

We were just kids when we first fell in love. We didn't know what that really meant and that lack of awareness broke us. We now have reached a beautiful part of our love story. The part where we truly decide to love each other despite the hurt we have caused each other. Despite the dreams that have been lived out and the dreams we had to defer. Despite being apart for seven years. I know in my gut that we will be all right this time around. I see my future in Noah's kind, emerald eyes. He's perfect.

God, I love this version of us so much better.

Noah and Evie 2.0.

22

Noah

I am in fucking heaven. I grab the top of the metal headboard and go deeper inside of her tight, wet pussy.

"I don't know if I told you this yet, Evie. But you look perfect tonight." Her hair is strewn across the pillow and her skin glistens with sweat. I lean down and lick her neck, and God, I missed the way she tastes. Her body writhes under me as I go deeper inside her. The way her pussy tightens around my dick makes my whole body tense with pleasure. I can't imagine doing this with any other person on this planet. She is fucking everything.

Her heels press against my lower back as she digs her nails in my shoulder blades. "You're perfect," she exhales. "You are so amazing at this. Don't ever stop what you are doing."

I groan against her neck as I drive deeper into her and she bridges her hips up to meet my thrusts. I throw one of her legs over my shoulder and go harder into her. "I will never stop if it makes you look the way you look right now. And just for the record, you are pretty amazing at this, too. Your pussy is so fucking wet."

"You make it that way." She lightly licks my neck right beneath my ear and I am two seconds from unraveling. "You're the only man who ever has."

Jesus Christ, this woman. That statement unleashes a primal need to be the one and only man to ever make her come. I observe her face for probably the millionth time in my life but it never ceases to amaze me that this beautiful girl would want to be mine. I will happily take it. Especially when her lips are full and puffy and her eyes are full of hunger.

I let go of the headboard and frame her body with my arms. I am not going to hold back anymore with her. I have been wanting to say this since the moment she stumbled into that kitchen during that ridiculous, fake interview.

"I will spend the rest of my life wanting you and loving the hell out of you. Out of all the things I am good at in this life, I am the best at loving you."

Her eyes flutter and her breath hitches. "You still love me?"

"I've never stopped loving you, Evie."

She kisses me deeply and we both breathe sharply. My declaration that breaks the stupid dam that held up all of our past. The dam we built out of our need to cope and try to forget each other. How could I ever forget her?

This kiss is soft yet demanding. She pushes against my chest and I roll over to my back. She straddles my body. I spread my hand across her back to stabilize her on me and my other hand grabs her ass, which is so amazingly toned. Her body is even more beautiful now than it was seven years ago. I love every curve she has developed over the years. Her ash blonde long tendrils frame her face and cover her breasts. I prop myself up, move her hair out of my way and suck her nipple, and the guttural low sound that comes out of her mouth sends shivers through me.

"Keep moaning like that and I am going to come inside your perfect tight pussy. I want to savor the sight of you on top of me for a little while longer." I spank her, knowing that the combination of me sucking on her nipples and spanking her drives her crazy. She nearly screams then twists her fingers through my hair and pulls back, causing me to stop sucking and look up at her.

"Maybe I want to feel you come inside of me already. I want your cum to drip down my thighs when I get off you."

She knows me too well. She knows that once we're through, I would've gotten a wash cloth and cleaned her up. But forget what I want to do. I want her to call all the shots right now. I give her a devilish grin and say, "You got it, boss." Her eyes meet mine and the air between us gets even more heated. Her hips move back and forth and I tangle my arms around her body and kiss every inch of her that I can. I let her tug and pull my hair all she wants because I will literally do anything this woman wants me to do. Right now it's all about her. She is a goddess and I am fully prepared to worship her in every way possible.

"Noah," she breathes out. I can feel her tighten against me and tingles shoot up my spine. I want to come with her. I slide my thumb between us and rub against her clit.

"Look at me," I demand. Evie looks down at me, lips parted, completely lost with me in this euphoria we created for ourselves. She kisses me and it's full of desperation. I can feel everything that she has been holding back in that one kiss. All the feelings of who we were and who we are now. I hold her tightly as we come together. Our moans get lost in each other. I sweep my tongue against her hot mouth and she does the same to me. God, I don't deserve this woman.

Once we come down from the high and our breathing slows, I say, "You are fucking magic, Evie Hawkins."

"So are you, Noah Pearson."

Evie lays down on top of me so I can feel every curve of her naked body against mine. Her skin is soft and warm and fucking perfect. She tucks her forearms beneath her boobs and props herself up. The sight of her flushed face, full lips and tousled hair is now in competition against all my other favorite memories of Evie. I run my hands through her hair and kiss the top of her nose.

"Mmm," she says. "I missed you doing that."

"Doing what? Making love to you like that?"

"Let the record show that you've never made love to me like that." She gives me a soft peck on the lips. "No, you kissing the top of my nose. You know I have always been insecure about my nose. It's too big."

I kiss it again. "It's not too big. I love your nose." I run my fingers along her arms and goosebumps develop under my touch. She giggles as I continue down the sides of her torso and grab her ass. "I've always loved everything about you." She kisses me deeply, inches her way up my chest, and grabs my hair. She pulls it and spreads her legs around my body. My girl wants more and I am not going to disappoint her.

I break our kiss. "As much as I want to make out with you, I want to do something for you. Is that okay? Can you give me a few minutes?"

A low whine emits from Evie's mouth. "Yes, that's okay, I guess." I give her a love tap on her ass and slide out beneath her. I search for my underwear that was strewn on the floor at some point during what Evie calls our sex-capade and honestly, that nickname is pretty accurate. I find them under part of the duvet that is on the floor. I quickly put them on.

"Shame shame shame," Evie says as she shakes her head.

I want to abandon my idea and climb back into bed with the goddess laying amongst the tangled sheets and blankets. Evie props up her head against her palm as she slowly untangles the sheet and drapes it over her body, not breaking eye contact with me at all. She is tempting me to get back into that bed, but I do my best to resist. "Now that's just cruel."

She cocks an eyebrow, acting oblivious to what she is doing to me. "What is?"

"You looking like that. Fucking irresistable."

"Well, then come back to bed."

My head takes over my heart and I resist the temptation wrapped in silky sheets. "I'll be back in two minutes. I promise it will be worth it." I run into the en suite bathroom and close the door. I start to run the large clawfoot bathtub, break the seal of the bath salts and bubbles, and scatter them in the warm water. In true Evie fashion, there are multiple candles around the bathroom and as a courtesy, she provided matches in a little clear jar on the vanity. I light all of them and the room fills up with a nice pomegranate scent coming from the bath salts I poured in. I fill the bathtub to almost the brim and once everything is set up, I open the door and see Evie in the same position I left her in.

"Are you ready for your surprise?"

She smiles and nods. I climb over the throw pillows that dispersed on the floor. I reach her, strip the sheet from her body, and lift her out of the bed. Once we reach the threshold of the bathroom, I say, "Just thought it would be smart to test out the products you have in here...You know, for research purposes only."

She nods in agreement, "Smart." Then smiles. "Noah, this is so nice. You really didn't have to do this."

"I want to do this, Evie. You deserve to be pampered and I want to take care of you. I lost so much time away from you. I'm making up for time I'll never get back."

I set her into the mound of bubbles and some splash over the edge of the vintage tub. I stay standing and she pouts. "Aren't you going to join me?" She looks up at me with a sultry expression. I thought I'd already witnessed Evie in her sexiest state. I am clearly wrong, because right now in that bathtub with bubbles up to her ears, she has never been so sexy.

I lean down and get as close to touching her lips as possible. As much as I want to close the smallest of gaps and kiss her deeply, I want to tease her a little first. "Well, that depends…"

Her breath hitches and she slightly inches toward me, and my body aches to get inside her again. "Depends on what?" She took the bait and now I am ready to claim her as mine. Again.

I reach down underneath the warm water and don't waste any time placing two fingers inside her pussy. She gasps and her head falls back against the edge of the tub. How is it that she gets sexier by the second? I am mentally kicking myself for ever leaving her side in the first place. Her moans fill the room and her hands grip the sides of the tub and I'm afraid I'm going to come in my underwear any second just by watching her.

"Is my trial period over?" I insert a third finger and she gasps even louder. Her knees spread apart even farther and she props her feet up so I can get deeper.

"Yes, Noah, yes. It's so over," she says almost incoherently. God, I need her now. I pull my fingers out. "What are you doing? Why are you stopping?" There is a hint of frustration in her voice and I cannot wait to fuck that right out of her.

I strip off the underwear I so foolishly put on before heading to the bathroom. "I'm getting in with you." I position myself behind her, feeling her body sink into mine. I'm not one for bubble baths, but this woman has such a strong hold on me that I will do just about anything she demands of me. "Isn't this what you wanted?"

"It's more than I could have ever dreamed of, Noah." She

rests her head on my chest and scoots her ass up against my erection. She laces her fingers through mine and guides one of my hands on her inner thigh, helping me push her leg out toward the side of the tub. Then she leads my other hand down to her very wet pussy. She moans, effectively unraveling me, as I insert my fingers one at a time until I have three fingers deep inside of her again. Each moan strengthens and fuels my need for her even more. I anchor her toward me with my free hand as I thrust deeper and deeper into her.

Her back arches and the back of her head digs into my chest.

"Mmm," I murmur. "I have never been a fan of bubble baths, but keep moaning like that and I think you might convert me."

"Keep doing what you are doing to me right now, Noah, and we will never leave this bathtub. And that's going to be a problem."

"Oh, is that right?" I adjust my fingers slightly inside of her and find her G-spot. I feel her body shiver and tense up. "Because I don't see any problem in giving you multiple orgasms in this bathtub." I nip at her neck.

"Noah," she practically purrs. Her leg props up on the edge of the tub and I see her toes start to curl. She completely releases and the sounds she makes nearly do me in, but I need to be inside of her when I come again.

"Mmm," I hum in her ear. "That's my girl." Before she has a chance to recover, I reposition myself so that I am propped up behind her and I bend her over just enough so she can rest her forearms on the other edge of the tub. I wrap my arms around her torso. "Are you comfortable?" I kiss her shoulder blade.

She nods as her head rests.

"Good." I gently rub my thumb over her clit and she shakes underneath me. I caress her more and then I take my dick and push into her from behind. I feel her widen her legs more for me and I hold her up with one of my arms, feeling her toned body underneath mine.

"Oh my god, Noah." The water sloshes around our bodies. Evie readjusts her hands so they are gripping the rim of the tub, her knuckles white.

"You're taking me so good, Evie." She presses her ass back into me and I fucking melt. "I swear, you've ruined me forever."

I ram into her and she turns her head and kisses me, tangling one of her hands in my hair. It's a soapy mess around us and I can't be bothered to care. The way Evie is kissing me and taking me right now makes it all worth it. She tugs my hair harder and explores my mouth with her tongue in a way she has never done before, and it almost sends me over the edge.

My entire body vibrates from the pure ecstasy that is Evie. I feel my knees slipping in this water and goddamn it I need some stable ground to fuck her properly.

23

Evie

"**G**et out of the tub, now," Noah nearly growls in my ear as he pulls out of me.

I whimper in protest. "Noah, that felt so good. Why did you stop?"

Water spills all over the tiled floor as he lifts his long muscular legs out of the tub. He offers his hand to me and I can barely catch my breath as I gain my own footing outside of the tub. He pulls me up against him and I feel how hard he really is. I reach down and grab his dick and start stroking up and down.

He grasps my wrist to stop me and when I look into his eyes, they are almost black. He shakes his head. "If you keep doing that, I won't be able to do what I want to you. I stopped because I need to have stable footing to fuck you the way I want to."

My pulse thrums against my neck. He leads me to the vanity, where a large gold-plated framed mirror greets our reflections. My face flushes. "And how do you want to fuck me?" My voice nearly cracks with anticipation and curiosity.

Without saying anything, Noah presses himself against my back, runs his hand over my stomach, and sinks down until he grazes me right beneath my navel. His other hand palms my breast and his fingers pinch my nipple. "I want you to watch me fuck you in this mirror." He lays small kisses along my collarbone, causing arousal to ripple across my body. "I want you to see what I see when you come." He spreads my legs apart with one of his knees. I lean forward over the counter and grab onto the edge of the vanity to brace myself.

"Are you ready, beautiful?" He kisses my shoulder and places his strong hand on my hip.

I am helpless against this man and he knows it. I nod.

"Words, Evie. I need you to say it."

"Yes, Noah."

I feel his huge cock ease into me and I immediately grip the counter harder. No matter how many times Noah has been inside me, this is a new position and a completely different angle. His hips grind into me. His fingers rub against my clit and my head falls forward. "Yes, Noah, yes. Please keep doing that."

"Look at me, Evie." His voice is low and animalistic and so goddamn hot I can't help but listen to his every demand.

When our eyes meet in the mirror, I can see a shift in Noah's face. I've never seen him so turned-on in my life and it brings me so much satisfaction that I am the one responsible for it. He pinches my nipple again and I rest my head on his heaving chest. The sound of our wet bodies colliding together is so hot and turns me on even more. Noah has never made love to me like this before. And I am loving how adventurous he wants to be with me. I feel completely safe with him—something I never felt with other men. That was the block all these years. The lack of safety.

He thrusts into me harder, hitting a new spot every time, undoing me with every movement he makes and every sound that comes out of his mouth. "Damn, Evie. This feels so good. I love feeling your ass against me when I fuck your tight pussy. You were made for me, baby girl."

"I'm so close, Noah." I see him smile in the mirror, satisfied that he is making me feel this way. "Can you do something while you make me come?"

"Anything, baby girl." My hips buck back into him as his words thrum against my already-heated skin.

"Tell me that I'm yours and that you'll never leave me again...ever."

Noah slows down, hitting every angle imaginable. He places his hand over my neck, lifts my chin and makes me look at him again.

"I will never leave you again and you will always be mine, Evie. Come with me, baby girl, please." His body jerks against me and a guttural sound escapes his mouth. He pounds me into the vanity so hard that it shakes. I finally release and since his hand is still around my throat holding my head up, I have a clear visual of us coming together. It's animalistic and raw and completely right.

"Told you that you look hot when you come." He kisses the side of my head. "Damn, you are beautiful." I lock eyes with him and this image of Noah will forever be imprinted in my mind. I'm pretty sure this whole night has altered my brain chemistry. I can't take my eyes off him. His tattooed arms are still wrapped around me and he is still inside of me. His hair is disheveled, some pieces falling above his eyebrow.

It's official. We are never leaving this suite.

24

Noah

White light shines through the sheer curtains. I slowly open my eyes and see a sea of golden blonde hair on the pillow next to me. Her left hand is laying on my chest and the way the light is hitting her, she looks like an angel. My angel. I grab my watch from the nightstand and squint to try and register the time. *6:00 a.m.* We didn't get much sleep last night, maybe three hours, but my body naturally wakes up at this time and my stomach is growling. I want Evie to keep sleeping, so I gently free my arm from under her body and tuck her back into bed. I throw on my underwear and go into the bathroom.

I look underneath the vanity for some mouthwash, and lo and behold, find a basket full of unopened travel-sized ones. I swish it around in my mouth and notice how messy the bathroom is. We left towels everywhere and the floor is still a little wet from the bath. I smirk when I look in the mirror. Images of me fucking Evie against this vanity invade my mind. My body is already aching for her, but I know how much she needs to sleep. I don't want to wake her yet.

My stomach growls again. When I go back into the bedroom, I find my cell phone in my jeans pocket and look at the battery life. It's at ten percent and I have a couple of missed calls from my old friend from culinary school, Trey. Before I can even think about what he would want, my stomach growls again. I need food and when Evie wakes up, I know she is going to be famished.

I run as quietly as I can down the stairs and push open the door to the kitchen. I throw some bacon in a frying pan. While that is sizzling, I get out all the ingredients for French toast. I plug in my phone in the extra charger Evie housed in the kitchen and open my music app. I feel inspired, so I put on a curated Christmas playlist that Evie herself created when we were dating. I keep the volume low.

I'm flipping the first round of French toast in the pan when cold, soft fingers graze the front of my bare abs. Evie's head rests against my back and I hear a sleepy, "Morning."

I smile, eager to see my girl. I turn my head and catch a glimpse of the beauty holding onto me. I remove the first batch of French toast onto a plate and turn off the burner so I can give Evie a proper greeting. Turning around, I note that she is wearing my shirt from last night. She is drowning in it, the hem reaching mid-thigh. Is she trying to kill me?

"Morning." I kiss the top of her head. "You look edible in my shirt."

She giggles as she jumps onto the counter. "What are you making?"

"French toast, eggs, bacon and sausage."

"Geez, who are you planning on feeding today? An army?"

"Figured we need some sustenance for the rest of our day, since by the looks of it, we might not be able to get out of the inn today either. Who knows what kinds of salacious activities will take place. I need you well-fed." I wink at her and she blushes and her thighs clench together. Then, I catch her beautiful blue-green eyes linger on my bare chest and slowly descend down the rest of my body, stopping briefly at my ass. She bites her bottom lip and it seems like she is devouring me inch by inch.

God help me, I want this woman. She is making me want to abandon breakfast by the second.

She takes a piece of bacon off the plate next to the stove and bites it. I turn off the burner, frame her with my arms and fall to my knees, completely prepared to recreate what we did last night in that suite.

The clearing of a throat stops me cold in my mission. "Well, well. What do we have here?"

I quickly stand up, almost knocking Evie off the counter in the process. She turns beet red and I press my lips together when I realize who interrupted us.

Gerard is standing at the kitchen entrance, arms crossed, looking immensely humored by the scene he just walked in on. "Let me guess... 'This isn't what it looks like'?" He smirks. "Don't mind me, even though I just survived the snowpocalypse to make sure you weren't dead."

"Sorry, G, I had my phone set on silent and it must've died."

Gerard holds his hand up to stop her from spiraling. "I'll tell your parents not to bother coming by the inn today. You two seem like you have everything under control. I was never here." He walks backward slowly and disappears into the hallway, not before shooting me a wink and a smile. We hear the front door finally *click* behind him, and Evie and I burst into a fit of laughter.

Evie covers her face and muffles, "I cannot believe that just happened. I am mortified."

"Oh, come on, it could have been way worse. Your parents could have walked in on us. Then we would really be in trouble." I take her wrists and lower her hands to her lap.

"You're right. That is worse. I wonder how he got through all the snow. The roads must be undriveable."

"Well, did you see him? He was dressed like he was about to brave the Arctic tundra. You heard him, he braved through a snowpocalypse in that outfit. He even had boots with fur, Evie. *Fur.*" I drench more bread in the batter and continue making breakfast.

"Gerard is anything but subtle. He is not afraid to be flashy or on-trend." Her legs swing back and hang over the counter's edge as she steadies herself once more next to where I am making breakfast.

"Caught that." I reach over to the plate next to the stovetop and grab a piece of French toast. I hold it up to Evie's lips and say, "Try it. You must be hungry." I give her a wolfish grin.

She softly licks her lips and takes a bite. A low "mmm" comes from her mouth and her eyebrows shoot up, seemingly impressed. "That's pretty good. But I've had better," she says playfully. She's teasing me and baiting me and I kind of love it.

I play along. "Is that so?" I clean off her bottom lip with my tongue.

The air is charged between us and I can honestly say that I will die a happy man if I am stuck in this inn forever with this woman.

"Where was I?" I return to my knees and trail her inner thighs with kisses.

Evie giggles. "Noah, what about breakfast?"

"I'm hungry for something else right now. Breakfast can wait."

25

Evie

I have been so busy with decorating the inn and engulfed in all things Noah, I have not decorated my own house for Christmas. It's a crime in my book. I am usually a decorate-before-Thanksgiving type of gal. We are two weeks into December and I have taken nothing out of my small guest bedroom a.k.a my extra storage space, which basically looks like a Christmas warehouse.

I pull down the first box from the closet when I feel a buzz in my back pocket. I grunt as I place the clear bin on the floor and reach back and get my phone. A text from Noah:

> Hey beautiful. What are you doing?

The cheesiest smile spreads across my face and butterflies fill my stomach. I missed him texting me.

> My house is about to look like Santa's workshop. And you?

> I just finished cleaning the kitchen at the inn. You haven't decorated your house yet? Are you ok?

> Haha. I've been a little distracted. With the inn and with a really hot chef who just bulldozed his way into town a few weeks ago.

> How about I head over and be a productive distraction. I will offer up my services.

> Thanks, but I have a system.

> I will make you dinner. Maybe some homemade pasta? I promise I won't get in the way of your very established system. I'll stay in the kitchen the whole time.

This man knows the way to my heart. Food.

> Fine, but if you keep feeding me like this, I am going to gain ten pounds.

> You'd still be the prettiest girl in any room. Plus more to hold onto. Win-win.

> The door will be unlocked when you get here. Just let yourself in.

A whole ten minutes later, I hear Noah's voice: "Evie. I'm here. Just want to make my presence known so I don't scare you again and you don't try to hit me with those murderous tongs."

I am on a step stool with a bin over my shoulder, struggling more than I thought I would with this final bin of Christmas magic. "Lucky for you, I left my tongs at my parent's house." I let out a laugh, which causes me to lose my balance. I feel my body falling back. Shit. Shit. Shit. Shit.

Just when I think I am going to be one of those old ladies on those Life Alert commercials – "Help I've fallen and I can't get up!" – I feel a strong hand against my back and another on my ass, holding me upright with ease. "Evie, what the hell do you think you're doing? You knew I was coming over. Why didn't you wait?"

Once I am stable on the step stool, I see Noah's arms grab the clear bin and take it down with the same ease as he held me with. "Where to, boss?"

I point in the direction of the living room. "This will finish up the living room. I kind of like that nickname. *Boss.* Maybe it'll stick." I descend the stool and wink.

"Finish up?" Noah chuckles as he walks down the hall to

my living room. "It looks like it's done to me. What else can you possibly add to this room?" He sets down the last of my decor and places his hands on his hips. I instantly want those hands on my hips.

"Hey hey, don't judge. This brings me happiness." I lift off the plastic lid and throw it on my couch that is already covered in festive throw pillows and blankets. I beam with pride at my work so far.

I sense Noah walking toward me and then, just like he can read my mind, he places his hands on my hips and pulls my body closer until it's flush with his. He kisses the side of my neck and my body gives in. I sink into my favorite nook against his chest. I place my hands on his and get lost in his invigorating scent: a mixture of freshly baked pastries and a hint of ambery wood. "I know it does. I just like to get a rise out of you. It's the cutest thing in the world. Especially when your nose crinkles up and you get those adorable lines between your eyebrows."

I slap my hand to my forehead and make the exact face he is talking about. He flips me around, pulls my hand away, and replaces my hand with his lips. He reaches under my fuzzy taupe sweater and tickles my lower back, knowing undoubtedly that is going to twist my insides like a pretzel and create a puddle between my thighs.

I move away from him because as much as I want him right now, I really want to finish decorating. Because once we start, I fear we won't be able to stop. This man is insatiable. "Okay probie, I thought you were going to be in the kitchen the whole time so as not to distract me."

"I kind of like you being my boss. Maybe probie will stick.

But fair warning, I may be probie in the grand scheme of things at the inn, but in the kitchen, I am the commander in chief. The kitchen is my favorite place to have control."

"Oh really? I would have thought your favorite place to have control would be in the bedroom."

"I don't need a bedroom to have control, Evie. I can promise you that. In fact, do you want me to teach you a lesson?"

I cock up my eyebrow. "A lesson in..."

"How to make the pasta you love so much."

My heart deflates. This is not going where I thought it was going to go. I guess finishing my task of transforming my house into a Winter Wonderland can hold off for a little while. I'll get to it eventually. Right now, I am starving. I follow Noah into the kitchen.

"Yes, please Noah, teach me how to make your famous pasta. I need to know what these Italian ladies taught you in between fawning over you." I lower my chin coyly at him, probing at his weakness–not being able to accept the fact that he looks like he got torn out of GQ magazine and plopped into the real world with us mere mortals.

Noah chuckles. "They were hardly fawning over me." He pulls out all the groceries from the multiple bags he brought with him, slightly blushing at my total spot-on assessment of what happened in Italy.

I prop myself up on my counter and cross one leg over the other, bobbing it up and down. "Oh, trust me. They were. Have you looked at yourself lately?"

His dimples deepen, as does the color on his cheeks. "Well, even if they were, I wasn't paying attention to that. I was actually trying to learn." He bundles up the plastic bags and tosses them aside. He presses his hands on either side of me on the counter. I have no choice but to uncross my legs and let him fill the space between them. I become breathless. I should be used to Noah's presence, but alas I come to the realization I may never be. He's pure magic and his spell will never waver. "And you are the only one I care about looking at me like that."

I clear my throat. We need to start cooking now because I am about to combust from all the heat this man is generating in my body. "Okay, what's first? Hangriness is starting to develop here."

He smirks, runs his hands up along my hips, and squeezes. "Again, patience." Then kisses my nose. "I am going to walk you through it." He reaches for an apron he must have purchased at the store, because I for sure do not own one, and hands it to me. "I have one condition while I am teaching you how to make it, though."

I hop down from the counter and put the apron on over my head. "What's the condition?"

Noah comes up behind me and ties the strings of the apron right above my ass. His fingers graze the small of my back and my body electrifies. He knows what he is doing. Especially when he leans in and whispers in my ear, "Say 'yes, chef' after every instruction I give you."

My breath hitches and my core is molten.

"You may run your little bed and breakfast, but I run the kitchen." He spanks me lightly. "You are going to do what I say."

"You still like to be in control, then?" His fingers brush a rogue strand of hair on the side of my neck. "You better stop,

Noah. I am legit getting hungry and you know I get hangry if I don't eat within a certain amount of time."

"Oh, I know all too well of your hangry state, Evie. Why do you think I wanted to be a chef? I wanted to make sure my girl was fed and satisfied...in every way possible. I'm willing to take the risk of you getting hangry. And as for control, that's why I worked so hard to become head chef. It's fun to order people around."

He pours a heap of flour onto my bare, clean island counter. "First, make a nest with the dough." He rolls up his sleeves and all I can think about are the veins protruding from his forearms and now I have the urge to stop this lesson and have a lesson in all things Noah. Explore every inch of him until there is nothing left to discover.

"Yes, chef."

He comes up behind me and traps me between his strong arms. "That's my girl." I make the nest he requests. Then he says, "Okay, now put the olive oil, eggs and salt in the middle of the nest, then use your hands to mix the ingredients together."

"Don't you want to demonstrate for me? I don't want to mess it up, chef." I then feel his hands play with the button of my jeans. My breathing gets shallow.

"My hands are going to be preoccupied." He unzips my pants and pulls them down in one fell swoop. "I don't know why you even bother wearing pants when you have the sexiest legs, and ass I might add, in the universe."

"Because no one wants to see me without pants. And it's freezing outside." My hands are shaky as I knead the dough and do my best to roll it together into the most dilapidated ball I've ever seen.

"That's not true. *I* want to see you without pants. And as for the weather, you are inside, so your point is moot. You have no excuse." I step out of my apparently pointless jeans. "New rule: when we are in the kitchen, alone, you are not allowed to wear any pants." His rough hands caress my inner thighs, taunting me. I press my ass back into him and feel how hard he already is.

I exhale. "Yes, chef."

"Spread your legs apart for me, Evie." I do what I'm told and he kneels behind me, playing with my panties. I can feel his breath against my blazing skin. "Keep kneading. Don't stop until I tell you to."

My heart is pounding in my ears. "Yes, che–"

I can no longer form words as Noah moves my underwear to the side and starts licking my pussy. He anchors me to him by grabbing my upper thighs and pressing me further onto his face. The only thing I can concentrate on is my hands digging into the dough. His tongue glides in and out voraciously. He is acting like a starved man even though he ate me out a mere few days ago.

"Noah..." I say breathlessly.

He momentarily stops. I groan in disappointment, wanting him to continue until I don't remember my own name. "You like me on my knees for you, don't you, Evie? Licking that perfect, sweet pussy?"

"Yes."

He lightly spanks me. "Yes, what? I need you to say it."

"Yes, chef."

His tongue finds my slit again and my moans fill my house. I completely stop kneading the dough, but I don't care. I work my hips back and forth and press into his face so his tongue can go deeper inside me. "Jesus, Evie." His voice vibrates against me and I release onto his face, totally letting go and giving myself completely to this man.

Noah stands up and I hear his own pants unbuckle and fall to the floor. He presses his hand against my back and lowers my torso onto the flour-laden counter. "I need you like I need fucking air, Evie. I want to come and when I do, you will again. I promise you that."

He rips my panties off. I squeal as he rams inside of me from behind. I grip onto the edge of the other end of the island and with each thrust, I continue to utter the words, "Yes, chef," which only encourages Noah to go harder and harder.

He clutches my upper thighs tighter. The sound and feel of him coming undone makes me unravel, too. Pleasure shoots up my spine and I fall like a pile of mush onto the cold kitchen counter. Noah breathes heavily with me, savoring what just happened between us. This must be part of the upgrade of Noah 2.0 and I am not complaining at all. If anything, I want more of it. He isn't as careful with me anymore. I do love when Noah is gentle, but I also love this new side. He always had this layer of dominance when he played football. He liked to lead—it's his strong suit so it doesn't surprise me that he ended up pursuing a career that would allow him to assert that dominance. He just never asserted his dominance on me too often, if at all. I'm so glad he is asserting it now.

He slowly pulls out and turns me around so I am finally facing him. He tilts my chin up and kisses me so gently, a direct juxtaposition of what just transpired between us, it throws me off-kilter. His kisses make my heart burst into a million pieces. His raspy voice sends goosebumps across my sensitive body. "Are you okay, Evie? Was that too much?"

"Noah, I promise that I am more than okay. It wasn't too much." I tousle my hair, still adjusting to the reality that this is now my life. The drought that was my sex life is now experiencing a damn monsoon. He is spoiling me and I am savoring every minute with him. I press my hands to his chest and then reach up to move his damp hair from his forehead. "I just can't imagine what else you can do to top that."

Noah's eyes darken and he lifts me back up onto the counter. The coolness of the granite shocks my system and disorients me even more. I assume Noah is going to clean himself up and then finish teaching me how to make this pasta. I'm proven wrong when he spreads my legs again and says, "If I learned anything in culinary school, it's the importance of doing a taste test." He inserts his fingers back inside of me and then says, "Open."

26

Noah

Evie does as she's told. Her lips are swollen and plump as I push my fingers into her mouth. She licks them off in a slow and controlled manner and my dick immediately hardens. I love seeing her at my mercy, doing exactly what I am telling her. I am happy she can handle it. Sex with Evie now is so much more meaningful and so much more fun.

She sucks my fingers clean. I take them out of her mouth and cock my eyebrow. "Well?"

"Delicious." The combination of her licking her lips and her starving eyes gives me all the go-ahead I need.

I drag her off the counter and into my arms. I have a stronghold on her ass with one arm and the other across her back, crushing her delicate body against mine. She giggles when I lick the side of her neck. "But what about the pasta?"

"Fuck the pasta." I pin her against the wall and kiss her. She opens her mouth and grazes my tongue with hers. "I'll feed you later, baby girl. Right now, I want to fuck you until you can't move."

Her toned legs tighten around me and she moves her hips against my bare chest and whimpers. She wants this just as bad as I do. We literally cannot stop. Ever since we first had sex at the inn, we can't keep our hands off each other.

I can't even wait until we get to her bed, which is a mere six feet away from where we are in the hallway. I press her harder against the wall as I enter her and her gasp nearly sends me over the edge. My hands wrap under her ass and upper thighs, providing the stability we need as I thrust hard in her.

"This feels so good, Noah. Don't stop." Her hands wander and scratch and trace my arms and when her fingernails dig into my back, my body twitches and I know I need to get her to the bedroom.

I unpin her from the wall and take the widest steps I can to get to her bed as fast as possible. Right before I lower her onto the bed, Evie decides to bite my bottom lip and that electrifies my entire body, especially my throbbing dick, which is still inside of her. "Shit, Evie." I bite her lip back and taste her cherry chapstick and she smiles. I will never get enough of her.

I lower her onto her pillowy soft pink duvet and before I drive into her again, I pause to take her in. Her blonde strands of hair strewn all around her head, her green eyes sparkling with mischief and sweetness all at once, her glowing skin. I am still falling for her every second I'm with her. This crazy love we have is the best kind of love I could ever ask for.

She plays with the hair along my neck and says, "Why did you stop?"

"Just admiring my girl. I don't know what I did in this life to deserve you, Evie. I still cannot believe that I was able to have a second chance with the love of my life."

She grazes her thumb over my scruff. With the other hand that's behind my neck, she pulls me down to her and kisses me slowly and deeply, making me lose myself within her. My body aches for her every second that I am not with her. She always had this ability to soothe any of my ailments: sore muscles, anxiety attacks, soul aches...she is the cure to everything.

My movements resume and she wraps her legs tightly around my back. I moan mid-kiss and feel her satisfied smile against my lips. I trace along the side of her body and stop at her upper thigh. I lift her leg until it is over my shoulder, spreading her wider for me. She gasps sharply at the new position and I revel in her body shuddering underneath me. Her back arches and she whispers, "Yes, Noah. Keep going."

"I don't plan on stopping until you come all over my cock. I want to hear the sweet sound of you coming for me, Evie. It's fucking music to my ears. It's a fucking song I play on repeat in my head." I kiss her cheek softly. "No wonder I am constantly hard for you. You walk into the room and my cock twitches in excitement and pure need to get inside of you." I drive into her, making her scream my name. "I want to feel your pussy tighten around me."

I grab onto her black metal headboard and drive into her hard and slow. "I love this headboard better than the other one at the inn. I can actually hold onto it properly while I fuck you."

She moans. "I love it better, too." Her nails dig deeper into my shoulder blades. "Now fuck me like you promised. I'm not supposed to be able to walk by the time you are done with me, remember?"

I lower my head until our lips almost touch, teasing her, driving her crazy. "Oh, don't worry. I am nowhere near done with you. I want to make a mess on these pretty pink sheets of yours. I want my cum to drip down your fucking thighs." She tightens and her body jolts. Her fingers dig into my back, which makes me lose control.

I am disciplined in almost every aspect of my life. Except for Evie. She is the one exception. She has this power over me that no other woman has. I might be in control in the kitchen and at this moment as I am fucking her, but she holds the reigns in my life.

"You're about to come, aren't you?" All she can do is nod and then she turns her head to the right, exposing her beautiful neck. I start sucking on her neck and driving into her faster and harder. Her breath becomes erratic and I feel her body tensing underneath me, making my own body ripple with jolts of pleasure.

We come together and I ride her until her body relaxes

under mine. I don't put my entire weight on her, afraid as always I will crush her. I kiss her forehead and I can feel her dainty fingers imprint a path up and down my back, sending a tingling sensation up and down my already sensitive body. My arm muscles tense and she clocks it, biting her bottom lip. Jesus Christ, I need her again as soon as humanly possible.

"I can get used to this." Her long eyelashes block my view of her gorgeous ocean eyes checking out my flexed, tattooed bicep next to her head.

"What's that, beautiful?" I play with her hair.

"Laying in bed with you." Then she looks up at me, giving me an unobstructed view of her eyes, which now have a filmy layer of tears. "Being someone you love, again."

I shake my head. "That's where you have it wrong, baby girl." She crinkles her eyebrows, apprehensive of what I have to say next. I ease her mind. "Not *again*, Evie. You have been someone I have loved forever and always."

A single tear streams down her face. I kiss it away and hopefully kiss away any fear of hers that she is anything but mine. I press my forehead to hers, ease out of her, and roll onto the empty space next to her. She immediately pulls the covers on top of her flawless body.

"That should be a crime." I let out a low growl as I place my right hand behind my head and outstretch my left as an invitation for her to curl up next to me.

"What should be a crime?"

"You, covering up your body in any way, shape or form. Seriously, it should be illegal."

"Oh, well you know what else should be illegal? Your perfect face and even more perfect body. I can't compete with all of that going on." She playfully pulls the duvet over her head. "Never could."

I chuckle. How does Evie manage to be sexy when she is doing something so goofy? I pull it down and say, "Come here, beautiful. There is no contest when it comes to you."

"I can't move, remember? You have made it impossible to do so." She raises her eyebrows and smirks at me. This woman is tapping into all my weaknesses and yet I feel the safest I've ever felt. It's easy with Evie. Even when we would get into little spats, we always found our way back to each other.

"Get your sexy ass over here, Evie Hawkins." I pull her toward me with my left hand and she giggles as she inches her way to her rightful spot next to me. Her head rests on my chest and she drapes her arm and leg over me, trapping me in the sexiest way possible. I glance out the window and notice a light snow falling. It's calming and peaceful. Everything this moment is. I can feel her breathing slow. Our exertions are catching up with us.

"I never want to leave this room. Do you think Lydia, Bill and Gerard could handle the grand opening without us? Hell, even running the whole damn thing for all eternity?" I rest my chin on top of her head.

"As great as that seems, absolutely not." She grips the side of my torso tighter and snuggles up closer to me so that I can feel the mess we made between her legs. "I don't like to give up control."

"Hmmm. It seems like you don't mind giving up control with me."

"I do have to confess: I like when you take control in the bedroom...and in the kitchen. Actually, I love it when you take control." Her body rocks into mine, making me shiver from head to toe.

"Hence my idea of never leaving this room."

Instead of feeding into my completely flawless and seemingly feasible idea, Evie says, "I have another confession."

"Tell me."

"Ever since my mom got diagnosed with cancer, I couldn't really sleep. I have terrible insomnia. I literally cannot turn off my brain. But, it is productive insomnia for the most part. That's when I planned out my ideas for the inn or I would drive over to my parents' house and work in the darkroom. There was so much on my mind and I couldn't silence anything. The intrusive thoughts haunted me and it sucked."

"I'm so sorry, baby girl." I don't know where she is going with this. But I am eager to listen to Evie's voice for eternity. I didn't realize how it feeds my soul. I have been deprived of it for so long, it's a long-awaited antidote for all my problems. She could do a TED talk about watching paint dry and I would be invested in every word.

"I thought my insomnia would stop after my mom was cleared and was officially in remission. I thought it would stop after I graduated or after we cut through all the red tape of purchasing and renovating a historic inn. It didn't stop. Until the other night at the inn."

My heart aches for her. It kills me that she had sleepless

nights with all the worries in the world. I hate that. But I am here now. The room starts to feel heavy, so I make a joke, even though some of it might be founded on some truth. "It's all the mind-boggling sex, isn't it? I'm wearing you out."

She huffs out a small laugh and I feel her head shake and then she climbs on top of me, her forearms resting on my chest, her naked body completely on top of me. I feel every fucking curve and suddenly I am starving for her again. Her face inches closer to mine and she says, "It's the fact that you are back in my life. You are my cure, Noah."

I grab the sides of her soft face and kiss the tip of her nose. My heart has never been so full because that's exactly how I feel about her.

"Trust me when I say to you, Evie Hawkins, that you are my cure, too."

She closes her eyes and smiles. "And just for the record, the sex helps, too." She reaches one of her hands down to my dick, making my breath hitch.

"Is my girl ready for round three?" My cock hardens immediately from her touch. My girl is insatiable and I wouldn't have it any other way.

"Only if you feed me first, chef." There is a devilish look in her eye I can't get over.

I sit up, wrap my arms around her back, place one of her nipples in my mouth, and suck hard. It's my turn to make her breath hitch. "You are such a little tease."

"I burned off a bunch of energy. I need to eat." As if on cue, her stomach growls and we both laugh.

I lay another kiss on her forehead. "Okay, okay, I'll finish making the pasta. You stay here and I'll come get you when it's ready. You are not allowed to move. You need to rest up for later." I throw on my underwear and start walking to the door. Before she can cover up her naked body, I pull all the sheets off and take them with me.

"Noah Pearson!" Evie shrieks.

I laugh as I head back to the kitchen.

27

Evie

I open my eyes and don't even know what time it is. I crashed out so hard. After Noah loaded me up on the most delicious carbs known to man, I got so sleepy I fell asleep on his shoulder on the couch while we were watching *Christmas Vacation*. At some point last night, Noah must've carried me to my bed. My head is on his sculpted chest and his arm is wrapped tightly around my back, his hand right above my ass. I look up at his face and he looks so peaceful. I notice that his other arm is propped up behind his head, showing off his crazy large bicep.

This man makes it near impossible to leave this bed. Maybe he's right. Maybe I should abandon the inn and stay cooped up in our little isolated love snowglobe we made for ourselves.

As much as I am craving him right now, I don't want to disturb Noah. He needs the sleep. He has been busting his ass ever since he got back into town. He has the best work ethic of any person I know. That is one of the many things that makes him so attractive. Noah does not rely on his ridiculous good looks to advance anywhere. He is so smart and so hard-working, he motivated me to be the best version of myself and to pursue something as wild as flipping properties and going all-in on running my own business. I remember his drive back when he was training for football, and it is obvious that work ethic has not waned over the years. If anything, it may have gotten stronger. He is overall a stronger person, mentally...and physically. It's the mental strength that sends all the butterflies to my stomach. I know how much he has struggled with his mental health and there is an ease in Noah's face now that brings me comfort. Once upon a time, sometimes with other people but never with me, his demeanor was so hard, it could cut glass. It's in moments like these, where the world is quiet and no one is asking for his autograph or picture and there aren't cameras filming him making a delicious dish, that he is truly the Noah I fell in love with. Relaxed Noah is my favorite Noah.

I weave my way out of the cozy cocoon that is Noah and grab his shirt. Once I throw it over my head, it falls about halfway down my thigh. I am drowning in it, but there is something about putting on a man's oversized shirt that feels so gratifying and possessive. He's mine and I am his. And this is how it was always supposed to be.

He shifts a little on the bed and as tempting as this half-naked man is, I go with my better judgment and tip-toe out of the room.

I turn on my bluetooth speaker and play some instrumental Christmas music as I brew some coffee and take out a mixing bowl, eggs, milk, and pancake mix. I throw bacon in a frying pan and start measuring all the ingredients to make pancakes. As I am stirring the batter, I sway my hips slowly side to side. Then I feel strong hands on my hips and the invigorating scent of Noah overpowers the heavenly scent of freshly brewed coffee. He moves my hair to the side and kisses the side of my neck. "Mmm, good morning, beautiful."

I slow the stirring, my core immediately tightening the moment his fingers touch me, and say, "Good morning, handsome. Hungry? I'm making pancakes."

He doesn't stop kissing all along my neck and the top of my shoulder, "Starving." I smile so wide my cheeks start to hurt. "Oh shit," he says. "I'm sorry about the hickey."

"What?!" I nearly tip over the mixing bowl and throw my hand up to the side of my neck. Noah starts laughing. "How is this funny? I haven't had a hickey since…" I run over to the mirror in my living room to inspect it. And yup, there it is, a purple mark on my neck. At least I can attempt to cover it with makeup and a scarf.

"Since the last time I gave you one?" Noah smirks as he walks over to the cupboard full of Christmas mugs and pours himself some coffee. "It's not that bad. You've had worse." He takes a sip, beaming at his work.

I point a finger at him. "Don't you dare give me that look."

"What look?" he asks, seemingly perplexed.

"That prideful look. You should not be proud about this." I go back to stirring a little more vigorously, slightly annoyed that I have this on my neck. I feel so exposed.

"I am immensely proud because I like the world knowing that you got properly fucked by me last night," he says nonchalantly as he turns off the bacon.

"That mouth of yours has indeed gotten worse."

"So has yours, sailor. But I'm not complaining. It's really hot." He resumes caressing my body and lifts the hem of his shirt I'm wearing, so that his warm hands are pressed on my hips. "I was looking for this a few minutes ago," he whispers against my ear. Tingles shimmy up and down my body. "I'm glad that you're wearing it. This is another good look for you in the kitchen. I love when you wear my clothes."

I turn and wrap my arms around his neck. "Good, because you aren't getting this shirt back."

Noah's lips crash into mine and God, he is delicious. He lifts me onto the counter and holds the back of my head, deepening our kiss. His other hand moves its way up and down my back, leaving a trail of fire along my spine, while his tongue explores my mouth.

Then Noah lightly spanks me and says, "As much as I love that you started breakfast, please let me finish. You have done more than enough. I'm the chef, remember?"

I hop down from the counter and start pouring the batter

onto the hot griddle before Noah can swipe the bowl for himself. "Nope, not this morning. This morning, I'm the chef."

He gives me an incredulous look and leans against my island. He looks like a damn underwear model. "Okay, I'll just sit back and enjoy the view." He sips his coffee and stares at me with devilish eyes. His phone pings and he goes back into the living room, where we apparently left both of our phones last night, and picks it up. I flip the first batch of pancakes and when I turn to look at him, his eyebrows are scrunched together. *Who texted him? What did they text him about? Is everything okay with Walter?* All these thoughts run through my head all at once and I get dizzy with possibilities that are likely not even the reality. Noah clicks the side of his phone and sets it on the counter. I exhale and transfer the cooked pancakes onto two plates.

"Everything okay?"

"Yeah. How many pieces of bacon do you want?"

I can't help but notice that his hard demeanor is resurfacing. Not fully. Just a hint. But it's there. Something is bothering him.

His phone starts to ring now and I see the name "Trey Preston" flash across his screen. "Um, two is fine." I lift up his phone and hold it out to him, "Trey Preston is calling you."

He doesn't take it. The two lines between his eyebrows reappear and he forces a smile. "I'll call him back." He hands me the plate and a fork. "*Buon appetito*, bella. Let me get the butter and syrup. I am assuming you still put a deluge of syrup on your pancakes until they are swimming in it."

"Haha, very funny. You keep talking to me in Italian, we seriously will never leave my house."

He winks at me while he places the newly purchased maple syrup in front of me, along with my vintage butter dish I found at Clay's a few years ago.

"Those Italian ladies taught me more than just how to make pasta, Evie." His phone rings again. Trey Preston.

"It clearly is important if he is calling you two times in a minute. Just take the call. It's fine. I'm in breakfast heaven right now." I pour the said deluge over my pancakes.

"Okay, fine." Instead of going into a quiet space to take his call privately, he swipes his screen and answers it. "Hey, Trey, I'm very busy at the moment. What's up?" I hear a muffled response on the other end. I stuff my face and while Noah is the chef in this relationship, my pancakes are seriously the best thing I make. I might even let him in on my little secret of adding cinnamon to the batter. It's the ingredient that makes everything taste better, in my opinion. Hence why I add it to everything.

"Got it," Noah says into the phone. "Well, I'll get back to you about my availability. It's kind of a busy time for me right now. And I'm kind of in the middle of something important. Can I call you later once I have a clear answer?" Noah studies my face and I must look like a satisfied chipmunk because his face softens – he is definitely holding back a laugh. "Great. Talk to you soon, man."

He places his phone down on the counter and drizzles a small amount of syrup onto his pancakes. "Enjoying your meal?"

I finally have the ability to chew comfortably and mumble, "I am, actually, thank you for asking." I swallow. "How can you possibly just drizzle the tiniest amount of syrup? Your self-control is something to be admired, Noah Pearson."

He finally lets out that knee-weakening smile of his and cuts into his pancakes. Even though he seems fine, my gut is urging me to see if he is covering up his real feelings. There is a reason he avoided Trey's calls and I don't think it's solely because of me. "Dare I ask again? Is everything okay?"

Noah chews and is clearly contemplating if he wants to expose exactly what he is thinking. "Trey is a restaurateur in New York. We both worked at the same restaurant for a little while. Now his partner has a restaurant opening in Midtown and he is insisting that I go. A lot of high-profile people in the industry are going to be there. It's a high-end restaurant that calls for a high-end look with a red carpet and press. It's a big deal."

I nod and sip my coffee, trying to curtail the panic invading the peace within me since we got back together. "When is it?"

"Next weekend."

We are only two weeks from our own opening. How could he even contemplate leaving to attend this event so close to our opening? I mean, sure, the menu is already meticulously planned out by both of us. The bedrooms are done. There are a few finishing touches we need to work out before our soft launch on Christmas Eve. I know the soft launch will be just people from our town, but still. I can't help but feel this large weight descend on the delicate bubble protecting our peace. There is a bad feeling in my gut that I can't ignore.

But it's not like he is going to miss Christmas Eve.

"That sounds fun. You should go." I am two seconds away

from stuffing another piece of pancake in my mouth, but he grabs my hand and makes me drop my fork against my plate. I look into his earnest green eyes. I blush nervously, "What?"

"Will you be my date? That's the only way I am going to attend this thing. There is no way I am letting you out of my sight. I've gotten used to seeing you every day and I don't know if I can bear going to New York without you. Plus, it's Christmas in New York. There's nothing like it in the world."

Flutters emerge in my belly. Christmas in New York is something I've always wanted to see, and now I have this chance of experiencing it for the first time with Noah. "Are you serious?"

"Yes, I am serious. I need you there, Evie." He squeezes my hand, reassuring me that this is what he wants.

Although he is saying everything I want to hear and more, there is a small tug in my stomach. There are still some things I need to get ready at the inn and the opening date is creeping up on me faster than I realized. "I would love to go with you, Noah. But – the inn. It's not fully ready yet and I'm afraid that if I go, something will fall through the cracks."

Noah holds onto my hand and that small gesture effectively sends shivers throughout my body while simultaneously calming my nervous system. "Please, Evie. I'm sure if you give your parents and Gerard that cute little list in your Notes app of last-minute tasks for the inn, they can handle it. They are your team, after all. I'm confident they'll have your back for a couple days."

I scrunch my nose. "How do you know about the list?"

Noah laughs and squeezes my hand a bit more. "Because when another task pops into your head, you get that exact expression and type veraciously on your phone." He leans over and kisses my forehead, making my insides twist even more. "I promise we won't be in New York long. Just for the opening and we will leave the next day. I just really need you by my side, Evie."

How can I resist this man? He's right. I need to trust that my parents and Gerard can handle the inn. I give in because it's Noah, and once upon a time he did what I thought I needed. Now he is the one needing me to do something for him. "Of course. Anything for you, Noah." I take another bite of my crispy bacon. "Now when you say fancy, how fancy are we talking?"

"Black-tie fancy." He takes another swig of his coffee.

I raise my eyebrows. "Wow. Okay, I definitely need to go shopping for this. I guarantee I have nothing in that closet that will pass for a black-tie event. It's either sweatpants, hoodies, workout sets, cozy sweaters, jeans or leggings. None of those would pass inspection. "

"I can have something arranged. Although, as we have discussed, I prefer you wearing nothing." He wiggles his eyebrows, eliciting a ridiculous reaction in between my legs.

I clench my legs together and clear my throat. "I'm pretty sure no one shares that sentiment with you. And just for the record, no one else gets to see me naked except you."

"Good point. I wouldn't want any other man gawking at my girl. I wouldn't want to fight someone at this fancy restaurant opening."

"Well good news! You wouldn't have to fight anyone because no one would be gawking."

"Everyone would be gawking," he says so confidently as he shoves his last bite of pancake in his mouth.

"Okay, change of subject." I shake my head and place the overly-saturated-with-syrup piece of pancake onto my fork and hold it up for him to taste. "I bet you can't guess the special ingredient I put in these pan–"

"Cinnamon." The pancake disappears in his mouth and he has a smug smile on his face.

My jaw drops to the floor. "Why would you spoil that for me?"

"Sorry, but what can I say? I have a very refined palate. It's kind of a prerequisite of becoming a chef. Plus, you put in an inordinate amount of cinnamon in the batter. Only a person who has zero tastebuds wouldn't be able to detect it. I love you but you, baby girl, aren't as sneaky as you think."

I pause. Did I hear him right? He just said those three really big words that have been a constant elephant in the room since we got back together. Noah continues eating as if he didn't drop the biggest bomb on me two seconds prior.

"What did you just say?"

"I said you aren't as sneaky as you think. I tasted the cinnamon before it hit my tongue."

"No, no. Before the sneaky bit."

Noah seems to understand what I am referring to because he grabs the leg of my bar stool and scoots it as close as he possibly can before it crashes into his. He cradles my face and says, "I said, *I love you.*" No hesitation. No frills. He says it with the quiet confidence that I have always loved about him.

It feels like he has been saying that for years but it also feels like he said it for the first time. Swirls of excitement enter my stomach and I'm tingly from head to toe.

"This morning. With you. Having coffee and overly-cinnamoned pancakes. This is paradise, Evie and it's everything I ever wanted."

The words coming out of his mouth are everything I have been longing to hear and I am incandescently elated that he feels this way. "I love you, too, Noah."

Relief sets in on his face. His worry lines are replaced with crinkles around his eyes when he smiles wildly. He brushes his thumb against my very sticky lips and leans in. We kiss soft and slow, almost delicately, not wanting to shatter everything we just rebuilt, which is a massive change of pace than what our MO has been the past few nights together. This kiss feels different. It feels like a glimpse of forever.

And here, now, in my small house, in our small town, in the midst of the magic of snow falling from the sky, I feel us truly begin again.

"Fine, I have another rule in the kitchen. Nothing but an apron for you." Noah takes the empty plates, rinses them, and places them in the dishwasher.

I raise an eyebrow and halfway scoff as I swallow the last bit of pancake in my mouth. "And, if I don't want to wear an apron? What do you have to say to that, chef?"

"I mean, I am not opposed to breaking the rules every once in a while. But only because it's you."

28

Noah

I am woken up by the sound of my phone vibrating. I squint as I raise my phone to see who is calling at 5 am. My alarm is set for 5:15 so I can work out before heading to the inn. I guess depending on who this is, my plans may be altered. I make out the name Grandad on my screen. I swipe the bar and answer, "Hello? Grandad? Why are you up at 5 am?"

"Oh, son, I am always up this early. Well technically, I have been awake for about half an hour."

Why? "Got it. I was going to wake up and work out soon anyway. What's up, Grandad?"

"I am wondering if you want to stop by today? I haven't seen you in a couple of days and there is something going on here today that I want you to see and be a part of."

I tear the sheets off my body and swing my feet to one side of the bed. I look over to the empty space next to me and my heart aches. My girl should be next to me when I wake up every morning. She has no idea how much I want our life together to begin now that we are officially back together. "Yeah, I'll stop by before I go to the inn. Do you need me to bring you anything?"

"Nope, just yourself. See you in a few hours."

Beep. Beep. Beep. There's my alarm.

AFTER I EAT BREAKFAST, get my workout in and shower, I head over to the senior center. I walk into the dining hall and see my grandfather talking to a vision in a bright red sweater, a Santa hat and jeans that hug every curve of her perfect body. A body I cannot wait to touch again later. Evie's hair is hanging down by her ass and she is laughing at something my grandfather just told her. Jesus Christ, I don't know if I'll be able to control myself.

I stride over to my grandad and Evie. My grandad notices my presence and diverts his attention from Evie to me. "Oh hey, son, you made it! What a coincidence that Evie is here at the same time you are."

My grandad thinks he is the smoothest man to ever live. I

have always been able to see through his antics. "A happy coincidence."

"Anyway, Evie here has been coming by and visiting me for, what, about five years?"

Now I am the one caught off-guard, but it makes sense why my grandpa never told me. He wanted to protect my feelings when it came to my girl. He knew how heartbroken I was when Evie and I broke up. He certainly didn't want to pour any salt in the already stinging wound.

Evie smiles and nods at Walter, confirming.

Grandad says, "I think she has been trying to humor an old man all this time."

"You know that's not true, Walter. I wanted to visit. Make sure you are okay. You mean a lot to me. Always have."

He takes her hand and kisses the top of it. My grandfather always had a soft spot for Evie and it warms my heart to see that hasn't changed and to know that she took the time to visit him while I was gone. It makes me love her even more.

"You asked me to bring you a Christmas ornament to use for this exchange," Evie says. "I couldn't leave you hanging. Plus, you know how much I love me a Christmas ornament, Walter. I literally cannot fit all of my ornaments on my tree. There are years where I have to pick and choose. I have been tempted to get another tree just to decorate it with whatever leftover ornaments I have."

"I am highly surprised that hasn't happened yet." I push up the sleeves of my sweater and catch Evie in the act of checking out my forearms...again. White-hot desire for this woman courses through my veins. I need to focus on my conversation with my grandpa. "Grandad, why didn't you tell me to bring you an ornament when I was on the phone with you this morning?"

Walter shrugs, presumably assuming some sort of innocence even though he was the one who instigated it. "Evie was coming by no matter what to drop off her delicious shortbread cookies."

Evie sets a large Christmas tin in front of my grandfather. "These are just for you, Walter." She quickly ogles me and I have the urge to throw her over my shoulder and take her back to my place. "Hey, Noah."

"Hey, Evie."

I give Evie a platonic hug and there is a flicker of disappointment in her face when I don't kiss her. She shrivels a bit and I know that look—she got insecure and unsure of the situation. Dammit.

"Oh you two are ridiculous, just kiss already. We already know that you got back together. It's written all over your faces." My grandad comments, "Plus, Miss Lizzie came by and told us."

I roll my eyes. This is typical of Hollybury. Your business is never your own. The very thing I despise in one moment, I love in the next. This is the community that I missed. No matter how backwards and invasive they can be, I know that they love and protect those that are in their circle. It's the very community that helped raise me. The same community that watched Evie and I fall in love in the first place.

I may overcompensate because I press my hand on her lower back and bring her closer to me, making her body flush with mine. "You look beautiful today." I kiss her gently. I keep it very PG because of our captive audience. I hear whoops and some whistles. We stop kissing and I see that Evie is blushing, like we are teenagers again, showing a public display of affection in front of our elders.

"Thank you." Evie leans in a little closer to me. "Oh and by the way, they were apparently in need of someone to run the ornament exchange. Their usual MC got a bad bout of the flu. I am stepping in."

"Wait a minute. You're telling me that you, Evie Hawkins, the person who was deathly afraid of doing any type of presentation in school, are going to stand up in front of a crowd of people and run an ornament exchange? Do you want another snowstorm to sweep through town?"

"Haha, you are so hilarious." She bumps her shoulder into my arm. "Walter asked. I can never say no to that man."

"I understand. He does have that effect on people."

"Oh and I volunteered you to assist anyone who needs any help walking up to the table. I thought you should put those muscles to use." She pats my chest and beams.

I wrap my arm around her tightly and pull her in. The combination of her vanilla scent and ruby-red lips challenges all my inner strength and willpower. "I think I've put these muscles to pretty good use of late, don't you think?"

"Don't start something you can't finish, Noah Pearson." She pulls a Santa hat from her back pocket and hands it to me.

I lean down and whisper in her ear, "Who says I am not going to finish it? You underestimate me again, Evie Hawkins. I am no quitter."

"I guess we will find out later." Evie winks at me and then

walks up to the front of the dining hall where there is a big black speaker and microphone. She taps the microphone. "Can everyone hear me okay?" She hands me a bowl of small pieces of paper with numbers scribbled on them.

There is a resounding "Yes!" across the hall.

"Okay, great. So, my assistant, Noah here, is going to go around and distribute a small piece of paper. On that paper, there is a number printed on it. We have twenty-five participants, so we should have enough to go around."

I put on my silly Santa hat and begin walking around, holding out the bowl and once the last paper is taken, I return to the front.

"Thank you, trusty assistant. On the table next to me, there are twenty-five ornaments in these festive gift bags. Now, the rules are, once you touch a bag, it's yours. You can't feel around and try to figure out what it is. It's yours. You do have another option when it is your turn, however. You can steal from another player and then that person has the option to steal or pick a new bag. Once the ornament is stolen three times, it is frozen. Whoever has number one, will have a chance to steal from anyone at the very end." Evie pauses for about ten seconds. "Does anyone have any questions?"

Phyllis, the forever instigator of Hollybury, raises her hand.

Evie smiles and says, "Yes, Phyllis."

"I think everyone wants to know, when exactly did you and Noah get back together?"

The room goes completely silent in anticipation of Evie's answer.

Lord, Phyllis. Evie and I exchange a glance and she clears her throat, "Any questions about the *game* specifically?"

There is a low buzz of disappointment that Evie is not willing to spill the tea. Evie syncs her phone to the speaker so she can play Christmas music during this event. If Evie had a choice, she would listen to Christmas music on repeat all year round. Some people might find that annoying but I find it fucking endearing. A low chatter fills the dining hall.

Evie claps her hands decisively. "Alrighty then, who has number one?"

THE CHRISTMAS ORNAMENT exchange lasts for almost an hour, and I honestly forgot how intense it gets. I had to assist about half the participants to the table and back to their chairs, and even volunteered to be the one to go and steal an ornament from another resident. These people are ruthless when it comes to Christmas decorations. This is Evie in seventy years. I start chuckling as I am cleaning up the red-and-green plaid tablecloth.

"What are you chuckling about over there?" Evie grabs the other end and folds her sides together.

"Just had a glimpse of the future."

We bring the ends of the tablecloth together and our hands skim. She looks up at me. "You think I'm going to be like this one day?"

"Going to be?"

She snags the rest of the tablecloth from me, finishes folding it, and throws it in a clear bin. "Ha ha. Very funny."

"I love making you laugh and seeing you smile. It makes my whole day."

I feel a pat on my shoulder and I turn to see my granddad, holding up one of Evie's cookies and beaming.

"Evie, dear, these are your best yet. What is your secret?"

Evie shrugs and says coyly, "You know I can't reveal my secrets, Walter."

"It's cinnamon," I say flatly. "In the actual dough."

Evie's nostrils flare and she attempts to push me away. When I don't budge, she smartly gives up and then stands with her arms crossed. She's fucking adorable.

"How dare you reveal my secret."

"C'mon. Walter's family. I think he deserves to know."

"You know, maybe I'll revoke your offer and continue your little trial run at the inn for exposing such a secret."

I advance toward her and cradle her face, "Go ahead and try, Evie. No matter what the result is, I'm staying."

Evie's whole body relaxes and that's when I notice the bags under her eyes are no longer as prominent as they were when I first got back to town. She is finally resting and sleeping for more than two or three hours and it thrills me. She is looking more and more like the old Evie. Softer. Vibrant. Even more beautiful than I remember. Her hands finally envelop mine and she leans even closer to me, finally accepting the fact that I am staying.

Walter chuckles behind us. "I'll leave you two lovebirds to

it. Evie, dear, thank you for running the ornament exchange and for the cookies. And Noah, I'm glad you didn't quit."

I glance over my shoulder to wave goodbye and see him wink before he walks over to his small group of friends.

"Since things are dying down, I need to get back to the inn." Evie exhales, clearly bummed she can't stay in our bubble. I hold onto one of her hands and pull her back toward me.

"Same. Maybe we can make dinner together there tonight and then after, do you want to take a drive with me?"

Her face lights up. "Always."

29

Evie

Noah and I spend the rest of the day finalizing everything for the soft opening and talking about our plans for New York. With his help, I actually successfully make fettuncini from scratch and Noah makes homemade cheesy garlic bread. I can't stop eating the bread. I am so happy I wore one of my favorite sweater dresses –I need the space since it feels like I ate my weight in bread.

After we finish cleaning up the kitchen at the inn, we head out to Noah's truck. As always, he opens his truck door for me.

Ever since we have officially been back together, he hasn't let me drive to work, let alone let me open my own doors anytime he is near me. I slide in and scoot over to the middle of the seat so I am as close to him as possible. He gets in and kisses my forehead. "Did you enjoy dinner, baby girl?" He turns on the ignition.

"Yeah. My pasta was okay. Not nearly as good as yours."

"I disagree. Your pasta is close to rivaling mine. But I want you to know that you better get used to me cooking for *you* every night. You will never be disappointed."

"Wow, you are that confident, huh? You never have an off day?" I use air quotes on "off day" because I know deep down that Noah probably never has an off day. That concept is foreign to the unstoppable Noah Pearson.

"Oh, I've had plenty of off days. I learned from those off days and perfected any mistakes." He rests his hand on the steering wheel and turns his right blinker on.

"I thought we were going back to my house? It's to the left. Not right."

"I know where you live, Evie," he responds with no explanation or inclination of where exactly he is going. Noah's truck vibrates as he drives down Main Street. Heads turn in our direction as we pass the citizens of Hollybury. *Noah and Evie are back together! Alert the town crier!*

"So, where are you taking me?"

"It's a surprise. I just wanted to take you on a drive, remember?" He turns up his radio and *Have Yourself a Merry Little Christmas* by Frank Sinatra plays through the old speakers.

"I love this song."

"You love every Christmas song."

"This is true. You know me so well." Flashbacks of us driving down Main Street appear in my head and it makes me smile. My feet hanging out the window, music blasting, and the sheriff shaking head at Noah. Noah smiling his perfect smile. Everything was perfect back then. Less complicated. But somehow I am still grateful for the people we have become without each other.

"Anytime I would hear Christmas music anywhere in the world, your face would pop up in my mind. Of course I was sad that you weren't next to me, but it also brought me joy knowing that you were listening to the same music, possibly at the exact same time as I was, and it was a connection I held onto tightly." He laces his bare fingers with mine and kisses the top of my hand. It still baffles me that he doesn't really wear gloves.

"How is it that you don't wear gloves? I never understood that."

"I don't need them. I run really hot." He winks and the crinkles around his eyes deepen as he smiles.

I shake my head against his arm. "How can you be so charming and cocky all at once?"

"You disagree with me then? You don't think I run hot?"

"You are a human heater. I can attest to that, being the one who usually cuddles up next to you when the blanket isn't a sufficient source of warmth for me." Suddenly, an intrusive thought pops into my head. I wonder if anyone else has cuddled up to him lately. I don't want to ruin this perfect night, but I also don't want to hold anything back from Noah, especially my innermost thoughts that will definitely cause me to spiral. "I know this is kind of out of nowhere, but did you ever take Blair on that date, you know, to Enzo's?"

Noah pulls over to the shoulder of the two-lane road. Places the truck in park and looks over at me intently. "Never in a million years would I take Blair on a date. I didn't entertain that for a moment. I didn't give her a second thought in high school and I am definitely not giving her a second thought now, Evie."

"Okay. I get it. Blair can be a little...on the crazy side?" I honestly am being nice. There is no little about the crazy.

Noah gets back on the road. "I can sense crazy from a mile away, trust me. I honestly think she prepared me for all the women who would try and get pictures with me on the street."

I shut down the small ping of jealousy that is currently attempting to make its way up to my brain and make me insecure. I deflect but am also genuinely curious. "Did you ever get panic attacks when that would happen?"

He drapes his wrist over the top of the steering wheel. "I felt them developing, but it never turned into a full-blown panic attack. Maybe my body was in self-preservation mode and knew I didn't have time to panic. I was so driven and motivated to get out of the chaos, that it suppressed any other symptoms. It felt like I was completely out of my body, smiling, conversing, ignoring all the tugs on my shirt or arms. When you become somewhat of a celebrity, all notions of personal space goes out the window. People don't respect the fact that you are a person and you might have issues and feel claustrophobic. But I never wanted to complain because I have a great life."

"Just because you have a great life doesn't mean you don't

deserve your own personal space and peace. I'm sorry you had to deal with that alone."

"You know what used to help me?"

"What's that?"

"It may sound cheesy..."

"I am a big fan of cheesy. Cheesy's sexy."

Noah laughs, then continues, "I would recite the lyrics of the first Christmas song that would pop into my head. And I would see your beautiful face and know that everything was going to be okay. I imagined your hands on my face and you telling me to breathe. Just like you did the other day in the kitchen." He turns onto a side dirt road and my heart starts to race because I haven't been out here since that one time. Probably the most important night of my life. "Evie, you saved me more times than I can count."

Noah slows the truck down as we approach a beautiful wooden cabin. The exterior looks like it has been redone in recent years, but whoever did it, kept it as close to the original as possible. The truck comes to a halt and Noah places it in park.

Suddenly, I'm having a hard time breathing.

This is the place Noah and I had sex for the first time.

I remember that night like it was yesterday. Noah decorated the entire cabin with white twinkly lights and made sure everything was perfect. It was awkward but so amazing all at once and I trusted Noah that he wouldn't hurt me. I knew that I wanted to wait until I loved someone before I slept with them. Unfortunately, because of that goal, I was known at school as a prude or tease, but Noah never pressured me. In fact, one of his teammates was talking shit that I wasn't giving it up to Noah yet and called me a "fucking tease" and Noah slammed him against a locker and punched him. Needless to say, Noah was suspended for that game. He told me it was worth it. No one had any business talking about me like that.

Noah unbuckles his seatbelt and I do the same. "Do you want to go inside? See if it still looks the same?" He unlocks the doors and reaches for the handle, but I climb over the seat and stop him.

"Not yet." I need him now and I don't care that we are in his truck, parked in front of the cabin.

His eyes get dark and the hand that was reaching for the handle finds its way to my calf. Noah slowly caresses my leg all the way up under my dress until he reaches my ass. He squeezes it and I let out a whimper. His other hand grabs the back of my neck and he slowly pulls me toward him until our lips are mere centimeters apart. "Evie, are you sure? Because there is more to the surprise."

"I'm sure."

Not even a second goes by before Noah's lips close in on mine. Both my hands are on the back of his neck now, pulling him closer to me. At some point, between our mouths crashing together and hands exploring each other's bodies, I climb onto Noah's lap and rock my hips against him.

He leaves a trail of kisses down my neck and on my collarbone, one hand grabbing my hair and the other grabbing my ass. My hands find a home on his broad shoulders. He is doing something so right at the gym because he has never been this fit in his life. I continue riding him, totally unaware of the world around us. "Are you going to ride me until you come, baby girl?"

I ride him harder and feel his dick get even harder.

"I'm so wet, Noah. Want to feel how wet you are making me right now?"

Suddenly the horn of Noah's truck goes off and makes us both jump. I cover my mouth to stifle my laugh because this has happened before. We were parked in front of my parents' house and the same exact thing happened. We were fooling around in the front seat of Noah's truck and Noah pressed me up against the steering wheel so hard that my ass pressed the horn.

His hand leaves my ass and he starts to inch my sweater dress up until it's resting comfortably above my hips. His hot fingers trace along my wet panties and as he does, I let out another moan. He proceeds to pull my hair tighter and kisses me along my collarbone. "Fuck. Oh my god, Evie if you keep moaning like that, I am going to come before you do. We can't let that happen." His grip loosens on my hair and his fingers graze down my spine, tickling me in the process. I giggle and he laughs against my delicate skin, "Mmmm. Still ticklish, I see. That's fucking adorable and hot as hell all at once. You always had that perfect combination going for you, Evie." He presses his hand against my lower back so I am as close to him as possible. He licks along my collarbone and god that little action nearly pushes me over the brink.

I cling onto his shoulders and I'mconvinced I am going to leave an imprint of my nails on his skin. My hips grind against his sculpted body and find a steady rhythm. His cock is so hard underneath his jeans and I can tell he is getting frustrated that his dick isn't inside of me. But I know Noah wants me to come first. His fingers slide inside the hem of my panties and find my slit. I gasp at the sudden sensation of his fingers inside me.

"Jesus, Noah." I lean my forehead against his. His fingers twist deliciously while his thumb presses against my clit.

"Come for me, baby girl. Come on my fingers so I can lick them clean," he whispers in my ear.

Just that image of him licking his fingers sends me over the edge and I ride his huge fingers until I collapse onto his chest. As promised, he pulls his fingers out and puts them in his mouth. "I love the way you taste, Evie."

I kiss him again, tasting myself in his mouth. I want him to feel just as good. "Now it's your turn." I unbutton his jeans and run my hand over his underwear, only to find they are already wet.

"Noah Pearson, did you come in your pants?" I smile at him devilishly.

"You bet your sweet ass I did. That's how turned on you make me, Evie. I don't even have to be inside you to come." He holds the side of my face and kisses me softly.

"What if I do want you inside me?" I lick his bottom lip.

"I can definitely make that happen." He moves some stray hair out of my face and tucks it behind my hair, not without kissing the top of my nose first. He quickly buttons himself back up and I shimmy my dress down my legs before he grabs the back of my head and kisses me deeply. He opens his door. "C'mon, beautiful." He takes my hand and I slide over the front seat and follow him to the front door of the cabin. There is a dim light coming from the windows. He pauses before he opens the same old wooden door. "You ready?"

I smile and nod. Noah leads me into the cabin that holds probably the most important moment in my life. It's like stepping back into the past. Not only are there multiple strings of white lights pinned to the walls, there are also tea light candles on almost every surface of this cabin. "Noah, I've been with you all day." I walk forward to investigate the scene: the old blanket he set down as our bed the first time is an actual mattress this time. And instead of an empty fireplace, there is a crackling fire in its place. The whole cabin is also decorated for Christmas, another upgrade from the first time. Just as our relationship got a reboot, so did this cabin. Still, I don't understand how he pulled this off since I've been attached to his hip since we woke up this morning. "How did you do this?"

Noah smirks. "I might have had help from a certain gossiping, fiery red-head, who loves to meddle in people's relationships and overall business." Miss Lizzie. "Now just to warn you, I owe Miss Lizzie multiple dinners until my debt is paid. She may drag this out for years."

I grasp onto his hands and lace my fingers through his. "Does that mean there will be nights when Miss Lizzie will hijack you from me for an extended period of time?"

"I'm afraid so." He wraps our arms behind my back and rests them on my butt.

I shrug. "I don't blame the woman for wanting you to cook for her and trying to steal you away from me. I hear that you are a pretty good cook, chef."

He pulls me closer so I feel every ridge of his body. "No

woman will ever steal me away from you. I dare them to try." He studies my face as if he is locking away every detail of who I am. He is piecing me back together again little by little. "I love you, Evie."

I stand on the top of my tip-toes to try and reach his lips. He unclasps our hands and lifts me from my upper thighs. I wrap my legs tightly around him and my lips land on his. We are leaping back headfirst into rekindled flames. The temperature changes between us and the air becomes so thick I can barely breathe. This time in this cabin with Noah already feels different. His kiss is the gentlest it's been since we started kissing each other again. He takes his time kissing me, his large hand tangled in my already tangled hair, and my pulse rushes to my ears. A flame ignites in my belly as I take hold of his sturdy, broad shoulders and match his gentleness with my own as I reciprocate the kiss. He lays me down softly on the mattress and I attempt to sturdy myself on my forearms.

Noah is the first one to break our kiss, but it is for a reason I can forgive. He pulls his sweater off from the back, revealing all the delicious muscles that lay underneath the garments he so ridiculously decides to wear every day. It still shocks me to see all his tattoos lace his arms. One of my favorites is a large husky on his right deltoid. That piece of Hollybury is permanently engraved on him forever. But my absolute favorite one I have discovered is the date he asked me to be his girlfriend inscribed along his left wrist. I noticed it one morning when he was still sleeping and all I could think was: *This man never stopped loving me.* Even though I hurt him deeply, he did the opposite of erasing what we had–he made sure he would never forget. I sit up fully and trace the raised lines along his arms. We were crazy to think we could ever live this life without each other. I was crazy to think that someday I would possibly find anyone who could replace this man, who is kissing down my neck onto my collarbone, sending sparks through every inch of my body.

Without any words, Noah finds the hem of my sweater dress and slowly inches it up my thighs. I aid him any way I can, matching my movements with his motives. He pulls the dress over my head and my hair is wild with static and tangles. I try to fix it, but Noah stops my progress. "Don't, you're perfect."

My stomach twists. This time it's not from nerves. It's not from the unknown.

It's from the realization that this man loves me unconditionally. Loves who I am at this moment. Loves who I used to be. Loves every single piece of me. Even the messy pieces. "I love the way you love me, Noah Pearson."

Without saying a word, he continues to do just that. Love me.

He unclasps my bra and slides my underwear off and I submit to him in every way. He does all the work. When I try to undo the button of his jeans, he pins my wrist above my head and shakes his head, his nose brushing against mine. He is taking control in the most unselfish way I can possibly imagine. It's all about me right now.

He lifts my body with ease until we are centered more on the mattress. He lowers his body closer to mine and pushes my legs apart with his knees. He throws a blanket over us. All the while, his lips never leave mine. He eases into me and I moan against his lips and he does the same back to me. Noah is so meticulous and intentional with the way he makes love to me. This time is so different from our first time at this cabin all those years ago. Now there is no awkward positioning or nerves. He knows exactly what he is doing and his confidence is overwhelming, but he is sweet on me like he was back then. My pleasure overrides his and that entices me to return the favor.

He steadily thrusts into me and his hands are taking their sweet time caressing every inch of me. At this rate, Noah's fingerprints are going to be imprinted on me forever. Like my own personal tattoos. Our silver chains clash, bringing my focus to something other than Noah's hands and tongue and dick. That distraction is short-lived when he reaches between our bodies and rubs my clit. My body writhes with overwhelming pleasure.

I bite my lip and smile and before I can say anything, Noah is expertly angling my hips upward, hitting a whole new spot. I clutch onto Noah's back and give into him again. Pleasure rolls through me and the same happens to Noah. Both our bodies tense and relax simultaneously and our breathing goes from heavy and erratic to steady and calm. Our bodies go limp and I wrap my arms and legs around Noah. He shakes his head and through heavy breaths, says, "Evie, I am seriously going to crush you if I lean on you for too long."

"Shhh." I brush some chestnut brown hair out of his forehead. I love his hair like this. Not too long. Not too short. He has the Goldilocks of hair. "No you are not. I am not as delicate as you may think. I can handle you."

His eyes sparkle with unshed tears. From the moment he told me of all of his trauma and demons and his panic attacks, I told him that I can handle him. I can handle anything he is afraid to tell me, anything he thinks I would possibly judge him for. Noah's vulnerability has always been so refreshing, and unexpected to an outsider looking in. To the public eye, Noah seems perfect. He seems like he has it all together all the time. He doesn't, and that's okay. No one has it all together. I always validated that for him because I can only imagine the pressure of being the wonderful man that he is.

He leans down to kiss me for the millionth time in our relationship. Still feels as magical as the first time he kissed me. Just like this time having sex felt every bit as magical as the first time. This kiss is loaded with all the promise of our future together, and for the first time in a long time, I allow myself to surrender to the possibility of forever with this man.

30

Evie

I zip the last packing cube and place it in my suitcase for New York. We are leaving bright and early tomorrow and I cannot wait for this quick trip before I am shackled down to the front desk at the inn for the foreseeable future. I have been freaking out about this red-carpet event we are attending, but Noah promised we will go shopping for my dress when we get to the city. Even in my excitement, I can sense there has been something on Noah's mind he isn't telling me. He has been getting texts and calls from that old classmate of his, Trey.

Apparently, Trey has been trying to ensure Noah will definitely be at the opening of their mutual friend's restaurant.

This little weight hasn't left my gut since Noah talked about this Trey character. I just can't put my finger on what about it is making me so uneasy.

After packing, I am planning to meet Noah at our old high school. He has a meeting with Coach Stanton about possibly helping out the team on a more regular basis. I can tell he misses football so much. He doesn't let his injury haunt him anymore. He definitely has a more healthy relationship with the game since those months following his ACL tear. That was one of the hardest things to witness, other than seeing my mom suffer through her cancer treatments. I felt so helpless.

I shake off those memories as I zip up my suitcase, relieved we are not in that terrible phase of life anymore. My phone buzzes in my pocket and I assume that Noah is the one calling me. But it's not him – it's my mom.

I swipe the bottom bar to the right and put the phone on speaker. "Hey, Mom." I pull Noah's old Hollybury Huskies sweatshirt over my head that he left at my house – I am now forever claiming it as my own.

"Hey, sweetie." My mom's voice sounds a little too measured. Too clipped and in control. Not like her natural easy-breezy tone. "Are you busy right now?"

I pull my hair out of the inside of the hoodie, adjusting the sweatshirt so it covers my leggings just above the knee. *Yup, this is mine now.* I take my phone off speaker and hold it up to my ear. "Actually, Mom, I am about to meet Noah at the football stadium and then we're going to head to the inn to make sure everything is ready for when I am gone these next few days. What do you need?"

There is a prolonged pause before my mom speaks again. "Would Noah mind if you come to the house instead?"

A lump in my throat develops. I close the door and lock it. "Um, sure. Let me shoot him a text. I'll be over in a few."

"Thanks, hon. See you in a few."

I JIGGLE my set of keys until I find the extra key to my parents' place. Once I open the door, I see both my parents are sitting on their lumpy old couch. My mom gets up to greet me with a big hug and the way she squeezes me scares me a little. She is holding me a little too tightly. It's slightly suffocating and then the next thing that comes out of her mouth sends chills up my spine.

"Evie, we need to sit down and talk with you." My mom rarely has that tone in her voice. She is usually so jovial and light. I look at her and then my dad and both of their faces catapult me back to the moment my whole life changed. The same vibes. The same grave looks.

"Okay, you both are freaking me out. What is going on?" I sit down and sink to the bottom of their couch.

And then I remember. I have an out-of-body experience where I can see a crash coming in slow motion, but there is nothing I can do to stop it. My mom had a doctor's appointment today.

My stomach sinks.

I already know.

"It came back," I choke out. It isn't a question. It's a fact. The nightmare that I tried so hard to forget the moment my mom was in remission is rearing its ugly head.

My mom slowly nods and holds my hand. "Yes. The good news is…"

"There's good news about this?" Tears well up and blur my vision. I was slowly getting back to my old optimistic self. I so desperately want to return to being that person who tries to see the light in the darkness, but at this moment, I can't see any light. It's pitch black.

Mom's voice cuts through the deep abyss I am falling into. "Evie, there was always a possibility it could come back. That's why I go in for regular checkups and screenings. They caught it early this time and they told me they can get all of it out."

"That is what they said last time!" I yell and both my parents jump in their seats. I stand up and start organizing ornaments on their tree that don't need to be organized. "And it came back anyway, didn't it?" I wipe away my tears, hoping that by some miracle, I can wipe away this reality, too.

"Evie," my dad says. "Please, honey, sit down."

I crumble onto the couch once more, pressing my hands over my face. I feel like I am going through all the stages of grief all at once. It's this ebb and flow of anger and sadness. I don't want to reach the last stage of grief – acceptance. Because I don't accept this. How can such an amazing, sweet, generous, nurturing person like my mom be dealt this card in life? Twice. *It's not fair.*

"I know it's not." My mom rubs my arm as she sits down

next to me. *Did I say that out loud?* "I know it's not fair. That's what you are thinking, isn't it? I know because I am in tune to your thoughts and emotions. No matter how old you get, you are still my little girl."

I bring my hands down to my lap and my mom's hands immediately cover them. I sniffle. "I always found that talent of yours freaky."

My mom lets out a small laugh. "I'm your mom. You can't escape my special mom superpowers."

"I guess not." There is only one other person who is so in tune with me and my thoughts, and I fear that the hope I felt back at the cabin is only temporary. He still has ties to New York and no matter how much he reassures me that he is staying, my instinct is to doubt him. Just when I am back on stable ground, the universe decides to throw a massive curveball and I can't shake the feeling that I am going to strike out again. I don't want to lose my mom. I don't want to lose Noah.

I just got him back.

Tears roll down my face again. There's no use trying to control them anymore.

And like the superhuman that she is, my mom says, "Now tell me why you are really upset. It's not just this news that is making you so upset. Tell me the truth, Evie. What's going on?"

I take a tissue that my dad has been holding out for me for I don't know how long and blow my nose. "Seriously, freaky."

"It's a gift." She rubs my back. "Now spill."

I clear my throat. "Noah has this old friend, Trey, from culinary school who won't stop calling him. He has asked him about a thousand times if he is for sure going to the restaurant opening this weekend and I can't shake the feeling that Trey has something else up his sleeve. An offer that he cannot refuse. And before you say anything, Dad, I am not quoting *The Godfather*."

My dad shrugs and gives me a sheepish smile. *The Godfather* is my dad's favorite movie of all time and I am sure he is having a proud dad moment right now that I inadvertently spoke a famous line from that film.

It provides temporary levity in this situation but I continue, "I just have a feeling he is going to return to New York and miss the life he had." I cover my face again. "Ugh this is so stupid. This is why I didn't want to let him back in. It hurts too much. Not everything turns out the way you expect it to. Look at what is happening to you, Mom. You got a second chance at life and you are back to square one with cancer." I criss-cross my legs onto the couch and bury my hands in the hoodie pocket. I shrug. "I don't know. Maybe it would be easier to just let him go back to New York on his own. I mean, that way I can focus on taking care of you and..."

"No," my mom states plainly, and to be honest a little more sternly than I ever heard her speak to me.

"No, what?" I ask quizzically.

"You are not going to stop your life because of me. I won't allow it."

I adjust myself on the couch cushion and turn my body so I am facing her head on. "But, Mom..."

"No buts, Evie. I am not letting you make that mistake again. I am not going to allow you to run away scared this time. Noah isn't going anywhere. Even if this Trey guy has an offer he cannot refuse, I know in my gut that Noah will not take it. When are you going to get it through that stubborn, thick head of yours that he is not going anywhere?" This is the most honest thing my mother has ever said to me. She is not fragile. She is brutal and brilliant all at once. "Evie, you have sacrificed too much in your life for me. I am not going to let my life and diagnosis stop you from pursuing the most important thing in this life."

Even in the midst of all that brilliance and sage advice, my intrusive thoughts take over and I start crying again. "That's noble of you to say, Mom. But don't be ridiculous. You and I both know, heck Dad even knows, that Noah is too big for this small-town life. He wouldn't want to stay, even if he did come back for me." I know Noah said that he came back for me. And I believe him, but I also don't want to stifle any opportunities for him. I don't want to be selfish. That's why I let him go in the first place. I may not have been in the best mindset when I made that decision last time, but that truth still stands.

Suddenly there is a mug filled with hot chocolate, whipped cream and cinnamon in front of my face. I look up and see my dad smile, with a hint of pain in his eyes. I can't imagine what's going on in his mind right now. To see the love of your life go through the scariest season in their life – again. I didn't even notice my dad leaving the room. I've been so wrapped up in this new reality and processing the plea from my potentially dying mother to not give up on someone I have loved since kindergarten.

"He came back for you, Evie," Mom says. "Even in the midst of all the success, he still wanted you. You need to instill it in your soul what he told you–he came back for you. That man loves you more than anything. He's not going to choose anything over you."

I press my lips together and rub my thumb around the rim of my mug. The warmth provides some comfort in this devastating moment. My eyes burn from the mascara mixing with my tears.

My mom continues, "You are making assumptions based on your past history. You both have grown a lot in seven years. Noah let you go because he was trying to respect your wishes. He didn't want to push you with everything going on. He let you go because that's what you wanted. Not what *he* wanted."

Then the tears come out in full force and I'm barely stringing together coherent words. It's all too overwhelming and this back and forth of my heart breaking, piecing back together, and shattering over again. It's too much. I don't know how much else I can handle. "That's the thing, Mom. I didn't want him to let me go. I was stupid and stubborn for pushing him away. And I knew he would do anything for me because he loved me. Loves me."

"Then let him, sweet girl." She rubs my cheek and I lean into it, letting my mom's words sink in: "Let him love you the way you deserve to be loved."

31

Evie

I tap my phone screen and notice the time. I am five minutes behind schedule. "I'm so sorry, Noah, I am almost done."

"It's okay. Take your time. I can be fashionably late to this. In fact, that's what all the cool kids are doing." I am surprised he isn't watching me get ready. We haven't left each other's side since we got to New York. He even snuck into the dressing room when I was trying on dresses and kissed me senseless. "Besides, it's kind of my fault we are running late."

This is true. When we got back to the hotel, Noah pinned

me against the wall and next thing I knew it was an hour later and we were tangled up in the sheets. Tangled up in each other.

"That is a true statement." I smile and I tug again on the zipper, which apparently hates me because it keeps getting snagged. "Ugh, I need help with the zipper." Before I leave the bathroom, I look in the mirror one more time. I decided to try a black cat-eye and red-lip look to offset the softness of the blue satin dress that I settled on at the shop. The soft baby blue brings out any blue that I have in my eyes. I turn and look at my bare back. The dress swoops down so low on my back, I am surprised the hem of my nude seamless thong isn't exposed. Some satin fabric criss crosses against my lower back and the long gown drags on the floor. I run my fingers through my long curls to soften them and then open the door to the bedroom, where I am greeted by the most beautiful man to ever exist.

Noah stands up from the messy bed and he presses his hand to his chest when he sees me. "You're beautiful." He should talk. He is also wearing a powder blue shirt with a black tie. His hair is quaffed up perfectly and his hungry eyes are glued to my body. My face gets hot.

I meet him at the side of the bed and feel the woven wool beneath my fingers. "It's nice to see you in a tux." I play with his lapel and adjust his tie. "It's been a while."

His hands find a home on my hips. "Blue is definitely your color."

"Really? You mean I didn't look good in your maroon Hollybury Huskies football jersey?"

"Oh, you definitely looked more than good in my jersey. I just like how the blue brings out the little specks of blue in your eyes." He kisses my temple and lightly brushes his fingers along my bare back.

Suddenly very aware of how much skin I am showing, I ask insecurely, "Are you sure this dress isn't too revealing?"

"No. If anything it's not revealing enough." He traces a finger along the lining of my dress that's right above my ass.

I reach behind me and attempt to stop his progress. "Excuse me. This is a classy event. I think I'm already going to get stared at given who I am with. I don't want to draw any more attention to myself than I have to. This night is about you." I turn toward the dresser to gather my ID and my lip stain, which I shove into a small clutch.

"Actually it's about my friend." Noah comes up behind me, zips up my dress, and wraps his arms around my arms, trapping me in the best cage. He kisses the side of my neck and says, "And I think everyone is going to have their eyes on you because you're you. I mean, look at you."

I change the subject before my body unwillingly caves to his swoon. I clear my throat, needing to address a possible elephant in the room. "Are you ready for all the attention, Noah? I know how anxious you get." I turn around, press my hands on his cheeks and look at him intently.

"I'll be fine. You'll be next to me the whole night, which will help." He presses his hand on the small of my back and pushes me into him. "Ok, let's go before I rip this dress right off you. You look so damn hot, it's excruciating." He squeezes my ass and lightly taps it before we throw on our winter coats and head out into the bitter cold night.

"Noah Pearson in the flesh! Nice to see you, my man!" A man close to Noah's height and build interrupts one of the many conversations we've had since we arrived at the restaurant twenty minutes ago.

Because Noah is Noah, he was able to bypass the enormously long line to get in. The exorbitant amount of press we encountered on the short red carpet was overwhelming and Noah's hand was clutching mine so tight, I thought he might fracture it. His smile for every picture, his answer to any question, his innate ability to be at ease even in the face of the chaos going on inside of him was a sight to see. It was both amazing and heartbreaking all at once. He deserves to have this attention, but I know Noah. He doesn't thrive on the attention. He thrives on the actual work. He likes to see when his effort has that immediate reward. He likes to see where progress and hard work leads him. That's where the true joy lies for him. Not people yelling a thousand questions in his direction. This level of celebrity is never what he wanted. He is just one of those people who has the perfect combination of natural talent and ambition, sans the cockiness that usually accompanies people with the same traits. He's an outlier.

To any other person, Noah seems like the most charismatic, laid back, coolest guy to talk to on the planet, but because they don't know him like I do, they can't tell that his shoulders are extremely tight, his fingers moving wildly, his jaw clenched so tightly I thought he might dislocate it. I was right by his side though, so happy that I got to experience this with him and support him in any way that I can. That's all I ever wanted.

Right after the red carpet, we checked our coats at the hostess stand, and an influx of people surrounded us. Only this time, we didn't have the luxury of the black crowd-control barrier blocking people from coming so close to us. The boundaries were completely gone. Apparently this lack of boundaries also applied to the one-and-only Trey Preston.

"Nice to see you too, Trey!" Noah shakes his hand and he holds me closer. "Trey Preston, I want to introduce you to Ms. Evie Hawkins." He looks at me and looks the happiest I've seen him since he came back into my life. "My girlfriend."

My stomach flips. I didn't realize until this moment how much I missed him calling me that. Claiming me as his. He said it with such conviction like he never stopped saying it. My heart swells and I have to actively stop myself from tearing up.

I shake his hand. "Nice to meet you, Trey. I can now match the face to the name I've seen on my boyfriend's phone as of late." I swear I see annoyance sweep across his beautiful face. He is just as charismatic as Noah. He has a similar stature to Noah. He has dark caramel skin and piercing dark eyes with sharp, meticulously manicured thick eyebrows that make him look intimidating. His jawline is almost as defined as Noah's, but he has a different confidence about him that throws me off a little. He almost has a smugness about him that is a major turn-off for me. He smiles at me and there is a flicker of recognition in his eyes.

"Wait, this is *the* Evie Hawkins? The Evie Hawkins you couldn't stop talking about while we were working together?

The Evie Hawkins you've been hung up on since you left that podunk town?"

My insides twist and my face flushes from an equal amount of flattery and anger. *Podunk town?* How is he even able to make that assessment? I love my little town. Sure, it's not as exciting and stimulating as New York, but there is something about seeing small businesses thrive and a community that supports each other no matter what grievances they have with each other. Those people are like family. It may be dysfunctional, but what family isn't?

Noah must feel my body tense up because he squeezes my side and he answers for me, "Yes, this is the one-and-only Evie Hawkins."

"Well, the pleasure is all mine, Evie. Noah has told me nothing but great things about you." Trey takes my hand and kisses the top of it. This guy reads as the type of person that can woo anyone into anything. Luckily, I have enough sense to not be so easily charmed by him.

He finally releases my hand and I take this opportunity to grab a glass of champagne off the tray of a nearby waiter. Noah and Trey take one as well, and then Noah's attention is snagged by what I can only assume is another one of his former colleagues.

He leans in and whispers, "Be right back, beautiful," then kisses me softly on my cheek. I watch him walk across the room. I can't help but notice most of the women's eyes are wandering from their own dates and landing on Noah. I can't blame them, but then white-hot jealousy courses through my veins and now I understand how Noah must have felt when he saw me with

Jeremy. I have the urge to run after him and glue my hand to his.

"So, how are you liking New York?" Trey asks.

"Oh, I love New York. It's been a while since I've visited so it's nice to be here, especially during Christmas time." I see Noah in the distance and he sneaks a glance at me and winks, which makes me smile again. I swear this man has me in a chokehold with that smile.

Trey brings me back to reality. "I bet. I reckon Noah is excited to return to the city soon. Are you coming back with him?" He takes a drink of his champagne.

My heart drops down to my stomach and I suddenly feel like I am wearing a corset. I can't fucking breathe. *Noah is coming back? What the hell?* "What?" I try to keep my composure as best as I can in the midst of this brand-new life-altering situation the love of my life has failed to bring up to me.

"Yeah, Noah is basically a shoo-in for my new restaurant that's opening early next year. I mean, he is the perfect candidate and he'd be crazy not to take this job and move back from that cute little town. He's there on a trial basis anyway, right? I am sure you love him enough to not want to hold him back. He's worked too hard to give up his career for someone who gave him up all those years ago."

I lock eyes with Trey, who within the past two minutes, has morphed into a malicious snake. My mouth turns dry and I catch Noah looking over at us. I can tell that he clocks my very obvious discomfort. His eyebrows scrunch together subtly and he tries his best to give the person he is talking to his attention, while also worrying about me.

I feel blindsided again and it's not a very fun place to be. The blood drains from my face and I feel like I'm about to pass out from this new information. "I guess time will tell." I gulp down the rest of my champagne, burning my throat in the process. "Well, Trey, it's been a real treat. If you'll excuse me." I place the empty glass on the very pretty white linen table next to me and head to the door. The walls are closing in on me and I feel like everything is crumbling—my mom's health and Noah are slipping through my fingers again and I don't know what to do about it.

32

Noah

I see a trail of blue satin exit the restaurant and I get a lump in my throat while the boulder from *Indiana Jones* sinks into my stomach. Why is Evie leaving? I need to go get my girl.

I have this gut-wrenching feeling she is slipping through my fingers and I am not letting that happen again. I put on a fake-ass smile and say, "It was so nice catching up with you all but I need to get back to my date. I'll see you soon. I'll reach out the next time I am in New York. We can grab a bite, yeah?"

I stride over to the table where I left Evie and Trey and

notice she left her purse behind. Something is definitely wrong. I grab her purse and sprint out of the restaurant. I step out into the frigid cold night and the city has never been more alive. In the corner of my eye, I see a beautiful blonde in a baby blue dress walking alone in the cold toward the direction of our hotel.

"Evie! Stop!" I yell after her.

She keeps walking.

Fuck. I left her alone with Trey for all of five minutes. What the fuck did Trey say to her?

Running after her, I can see my breath in front of my face. Damn it's cold. If I'm cold, Evie must be freezing. She is basically wearing the equivalent of a silk nightgown. I quicken my pace and finally catch up to her.

I grab her arm. "Evie, stop. What's wrong?"

She is on a mission and does not slow her pace once I reach her. Silence is never good when it comes to Evie. She shuts down and locks everything inside and I don't want her to suffer in any way.

"What the hell did Trey say to you?"

"Look, I'm sorry I left. I just felt so suffocated – I needed some fresh air. Go back, Noah, people are waiting for you. They are expecting you to go back."

"Fuck those people, Evie. All I care about is you."

Evie doesn't even attempt to avoid running into people, so angry New Yorkers are staring her down and looking at me like I might be the problem that she is running from. I hope that I'm not.

I try again. "What's wrong?"

She turns around quickly and I nearly run into her. "When were you going to tell me about the restaurant, Noah?"

Dammit Trey. I was waiting to have a proper sit-down with Evie and mention it to her. It's a giant opportunity for me and my career, but I'm not making any decisions without her. If she is not okay with this, I am not okay with it.

I remove my jacket and wrap it around her. "Evie. Please. Can I please go get our coats and we can get out of here? Trey will understand that I left early from his party. This is more important."

She wraps the jacket tighter around herself and nods, though the line in between her eyebrows is deep with hurt and confusion and clearly anger.

I brush a strand of hair behind her ear. "Okay, I will be right back. Don't move."

I sprint back to the restaurant and approach the coat check attendant. She gives me a once-over and says, "Leaving so soon, chef?"

"Yeah," I say, clipped. "My girlfriend had an emergency and we need to leave. My coat is black and hers is teal. If we can rush this, that would be great." I don't want to be a dick to her but I also just want to get back to Evie and I also want to pummel Trey. I hand her the tickets and she disappointedly turns toward the coats and starts rummaging through the racks.

I feel a hand on my shoulder. I look to my right and am greeted by an obnoxiously jovial Trey. "Noah, there you are, man. C'mon, I have an interior designer waiting to talk to you about the restaur—"

"Where the hell do you get off telling Evie about the

restaurant?" I square my body to him and take one step in his direction. Suddenly his charismatic demeanor changes into a defensive one.

"I assumed you'd already told her. I thought you talked to her about everything. She is your *girlfriend,* after all. Since when did that happen again? I remember how much she fucking destroyed you, man. Why the fuck would you get into that again?"

The attendant comes back to the counter with two coats and I can tell she senses the tension between us since she places the coats on the counter and returns back to preoccupy herself among the racks.

I clutch both coats with one hand and point at Trey with my other. "You don't know anything about it. It's none of your goddamn business when she became my girlfriend again."

"Well, I think it is my business if she is a fucking distraction to your future. More like *our* future. I'm your business partner."

"Not yet, Trey. We've been discussing the possibility of us becoming partners but if this is how it's going to be, then fuck this. I don't need this. I have everything that I need in Hollybury. And Evie is never a fucking distraction. Leave her out of this."

I head out the door when I feel a strong hand pull me back from my shoulder.

"You're making a mistake. This is all about her, man. Always has been."

"Exactly, Trey. This is all for her. And if she is not a part of the equation, I don't fucking want it." I lift my arms up, exacerbated that this is the current situation. How the hell could a friendship blow up so quickly? I guess that is how I felt when Evie and I broke up. It's like I blinked and my whole world crumbled. Except this time, I blinked and everything snapped into focus.

"Don't do this, Noah. You're making a big mistake."

"No, my mistake was thinking you were my friend. I thought since you knew mine and Evie's history you would be happy for me that we are back together. You'd understand that I want to stay with her."

"I don't understand why she has to be the one to call all the shots. Jesus. Be a man and tell her to come with you to New York. This restaurant is more lucrative than her small little bed and breakfast or whatever the hell she is opening. This city..." He looks around at the city that is enveloping us and for the first time in a long time, I feel so small in the city that gave so much to me. This city gave me everything except *her*.

"I want you to listen to me, Trey." I approach him until we are practically touching noses. My jaw is clenched so tightly that my teeth are starting to hurt. "I'm not taking the deal without Evie. And for you to say 'be a man' and just tell my woman what to do – well, that makes you less of a man."

Trey's eyes turn dark and his eyebrows furrow. Based on his own jaw clenching, I know he's pissed. He'll get over it.

"I'll be in touch if I'm ready to move forward. You better go back to all your other friends." I turn and start walking toward the direction of my girl.

"Damn, her pussy's that good that you would risk your fucking future?"

My body reacts before I can process what I am actually

doing–and that is punching one of my friends in the face. I cannot believe he has the gall to talk about Evie like that. He falls to the ground and grabs his jaw and I see a glimmer of blood fall from the side of his mouth.

"Fuck you, Trey. And you better stay down there on the ground because you really don't want to know what I'm capable of, asshole. Forget about that phone call. I'm out."

As I walk away, I hear a very distant, "Well then, fuck you too, Noah! See if you ever get an opportunity like this again."

"Well, I guess that's my problem, not yours!" I yell back, knowing that I have bigger connections than he does and I am not afraid of my future because I'm walking toward it right now.

Evie is standing on the sidewalk right outside of the restaurant, crossing her arms, looking stunning as ever in my coat jacket that is drowning her frame. Her nose is turning the faintest shade of red and she has a smirk on her angelic face. Her eyes are gleaming with something I can't quite decipher.

"Here's your coat, beautiful girl." I wrap it on top of my tux jacket and kiss her forehead.

She looks up at me and says, "What was that all about?" She nods toward the restaurant, where I see that Trey is gone. He must have retreated back inside to clean himself up before schmoozing the higher-ups of the industry.

"He said something I didn't like."

She cocks an eyebrow. "And what exactly did he say to elicit such a strong reaction? Punching people? That's not the Noah Pearson I know. Well I guess except for that one time when you got suspended in high school."

"Ha ha, very funny. Maybe it's part of the Noah 2.0

package." I snake my hands around her lower back and pull her towards me. I suddenly know where I need to take her.

She tugs on the back of my coat, pulling me out of my thoughts. "Hey, where did you go?"

"I want to take you somewhere before we go back to the hotel. Is that okay?"

She smiles and nods.

We walk for about fifteen minutes before we reach the southern end of Central Park. There at one of the entrances is a horse-drawn carriage and a hot chocolate stand. Perfect. "This is the last Christmas-y thing we are doing in New York before heading home tomorrow."

She smiles so wide that my heart melts. The sparkle in her eyes remains and if that's not my favorite fucking thing I've ever seen, I don't know what is. I want to make her smile like that for the rest of my days. I buy us each a hot chocolate and pay the carriage driver $200 for the ride. We climb up into the carriage and snuggle close. The driver signals the horse to go and I pull Evie as close to me as possible to keep her warm.

As we head over a small bridge, Evie breaks the silence. "So, about the restaurant. Can you tell me what that is all about?" Evie tickles the inside of my palm. She's finally calm. I wish I could say the same for my heart rate because it's going a million miles a minute. Not because I am nervous to tell her any of this. My heartbeat quickens every time I'm with her.

"I will always be honest with you, Evie. Opening a restaurant has been my dream ever since my dream of football was obliterated. Being the head chef of a potential Michelin star restaurant–that's the ultimate dream. I worked so hard for this that I told myself if that dream ever came into view, I would take it no matter what."

Evie swallows hard and looks down. "Until I came back into your life. I am blocking you from that dream. Noah, you should take it. I know that Trey is an asshole, but I've always told you to go after your dream. I told you that seven years ago and I am telling you that now. I'm not interested in holding you back. Take this job. This is going to take you to places that Hollybury will never take you."

"No, Evie." My heart sinks because this sounds way too fucking familiar. "Stop. Don't go to that place in your head."

"How can I not, Noah? You staying in Hollybury makes no sense. Just take this opportunity. We can figure it out." She sighs. "Letting you go – helping you become the man you were meant to be – that is one of the best things I've ever done. I missed you. Of course I missed you. But, look at you now. Noah. You deserve more than me."

She is pulling away and I need to know why.

"Why are you doing this? You have it all wrong, Evie. I am not leaving you again. I'm not doing anything without you by my side. I want you to be okay with all of my decisions. I want you to be fucking selfish! Because I sure as hell am. I am being selfish as hell not wanting to leave you ever again. Not wanting you out of my sight. Not wanting you out of my arms. If I could hold you forever, I would."

She chuckles a little. "As amazing as that would be, Noah, I will feel guilty if I know you have an opportunity to be a chef at a potential Michelin-star restaurant and you don't take it because of a job as a head chef in a tiny little town at an insignificant inn that is a passion project for your girlfriend. I want to be selfish. Trust me, I do, but it's not fair to you." She looks down at her lap, shoulders somewhat slumped.

"Look at me, Evie." Her eyes are watery and her mascara is a little smudged. "It's not fair to us if I take this. I'm not leaving you again. I promise." She looks like she still isn't fully convinced. "Now, tell me what else is bothering you."

She sniffles and wipes her nose with the back of her hand. "How can you tell?" She tries to flippantly laugh it off. Uh-oh. This is bad.

"Tell me, baby girl. I swear there is nothing you can say to me that will make me love you any less or not be there for you."

Then the water works come in full swing and I stay as stoic as possible. I pull a handkerchief out of my pocket, a trick that my grandfather taught me a long time ago because *"You never know when someone needs it."* Evie likes to tease me for my old man tendencies but they do come in handy sometimes.

She crumbles and buries her face in her hands. "Gosh, it's like we are back on that damn football field."

"Baby, what do you mean?" I rub her back and I am gutted. There is a massive piece of information I'm missing. I know it. There is a huge weight she is carrying and I want her to pass it to me. I'll bear all the weight for her. "Tell me. Please, tell me."

Her eyes are red and her face is blotchy and her body is shaking uncontrollably. It's my turn to hold her. I get to hold her in all the happy blissful moments and the terrible, unspeakable ones. Unfortunately, this moment is one of the latter. "Breathe, baby girl."

"It's back," she barely whispers.

"What is?"

"Mom's cancer." Tears are rolling down uncontrollably now.

I am at a loss for words. That's why Lydia was acting a little off. She still had her classic smile and her happy demeanor, but I can read a room and underneath the facade. I just didn't know what it was about. As much as I am intuitive, I can't read minds.

I do the only thing I know will ease some of her pain. I hold her in the biggest bear hug I can without crushing her. "I'm so sorry, baby."

"I got overwhelmed when Trey told me about your plans and I just found out about my mom's cancer coming back right before this trip. You know my mom, always with positive energy. Has no worries in the world. I wish I had inherited that from her. Instead I'm cursed with perpetual anxiety and worry." Her breathing slows down slightly. I rub her back and run my fingers through her hair.

"Why didn't you tell me the moment you found out?"

"I didn't want to ruin our trip."

I kiss the side of her head, "Baby, I am here for you. Forever and always. I'm here for the highs and lows. What kind of partner would I be if I was only in it for the highs? That's a bunch of bullshit."

The carriage slows to a stop and I generously tip the driver. I'm sure he was not in for a night of tears and confessions. I get down first, then hold my hand out for Evie to take and my God, if she isn't still painstakingly beautiful, even after crying. I'm in trouble with this woman. Always have been.

The carriage drives away and we're back where we started.

And right there, in front of The Plaza Hotel, I hold the girl of my dreams. "It's going to be okay, Evie. I know it is. Your mom is a fighter and she's not going anywhere. And neither am I."

She shifts under my embrace and I feel a tug on my jacket. She looks up at me. "They were right." Finally a small smile, but I'll take any smile from her.

"Who's right about what?" The wind blows some hair in her face and I move it away and tuck it behind her ear.

"My parents. About you." She touches my scruff and rubs her thumb alongside my jaw. "They said you aren't going anywhere." She grazes my lips with her soft fingers. "And that you love me more than anything."

As much as I want to kiss her senselessly, I kiss the top of her head and hug her. Her head rests on my chest and she digs her hands into my back. I know this is what she needs more than anything right now. Stability. And I am here to provide whatever stability she needs. "They are more than right, Evie Hawkins. I am so in love with you it hurts. Let's go home. And let's go kick this soft opening's ass in a few days."

33

Evie

"Here it is. Homemade apple pie – your favorite. Save for hot chocolate and fettucini."

I have not stopped moving since I came into the inn at 5 a.m. Last night was my worst night of sleep since Noah and I got back together. Thankfully, I'm pretty sure all my tossing and turning didn't disturb Noah one bit. He slept soundly the entire night. Apparently, the only thing not affected by the Noah Pearson insomnia cure is the concept of opening up a historic inn that one has fully renovated and is ready to present to the world. I wonder if this is what Noah experiences when he presents a dish to a food critic. Do all the possible scenarios of how it could go wrong ping-pong against the walls of his brain without any end in sight? I ponder if the concept of failure is in Noah's vocabulary because in all the years I've known him, he never let any setback define who he is. He just powered on.

Well, I took that energy of powering through my anxiety and worry and did not stop once, even to eat. Anyone who saw me today would probably describe me as that little roadrunner on the *Looney Toons* desperately running away from the coyote. But Noah saying the words "homemade apple pie" stops me in my tracks. He places a cake stand displaying an impeccable apple pie on the counter as if I'm a new cooking show judge he is trying to impress.

I smile and shake my head. "You did not have to make this, Noah. The menu is already full enough. It's too much."

He lifts the clear cake stand topper and gently positions it on the counter. He cuts a slice of pie and plops it onto a small plate, then digs into it with a fork and holds it up to my mouth. "Nothing is too much for my girl."

I smirk, then open my mouth. The moment the exquisite taste of apples and cinnamon hits my mouth, I am in heaven. It's the serotonin boost I desperately needed. "This is the most delicious thing I think you have ever made."

"Really?" he says, beaming. "That's the highest compliment, especially coming from you."

I chew the rest of the pie and swallow. "Somehow I don't believe that I am your toughest critic. I know nothing about food other than I love to consume it." I confiscate the fork from his hands to scoop up more pie and stuff my mouth.

I must have some crumbs from the butteriest and flakiest crust in the universe because he grazes his thumb against my bottom lip, effectively removing said crust. "Your opinion is the only opinion that matters. Everything else is white noise."

He leans in closer and presses his lips onto mine. Usually we like to keep things as professional as possible at work, but it's Christmas Eve and I can't help it. I soak up every second I have with Noah and kiss him anytime he's around me because I know what it's like to not have him in my world and that deprivation is something I have no interest in going back to ever again.

"Ew, you two are disgustingly cute. You both need to calm down. Not everyone is boo'd up this Christmas." Gerard's commentary puts a halt on our kiss, but not before Noah places little kisses all alongside my jaw, then my nose.

"Can you blame me, Gerard? My girl is looking extra beautiful today."

Gerard rolls his eyes and continues rolling the last few sets of silverware in white linen napkins.

"You say that everyday, handsome. By all means, don't stop on my account." He puts the last bundle of silverware in a wicker basket. "In all seriousness, it's giving me hope that I can find the same thing someday. Well, apart from pining after a love that's lasted almost an entire lifetime."

Noah squeezes my waist. I smile up at him and rest my head on his chest.

"And Evie," Gerard adds. "I have to agree with Noah, that cream-colored sweater dress is everything, honey."

"You were the one who insisted we color-coordinate and you were not budging on your, may I say, *fabulous* cream pant suit."

Gerard poses to show off his suit and I chuckle at my best friend.

"But, thank you both for saying that I look nice." I notice the time on the clock above the kitchen door and become a bundle of nerves and anticipation. "Shit. Okay, the guests are about to arrive. G, did you double-check that all the rooms are ready and spotless and the beds are made perfectly and all the toiletries are in the bathrooms and..."

Gerard comes over and grabs my shoulders. He looks me square in the eyes. "E. I triple-checked. Now, let's go out there and show this town what you're made of."

I take a deep breath and nod.

"And if I haven't said this yet," Gerard says, "thank you for bringing me along for this journey. You are a boss babe and I am ready to shine right there alongside you. You brighten up everyone's world, Evie. Although I give you crap about you and Noah, it's all in good fun. I am just happy to see you so happy. I was there for the years when you were trying to heal and grow for yourself and it's been one of the best things in my life to see a friend shine so brightly and see love come back into your life. Like I said before, you are glowing, girl. Never stop glowing." Gerard has tears in his eyes and the water works are starting for me too.

I hug Gerard tightly. "Thank you, friend. You have been my

light all these years and I am sorry if I haven't said that enough."
It's my turn to grab his shoulders. "And before this soft opening gets underway, I have a gift for you." I reach into one of my pockets and pull out an envelope. "Here. Open it."

"What is it?" Gerard looks at me suspiciously.

"Your Christmas present. I can't wait until tomorrow."

Gerard rips open the white envelope and his eyes widen as he reads the document enclosed. Noah wraps his arms around me from behind and rests his head on my shoulder. He knows how excited I am about giving this gift to Gerard.

Gerard looks shocked. "Wait, are you serious?"

"Very serious. I want you to be a partner in this business. You would have a say in all the business decisions. This is something I have been discussing at length with my parents for a while, but this decision was escalated when my mom's cancer came back. They are still going to own 25% of the business, but we want you to be a partner. I value your input so much, Gerard. You are the one I always go to for design, business questions... pretty much everything. You are part of the fabric that made the Evergreen what it has become."

"Evie, I don't know what to say."

"Yes would be the obvious answer, duh."

Gerard's tears stream down his face as he nods in agreement.

He whispers, "Thank you," in my ear and it's official. This is the best gift I've ever given.

I whisper back, "You are so welcome. You deserve to glow, too."

"Ooooh, this means I'm your boss now, too." Gerard points

to Noah and says in a flirty tone, "I'm going to have such a good time bossing you around."

"Looking forward to it, boss." Noah winks at Gerard, flirting back. These two have become fast friends and have the friendliest, albeit flirtiest, banter.

"Good lord, you're lucky you are taken and straight," Gerard comments before he leaves the kitchen. "Don't tempt me, Noah Pearson."

I turn and look up at Noah's piercing green eyes. "You are very tempting." I walk my fingers up his exposed tattooed arms. Forget a football uniform. His chef uniform is a thousand times hotter.

"That was nice of you, Evie."

I shrug and reach around Noah's waist, feeling his hard torso in the process. "He deserves it. He works his ass off and it's a natural partnership. He's wanted this for so long."

Noah sweeps a piece of hair out of my face and tucks it behind my ear. "So have I."

I melt into his arms. Although my mom's cancer came back, I can't help but feel so incredibly grateful for everything I do have. Life isn't about being jolly all the time. Life is going to throw curveballs and darkness does set in at times. But, there's a balance to everything. There is no light without darkness. And for once in my life, I am not going to focus on the darkness. I am going to embrace all the light instead. No matter what happens with the Evergreen, I have my family and friends and the love of my life back. That's all that matters.

Noah laces his fingers through mine and leads me out of the kitchen. "Let's go out and greet your guests, Evie Hawkins."

We meet everyone in the foyer. "Doors open in one minute. Is everyone ready to greet our customers?" My heart is pounding against my chest.

"You mean the townspeople that we see daily?" Gerard sarcastically pipes in.

Classic Gerard. Always attempting to lighten any situation with his witty sarcasm. I shoot him a look. "Hey. Attitude. Change. Now. For tonight, they are no longer the people we see every day. They are *customers* and we need to run everything like we normally would so we can get some honest feedback before our grand opening after the New Year."

Noah pulls me in so my body is flush with his, kisses my temple and says, "Breathe, baby. Everything is going to work out."

I exhale and then remember. "Hold on! I need to go get something!"

Before anyone can question or comment on what I'm doing, I scurry back to the kitchen where I left my tote. I reach into the bag and pull out the camera Noah bought me at Clay's shop. I want to document as much of this night as I can. I gesture for everyone to gather in a cluster. "Say Evergreen!"

Everyone does what I say and then Gerard comes over and holds out his hand. "Evie, you need to be in one."

I reluctantly hand the beautiful camera over to him. "Okay, but please don't drop this and you need to look through this part..."

Gerard slaps my hand away. "Go stand over there by your hunk of a man and let me operate the damn camera. This is your moment. It needs to be documented, too."

Noah wraps his arms around me and we smile. Gerard captures this perfect moment. Noah begins to tickle my sides and I giggle uncontrollably as I hear the camera click multiple times. "Got some good ones. I think the candid ones are going to be my favorite."

Gerard places the camera back in my palm and joins everyone else in front of the door, eagerly awaiting our first guests.

Noah lifts my chin and brushes the smallest of kisses on my lips and whispers, "You ready?"

The clock strikes at 6 p.m. "Ready. Here we go." I open the large wooden door and am greeted with snow flurries, which always cure any worries I have. And in this moment, I know everything is in fact going to be okay.

***

THE SOFT OPENING goes off without a hitch. Everyone comments on how beautiful the interior design turned out, how amazing the food is and how wonderful it is to see a town staple revived and better than ever.

"Congratulations, Evie dear! The Evergreen looks fantastic. I'm so proud of you." Miss Lizzie captures me in a huge hug.

"Aw thank you, Miss Lizzie. Thank you for showing up and supporting us. It means a lot to me." I hug her back. *Joy to the World* resounds throughout the inn. This is the perfect night and I can't imagine it going any better than it has. Every room is booked. Not everyone is staying the night, but they wanted to come for the overall experience.

"Oh absolutely. I wouldn't miss this for the world!" She cups my face. I have been blessed with so many extraordinary maternal figures in my life and Miss Lizzie is no exception.

She studies my face. "Remember what I told you all those years ago when you were in the midst of the breakup and your mom's cancer treatments?"

Honestly, that time was a little hazy. I wasn't myself and was so wrapped up in all the sadness, I blocked out any new information coming at me. I shake my head.

"I told you that whatever is meant for you will always find its way back to you." She directs her gaze onto Noah, who is genuinely laughing at something his grandad just said to Coach Stanten. I'm so happy his grandad is able to see Noah this happy. The crinkles around his eyes and dimples deepen. His hand presses against his torso as he laughs. He looks completely in his element. Charismatic and wonderful. Miss Lizzie's cool hand lands on my forearms, bringing my attention back to her kind eyes. "He found his way back to you."

34

Evie

As the party starts to die down and the guests head up to their rooms, Noah interlaces his fingers with mine, leans down and whispers in my ear, "Do you want to go on a ride with me, Evie Hawkins?"

"I'd go anywhere with you, Noah Pearson."

We escape the inn without anyone noticing. Noah drives a whole five minutes before he puts his truck in park and turns off the ignition.

I turn to look at where we are. It's my dream house. Mrs.

Johnson's house. The one that was taken off the market about a month ago. The lights illuminating the downstairs floor are bringing some life back into a house that was discarded so recklessly. Those Johnson children don't understand the gem they lost.

I look back at Noah. His forearm is resting on the steering wheel. He is still in his white chef's uniform and no matter how many times I've told him that he doesn't have to dress like that, he refuses to listen and claims that he is a professional and knows no other way to be. I am not complaining about it now, though. The contrast between his rough-around-the-edges sleeve of tattoos covering both arms and the stark white classic traditional uniform, makes me all tingly inside.

The perfect combo of Noah Pearson: classic and edgy all at once.

He has the goofiest smile on his face. I chuckle. "What are we doing here?"

Without answering me, he climbs out of the truck, strides over to my side, and swings open the heavy metal door. He holds out his hand and I repeat, "Seriously, Noah, what are we doing here?"

"I'll tell you in a second. Patience, Evie, remember?" He leads me to the covered wrap-around porch that has been beautifully redone. I swear whoever owns this house did a great job remodeling. They still kept the integrity of the space and no matter how much I want to hate whoever bought my dream house, I respect that they decided to keep the elegant beauty of this place intact.

Who knows about the inside, though. With the amount of

workers going in and out of this house for the past month, I can only assume they changed everything to make it more modern. "Are we here to torture me? Because you know how much–"

"You've wanted to live in this house ever since you were a little girl?"

I cross my arms. "Yes. Hence my question. Are we here to torture me?"

Noah shakes his head and cradles my face. "No."

"Really? Because this seems like a special kind of torture." Snow is starting to fall around us which softens the blow a little. "Isn't the owner going to be mad that we are standing on their porch?"

Noah shrugs. "I don't know. Let me ask."

My heart drops and suddenly my throat turns dry. He knows who bought this property? I feel like the rug has been ripped out from under me again.

Noah pulls out his cell phone and starts calling someone.

My phone buzzes and I think it's my mom or dad calling me to come back to the inn but when I look at my screen, it flashes NOAH. I'm so confused.

He raises his eyebrows and smiles. "I think you should answer it."

I tentatively swipe the bar to answer and raise my phone to my ear, my hands shaking in the process. "Hello?"

"Hi, um, I was wondering, well my girlfriend was wondering if you would be mad about us standing on your porch?"

I laugh nervously. "What?"

He hangs up his phone and I follow suit, nearly dropping it

on the wooden surface beneath my boots. He reaches into his pocket, pulls out his keys, and unhooks a single key from the chain. He hands it to me. "Welcome home, baby girl."

There are so many thoughts running through my head, so naturally I say them all at once, not before hitting him in the chest. "What? Noah, *you* bought this house? When did you do it? Why didn't you tell me? Please tell me you didn't renovate it to make it look like a glammed-up modern house." Then I get on my tiptoes and point in his face, ensuring he knows how serious I am. "Please tell me you didn't rip up that beautiful fireplace mantle! That was literally my favorite thing about this place!"

"Evie, breathe." Noah laughs my favorite laugh in the world. His eyes are sparkling as he looks down at me, and just like that, I realize that it doesn't matter. None of it matters. The man of my dreams is standing right in front of me and he bought a house for me. In what world does something like this happen? Maybe I don't need all the answers. Maybe I need to just be in the moment.

He opens his mouth to start his explanations but I press my hand to his lips and shake my head. "Never mind. Noah, you don't have to explain."

He gently grabs my wrist and places my hand back onto his chest. "Yes, I do. I will answer all your questions. Yes, I bought this house. I bought it the week I came back. Before I left all those years ago, I told Sheryl to contact me if this house ever went on the market. Through the years, I saved enough money for at least a down payment, not knowing what the future would look like for me. I didn't expect to be where I am today with my career. I knew deep down that I wanted to come back home. I wanted to come back to you. I knew that you always wanted this house and I knew in my heart that I needed to be the one to give that to you. And not in an anti-woman empowerment type of way. I wouldn't dare."

We both laugh because he knows me too well and it's so refreshing and easy that someone knows me like he does.

He continues, "I didn't tell you because I wanted to make sure it was ready for the magic that only you can provide, Evie. I wanted all the demo done. I wanted a clean slate so you can put your one-of-a-kind Evie touch on the place. I didn't ruin it, Evie. I improved anything that came back damaged in the inspection report. I did not touch the fireplace. But, I did gut the kitchen and the basement."

I cock an eyebrow. "The kitchen, huh? You know that I don't need a fancy kitchen to make my boxed macaroni and cheese."

He gives me a pained look. "Who is torturing who now?"

I laugh. "And the basement?"

"It was a complete mess and I wanted you to have a space to make your dream studio and we can put up some walls to make a nice darkroom for your photography."

I didn't think this man could be any more perfect but I stand corrected. This man is perfect and he is mine.

"Thank you, Noah." I turn the key over and over, thinking if I turn it three times it would send me back home and this world of technicolor would return to a world of sepia. I don't want to leave Oz. This is too good to be true.

As I'm turning the key, I feel an inscription on the top of the key and I bring it up to my eyes so I can see it clearer. "N&E?"

"N&E. The way it was always meant to be," Noah says without any hesitation or fear. He never gave up on us. "Do you want to go inside and see your new home, beautiful girl?"

The key feels heavier somehow as I turn it in the lock. The gravity that this house belongs to *me* is settling in. I push open the front door and step across the threshold. My breath catches in my throat. The house is just how I remembered it from all those years ago when I would come by and dog sit for old Mrs. Johnson. I fell in love with this house the moment I first walked in, and my feelings haven't changed. It's the same way I feel about the man who bought me this house.

I walk past the beautifully ornate mantle that frames the wood-burning fireplace and I can't believe that I get to live here. I step into the completely gutted kitchen and instead of sadness, excitement fills me. The new and old are merging and are going to turn into something so exceptional and unique. My fingers run over the blank space that makes up the walls in the kitchen. A clean slate.

"There is still some foundational work to be done, but they are waiting for the snow to clear to do whatever work is needed. Other than that, this house is in pretty good shape for how old it is." Noah places his hands in his pockets, the veins in his arms protruding, making me weak at the knees. He's not even flexing and his arms look like *that*.

Before I let my emotions get the best of me, I address the big elephant in the room: "Noah, are you sure about all of this? I mean, technically this is *your* house – it's your decision to do whatever you want with it."

"True, I am the owner, but I already have an appointment

set up with the title company after the holidays are over to add your name to the deed. The real question is, are *you* sure about this? I know I did this without asking you, but I also know you. I knew how badly you wanted this house. I knew that you wanted to reignite the spark this house once had and eventually create a life here. And maybe I was presumptuous in thinking you would want me to live that life with you..." Noah's voice trails off as he rubs the back of his neck and for the first time in a long time, he looks unsure of his next words. His next move. I can sense the anxiety creeping up on him like a villain that refuses to leave the hero alone.

Without skipping a beat, I run up to him and jump into his arms. My lips press against his and I tangle my fingers in his hair. My legs wrap around him tightly as I finally come up for air. "I have never been more sure of anything in my life, Noah Pearson. Anything that directly involves you is an easy yes for me. This is how I always envisioned it. You and me. Noah and Evie. Building a life together in this house. This is my dream come true."

Relief sets in on his perfect face. "Well, *you* are my dream come true, Evie. If you are happy, then I'm happy. I can't wait to see what you do with your house."

I graze my thumb along his scruff and a tear rolls down my cheek. I have waited all my life for this moment. The moment where all my dreams come true. I thought fairytales were for little girls who know nothing about the tragedy that life can contain. What I have come to discover is that the purpose of fairytales and all great love stories is to give me high expectations of how I should be treated. How I should overcome challenges. How I should be loved. And I am so lucky that I get to love this man in equal measure because he deserves to be loved just as hard and just as much as he loves me. "*Our house.*"

His hand reaches behind my head and he brings my lips back to his and we kiss in our completely demolished kitchen. I break our kiss and say, "Too bad there aren't any counters in here."

His eyebrow arches, clearly intrigued by what I am suggesting. "What makes you think I need any counters to do what I want to do to you?"

Flutters fill my stomach and I give him a small kiss on his neck.

He whispers, "All I need is for you to spread open your legs and let me do the rest." He squeezes my ass before setting me down on the hardwood floor, then removes his chef coat and lays it on the ground behind me.

He unbuttons my teal coat, unwraps my lucky red scarf from my neck, and tosses them to the side. He kneels in front of me and takes his time unzipping my boots and slowly removing my knee-high wool socks. The coldness of the hardwood shoots chills up my spine – or maybe the chills are from Noah caressing my inner thighs and inching his way up my dress.

"So you did bring me here to torture me," I breathe out.

"How exactly am I torturing you right now?" Then his hand rubs against my very wet panties and my gasp echoes in our empty house. "By the feel of it, I would say I am doing the exact opposite."

I run my fingers along his veiny arms and bite my bottom lip as my hands travel up to his very sculpted shoulders. I will spend the rest of my life indulging in everything that is Noah. "You are teasing me, chef."

He continues to caress my inner thighs, "How insensitive of me. I always aim to keep my customers nice and satisfied." He grins up at me like a devil as he pulls my panties down and the moment I step out of them, his mouth is right where I want it to be. I grab onto his hair and one of his hands grips my ass to hold me in place. My legs are shaky and I know the only thing preventing me from falling onto the floor is Noah's arms. My moans and his licking and sucking fill the house and everything starts to feel hazy. He stops for a second and I release a dissatisfied moan.

"Lay down, Evie. I'm starving and I need my strength to pin you down to this floor."

I heatedly follow his orders and lay on the floor, my head resting on his white chef's coat. He finally takes off his tight, white undershirt and now he is there shirtless, showing off his taut chest. The only thing distracting me from getting lost in the deep ridges of his abs is the long chain still hanging from his neck. My heart tugs as I reach out for the necklace and pull him closer to me. "You know you don't have to wear this, right?"

"I'm always going to wear it, Evie. It's a reminder to never let you out of my sight again because you are half of my heart. You gave it to me as a gift and it holds more value than this fucking house to me." He kisses me until my toes curl. "It's never coming off. Now..." He spreads open my legs and inches downward, and the tingles return to my body in full force. "Like I said, I am a starving man and need you more than I need fucking air, Evie. I want to savor you. It is my kitchen, after all. What do you say to me in my kitchen?" He anchors my legs and hips down the way I like and pure ecstasy rolls through my body as his tongue dips inside me.

"Yes, chef." Tension gathers between my legs again as those words roll off my tongue. I attempt to shift my hips up against his face and his tongue goes even deeper. He props one of my legs on his shoulder; my body jolts and I whimper when his thumb rubs against my clit. It's so intense that my breath hitches and a force stirs every inch of my body and I release the pressure stirring inside of me.

"Fuck, Evie," I hear him whisper as his fingers slowly glide in and out of me, as if they are an acceptable replacement for his tongue. "Is my customer nice and satisfied?" He climbs on top of me, setting his forearms on either side of my face.

My breathing is slowing down a bit and I start coming down from the biggest high yet. Meanwhile, the culprit is trying to destroy me with his muscles and his sharp jawline and emerald eyes. I am completely undone from his mouth. His touch. All of him, really. But I can't help but tease him back. I shrug and say, "Eh, I would give it four stars." I grin and immediately press my lips together, hopefully masking my terrible attempt at being unsatisfied.

His eyebrows tug together. "Interesting..." Then his fingers slip inside of me again, making me gasp. My body is betraying me right now. Any attempt to play it cool is quickly unraveling, but Noah is game to play along. His fingers circle inside of me, hitting every possible spot imaginable, leaving me breathless again. "What would get me to a five, boss?"

I trace his veins again, admiring every inch of him. "You… coming inside me. In this kitchen." I kiss his earlobe, then lick the side of his neck, knowing it will drive him wild. "Our kitchen."

He growls and then rams his fingers in deeper. "You mean *my* kitchen." He expertly hovers over me while he unbuttons his pants and slides down his underwear. His hard dick springs out and my need for him intensifies.

I can't pry my eyes away from his beautiful body. "Yes, your kitchen."

"Yes, what?" He angles his dick so it is barely touching my entrance.

The power he has over me is too much to bear and I impatiently grab his back and push him down so he is on top of me. "Yes, chef."

"That's my girl." And before I can say anything else, my words are taken ransom by Noah's overpowering kiss. He pushes into me with an ease that brings forth the thought: *This is us. Together.* We are permanent, just like an engraving on a tree or initials carved into wet cement. Except with us, we don't need any external reminder that this is how we were always meant to be. We have each other to be the ultimate reminder.

I will always remember us like this. Completely lost in each other. Completely in love. Completely together. Pieces of who were were, who we are, and who we are yet to be are finally fitting back together to make the most perfectly imperfect puzzle whole again.

Evie

Six Months Later

"Do you think they're going to like me?"

"Evie, they are going to fall in love with you almost as fast as I did." Noah kisses my temple as the summer breeze hits my skin.

We continue walking along a cobblestone path in

Gargnano. The buildings are nestled near the beautiful clear blue water. Noah was so insistent that he take me back to the place where he learned how to make pasta. Plus, he promised the ladies who taught him that he would visit them one day. I know these women aren't actively a part of our lives, but I still have butterflies in my stomach. It's as if I am meeting his family for the first time. Maybe because I've known Noah since we were young, I never felt those classic "meet the parents" jitters. His grandfather loved me from the start.

This moment feels significant.

This whole trip feels significant.

My palms are sweaty. I let go of his hand that hasn't left mine practically since we got back together over six months ago. My insomnia has also been completely cured since Noah came back into my life. He was my missing piece all this time. I rub my hands against my white linen dress and try to fix my hair since the wind decided to pick up and blow strands in all directions. I adjust my camera bag on my shoulder. I have been bringing the camera he bought me at Clay's everywhere. Most of my content has been Noah-related. I never miss an opportunity to capture how amazing this man is.

Noah looks like he was meant to live in Italy with his khaki linen pants and white linen shirt. His tan has deepened since we have been basically living on the beach this entire trip. We are definitely not in Hollybury anymore. No more flannel for these Connecticut natives.

We reach the quaint villa and I immediately fall in love with the architecture. I love everything about the stucco and stone blending harmoniously, how the exterior is adorned with ivy, almost mimicking the cracks along the aged stucco. The arched windows look hundreds of years old and there is an arched doorway we stop in front of. Noah knocks on the old wooden door and this little old Italian lady opens the door. She is wearing a pretty floral dress with a well-loved apron tied around her waist. A huge smile spreads across her face and her eyes light up when she registers that it's Noah. "Bello, Noe! E un piacere vederti, tesoro."

He leans down and hugs the woman. "It's nice to see you, too, Greta." She beams up at him. He has to be a full foot taller than her. Noah gestures out to me. "Greta, this is-"

"Evie!" She does not hesitate to give me just as big a hug. It makes my heart ache because it reminds me of how my grandma used to hug me when I was little–fully, tightly, and completely full of love. Once she loosens her embrace, she places her hand on my cheek and looks back up at Noah. "Quanto e bello." And then looks back at me. "You are even more beautiful in person. I've heard so much about you. " His face turns a faint shade of red.

I sheepishly smile. I can feel myself blush as I tuck a strand of hair behind my ear. "Thank you. You are too kind. Noah has told me a lot about you, too."

"Well, benvenuta, come on in."

Noah laces his fingers through mine and guides me inside. Greta leads us into an old Italian house, filled with beautiful arches over each entryway, warm neutral orange-brown tones and lots of talking and laughter coming from the kitchen. My nerves take hold of me and I take a deep breath as we step into the kitchen. A group of five women are in what seems like a heated discussion. Hands are flying in all kinds of directions and others are kneading dough intensely. Greta raises her voice to get the group's attention.

"Guarda chi c'e!"

Everyone in that kitchen turns their attention to where we are standing. I tighten my grip on Noah's hand and place my hand on his bicep to stabilize myself. Being the center of attention is not my strong suit. Then all at once, the women come toward us, and we are greeted with hugs and kisses on the cheek at every turn.

In the midst of this ambush, Noah never lets go of my hand. He forgoes the big bear hugs he normally gives to people, instead wrapping one arm gently around each small lady. He towers over all of them and he is equally happy to see these women. My heart fills with warmth knowing how much of an impact these ladies have had on him. He carried that impact all these years and always kept his promise to come back. I capture amazing moments of this reunion with my camera.

Noah eventually escapes the menagerie of women and draws his attention onto me. He takes the camera out of my hands and places it on a counter. "C'mon. Make some pasta with me."

AFTER SPENDING an afternoon with the sweetest women I've ever met, Noah and I head back to our villa off the Amalfi Coast. Though today has been one of the most fun days of my life, a black cloud is threatening my sunny disposition.

My heart plummets. I have been dreading telling Noah a scary truth: I lost my necklace at the beach this morning. The necklace that meant so much to our relationship and the bond between us. My half is gone. I am gutted.

We sit on the beautiful balcony of our villa, overlooking the ocean. The reflection of the moon is fractured by the constant ebbs and flow of the water. Waves crash against the sand, I look up at the stars and for a moment, my worries are swept away.

Noah laces his fingers with mine. "Hey, baby girl. Is everything okay?"

"Yeah! Why wouldn't it be?" My voice squeaks. *Smooth, Evie.*

Noah prods further. "Are you sure? Something seems a little off. Did you enjoy yourself today with the ladies?"

"Yes. Of course I did." I tuck hair behind my ears to tame what the wild ocean breeze is doing to my hair.

"Tell me what you are afraid to tell me."

Dammit. I cannot escape the mirror that is Noah Pearson. "Well, I've been so scared to tell you..." I reach up to my empty neck out of habit, and sigh. "I lost my necklace. This morning, when we went into the water. I took it off and when we came back, I noticed it wasn't there anymore." I shake my head because I should have left it in our villa instead of on a public beach where someone could have taken it or where it became buried in the sand. "I didn't want to admit to you that I lost it, so I didn't mention it, hoping you wouldn't notice. But you notice everything about me. So I don't know why I tried hiding it from you." I shrug and give him a sheepish smile. "I'm so sorry, Noah. At least you have your half still."

His delicious dimples appear as he nods. "I do notice everything about you." He takes my left hand in his. "It's just a necklace, Evie."

I shake my head, tears welling up. "But it's not just any necklace, Noah. It's *our* necklace. It holds so much weight in our relationship. It represented the other half of me." I keep my head down. "And I lost it."

He lifts up my chin. "Look at me, Evie." I do as I'm told and he grazes my bottom lip with his thumb and continues, "I know the significance of that necklace. Trust me. I wore it around my neck too for years, aware of the fact that it was the only piece of you that I could actually take with me. It represented the other half of me, but now I have my other half right in front of me. Okay?"

I nod and when I really look into his green eyes, he is teary eyed too. He is giving me the same look that he gave me the moment we met. Completely zeroed in. Completely into me. Completely in love with me. I recognize that look because that's how I feel every time I look at him.

"Stay right here," he says.

He goes back into the house and a minute goes by before he comes back with a brown bag in his hand. Greta handed him this bag right before we left her house and told him to keep it chilled.

"What did Greta give you?"

He sits next to me and pulls out a fork from the bag and places it on the table. He proceeds to take out a clear container with what appears to be one of my favorite desserts ever.

I point to the container. "Is that?"

"Tiramisu. Greta's famous tiramisu. I swear between all the pasta and the tiramisu, I gained at least fifteen pounds when I stayed here."

"Of muscle, apparently."

He snorts. "Not of muscle."

I snort back. "Yeah, right. You are too modest, Noah Pearson. You cannot deny you bulked up over the years."

"True. But my diet of pasta and tiramisu didn't help with that. Protein and strength training helped with that. That's what I would do in my spare time. Spend it in the gym, trying to distract myself."

"Distract yourself from what? Other women?"

"From my thoughts of you." He flips open the clear plastic container. I'm about to grab the fork and he stops me. "Hold on. There is something missing." He reaches into the bag again and pulls out some candles and a lighter. One candle says two and the other says five.

This man. He spoils me too much. "Noah, I told you that I didn't want anything for my birthday. This trip is enough."

"This isn't from me." He places the candles into the layered deliciousness. "It's technically from Greta. I had nothing to do with this. I guess other than the fact that I told her that it's your birthday tomorrow." He looks at his watch. "Actually, we are about two minutes from midnight." He lights the candles. "Make a wish, Evie."

I close my eyes to humor him. Noah has always been big on celebrating my birthday. He always did these elaborate stunts and grand gestures. I can safely say a trip to Italy is his grandest gesture to date. Well that, and the ginormous gesture of him buying my dream house for me. For *us*. I don't know what I did in a previous life that caused me to deserve a man like Noah Pearson.

I blow out my candles. The smoke twirls around and disintegrates into the cool Italian breeze.

Noah checks his watch again and smiles at me, "Happy Birthday, baby girl. What did you wish for?"

I lean forward and kiss the tip of his nose, "This." I play with the hair on the nape of his neck. "You." My fingers touch the silver chain around his neck and it takes me out of this moment. I want to still be honest with Noah about all of my feelings. I'm not holding back just because I'm scared. That's how I lost him in the first place. "And for my necklace to magically reappear."

He pulls the leg of my chair closer to him and I squeal when he lifts me out of my chair and places me on his lap. My legs drape over him and I wrap my arms around his neck. My forearms rest on his broad shoulders and my core warms up from how amazingly strong he is. He kisses me softly on the lips.

This.

This is what I wished for.

For Noah to be back in my life and for him to kiss me like he is kissing me right now. I readjust my body so it's more square with his and tug on his hair. He smiles against my lips and pulls away. "Wait, beautiful." Now he is the one who looks sheepish, which is a foreign look on Noah. "I lied to you."

My stomach twists and I loosen my hold on his hair.

He notices my eyes have turned from amorous to worried,

and he hurries to reassure me. "I did get you something for your birthday."

Relief cascades through my body as I exhale. I push against his hard chest. "Geez, way to bury the lead. Noah, I told you that this trip was enou—"

He reaches into his pocket and light ricochets off a silver chain. My necklace. "Oh my gosh, Noah! You found my necklace?"

"Well, technically, I stole your necklace."

I push off against his chest. "What? I'm so confused. Why would you do that?"

He hands the necklace to me and I snatch it from his hand. I fiddle with it and say, "Wait, that's why you wanted me to take it off at the beach. Before we got into the water."

"I needed it for this moment."

"What moment?" I laugh, and then my fingers feel something that is not the solitary half-heart pendant that I'm accustomed to feel. I look into my palm and see a large center-cut emerald diamond ring. The platinum band has small diamonds around it. It sparkles at every angle I move it in my hand. I am speechless.

"I thought it was about time for something else to represent my love for you."

I can't stop looking at it. This is so much bigger than I ever imagined my engagement ring to look like.

"I wanted to marry you the moment I laid eyes on you, Evie Hawkins. I knew that our story would never end. Even all those years apart, I knew you were it for me. We had to set each other free to eventually come back to each other." He kisses the top of my hand. "I know that now. At the time I didn't understand it. But now, I know that we aren't just together because we are afraid of what else is out there or that we are too comfortable to try and find other people. I've seen what else the world has to offer and none of it compares to you."

And just as easily as he placed me on his lap, he sets me back onto my chair because heaven knows I can't stand on my own two feet right now. Not with what this man is doing and saying to me. He gets down on one knee and takes the necklace back into his hands. He pulls the ring off and pockets the chain.

My heart is pounding so hard against my chest and I don't know when the tears started rolling down my face, but I am pretty positive that mascara is making small lines down my cheeks. But I don't care. Nothing else matters except for the man in front of me, telling me that he has wanted to do this since he met me. That he waited all this time to make sure I had everything *I* ever wanted.

"When we were teenagers, you said that you didn't want to get married until you were at least twenty-five. So here we are, baby girl. I waited and it was worth every second." Noah takes my left hand in his. "I plan on loving you for the rest of my life. I have waited too damn long to call you mine forever. I want to live our life together with you. Always with you, Evie. Will you marry me?"

I meet him on my knees and cup his jaw in my hands. I whisper because right now, this moment is just for us. "You better put that ring on me right now, Noah Pearson."

He slides the massive ring all the way on my finger and it's a perfect fit. Then he kisses me. I sink my fingers into the back of his brown wavy hair. I am in total bliss and the way he is kissing me right now is ruining me forever. But I don't mind being ruined by Noah Pearson. Our sweet kiss transforms into an all-consuming kiss. It's years and years of kisses we never shared, wrapped up into this one.

He breaks the kiss for a moment and presses his forehead to mine. "I'm so happy you said yes." His fingers wrap around my wavy hair. He tilts my face up and brushes his lips on mine.

"There was never any other option. You were always it for me. N & E like it was always meant to be. Like it always will be."

He licks my bottom lip, sending chills through my whole body. I love that after all these years, any time Noah touches me, it's like it's for the first time. It's electrifying. I open my mouth and his tongue glides over mine and my core is molten. I play with the buttons of his linen shirt and unhook the first button. He lowers me softly to the ground and the warm concrete of the balcony touches my exposed shoulder blades. His hard body hovers on top of me and I pull him down so every plane of his body is on mine. I can be here on this balcony forever with Noah, and luckily forever is all we have.

AFTERWORD

Dear Reader,

I hope that Noah and Evie brought you so much love and comfort during this holiday season. I hope that you fell for Noah Pearson almost as hard as I did. These two characters were a joy to write and I loved writing about a couple that had such a deep history, it was embedded into the very town they lived in. I wanted to write a love story that showed that love isn't always easy and life sometimes gets in the way of what you planned. I wanted to write a story that encapsulated every aspect of life and didn't want to shy away from difficult topics, like cancer or panic attacks. I hope that if you are going through a tough time, Noah and Evie helped you through it.

Second chance is such a beautiful trope to me. I love the concept that two people had to let each other go in order to find their way back to each other. That their love was so strong, their only choice was to be together. I love the idea of living in a small town, where everyone knows your secrets and they are also your greatest supporters no matter how much you screw up. That sense of community is something I have longed for ever since moving to one of the biggest metroplexes in the country. Luckily, I have found my people and the village I need to survive this life. It may not be Hollybury, but it's my home.

I find myself continuing to return to this notion of success and what it means–maybe because I am coming to terms with what it means. There are so many ways of achieving and defining it and what I have come to realize is that it doesn't matter what anyone thinks–as long as I love what I do, that's success. I wanted Noah and Evie to achieve and define success on their own terms and even if that meant breaking up for a short period of time to figure it out, everything would still work out the way it was meant to work out.

Although this is a romance, I always want my female main characters to be strong on their own first and foremost. They don't need a man to be successful or happy or worthy of anything. A man is just a bonus. In the same vein, I always want my male main characters to not be intimidated by strong women and be so supportive of their partners because that's how it should be. In the end, I wanted Noah and Evie to choose each other for the right reasons and not just because it was easy. I wanted them to choose each other when it was hard.

Always choose yourself first. Love yourself first. I promise what is meant for you will always find its way to you.

What did you think about it? I would love to hear!

It would mean so much to me if you take a couple minutes to leave a review on Amazon or Goodreads. You can also follow me on my socials and join my mailing list to find out about upcoming books and bonus content.

XO, Leslie

ACKNOWLEDGMENTS

This book has been so special to me. It's the first book that I have published since making the leap of being a full-time author and I can't even believe I am here again. The holidays are my favorite time of year so naturally, I wanted to write a book that took place during the anticipation of the holiday season. I can't tell you how many times I have thought to myself, "How is this real life?" I am so incredibly blessed to be able to bring these characters to life and I want to thank you, dear reader, for taking a chance on me. I hope that Noah and Evie's story made you laugh, cry and make you believe in the magic love can bring. I hope that it healed a piece of you that has been needing mending. I hope that you always feel seen and safe every time you open the pages of my books.

Now, to the incredible team at Breakthrough Books! To my marvelous editor and book doula, Dallas, I am so grateful for your constant support during the publishing process. I know that when I hand over my book baby to you, it is in the most capable hands. I am so lucky you are in my corner, challenging me to grow as a writer and being the most genuine person on this planet. I don't know what I would do without your guidance.

And to my girl Andi. I would not be where I am today in my author journey without you. Every voice note. Every text. You are my life line in this intense and sometimes tumultuous ride of the book world. You are the best PA a girl could ask for and you aren't getting rid of me. My social media would be nothing without you. Not only are you so amazing at your job, you are so fun and encouraging when I am in the middle of tenacious and crippling self-doubt. You make me feel like a best-selling author every day. The way you believe in me is everything and I do not take that granted. Love you girl.

To my beta readers–Michelle, Jenn, Anahi, Charisse & Nicole. Thank you so much for your honest feedback and for being willing to take the time to read my book and make it the best book it can be. You are investing your precious time into assisting me during this process and I do not take that investment lightly.

Now, for my family and friends. Y'all are the ones who are behind the scenes, watching me with the joys and struggles of writing and you stand by me every step of the way. Especially to my husband, Casey, who encouraged me to become a full-time author in the first place. You never stifled my dreams of being an author–you ignited them. You are showing our boys what a supportive partner looks like and I love you immensely for that.

I look forward to seeing you again in the next book. Until then, bye lovelies!

XO, Leslie

BOOK CLUB DISCUSSION QUESTIONS

1. What is the significance of the title? Did you find it meaningful? Why or why not?
2. What did you think of Noah and Evie at the beginning of the story? What about at the end?
3. Were there any quotes (or passages) that stood out to you? Why?
4. What did you like most about the book?
5. How did the book make you feel? What emotions did it evoke?
6. Who was your favorite character? Why?
7. Who would you cast to play Noah in a movie? Who would you cast to play Evie in a movie?
8. Were you rooting for the couple to get together all along? Why or why not?
9. If you could talk to the author, what burning question would you want to ask?

IMMERSIVE READING KIT

SMELL: Pine, Fir, Cinnamon, Clove, Vanilla

EAT/DRINK: Hot Chocolate with Redi Whip and Cinnamon, French 75, Fettucini Alfredo, Horchata Eggnog, Biscochitos

WEAR: Cable Knit Sweater, Red Scarf, Beanie, Heart Necklace

LISTEN:
Together With You Playlist- Top 25 (in no particular order)

"All Too Well" by Taylor Swift
"Someone You Loved" by Lewis Capaldi
"Christmas Tree Farm" by Taylor Swift
"Too Good at Goodbyes" by Sam Smith

"Sleigh Ride" by Ella Fitzgerald

"Unchained Melody" by The Righteous Brothers

"Always" by Armaan Malik, Calum Scott

"This Love" by Taylor Swift

"Seven Years" by Norah Jones

"Naked" by James Arthur

"Begin Again" by Taylor Swift

"It's Beginning to Look a Lot Like Christmas" by Michael Buble

"The Sweet Sound of You" by The Paper Kites

"Have Yourself A Merry Little Christmas" by Frank Sinatra

"Christmas (Baby Please Come Home)" by Darlene Love

"Love Like This" by Ben Rector

"Those Eyes" by New West

"How To Be Lonely" by Jake Scott

"Loml" by Taylor Swift

"Like It's Christmas" by Jonas Brothers

"Always Been You" by Shawn Mendes

"Out of the Woods" by Taylor Swift

"How Did It End" by Taylor Swift

"All I Want for Christmas Is You" by Mariah Carey

"Us" by James Bay

For the full playlist, search for "Together With You Playlist" on Spotify

ABOUT THE AUTHOR

Leslie McElroy was raised in Santa Fe, New Mexico but currently resides in Dallas, Texas. She loves her family, cozying up with a good book and coffee, and watching sports. Leslie has always dreamed of becoming a writer since she was a teenager, but she finally wrote her first novel, *Stuck with Me*, after being inspired from reading other contemporary romance novels and knowing that she had a story to tell. She is also the author of the fake dating rom-com *The Expiration Date* and the hockey, enemies-to-lovers romance *The Sweetest Risk*. Leslie loves watching movies, listening to music, and is an introvert at heart. She is a mom of two boys and is married to her college sweetheart. Leslie hopes that through her writing, she can connect with people around the world and spread happiness with the characters and stories she creates.

Follow Me on Socials & Let's Be Friends
authorlesliemcelroy.com
Instagram: @authorlesliemcelroy

ALSO BY LESLIE MCELROY

The Sweetest Risk

The Expiration Date

Stuck With Me